Marianna Morgan, Private Investigator

Double Trouble

The case of a Cold Trail and a Hot Musket

Janet Christian

Plum Creek Publishing
P. O. Box 29
Lockhart, TX 78644
www.PlumCreekPublishing.com

This is a work of fiction. All of the characters and incidents are products of the author's imagination or are used fictitiously. Any resemblance to actual events or people is purely coincidental, unless the person begged to be included, in which case they're stuck with the author's depiction.

Please visit Janet's author's page at: www.JanetChristian.com

ISBN-10: 0692716688
ISBN-13: 9780692716687

A TROUBLED PAST

He is a fine friend. He stabs you in the front.
~Leonard Louis Levinson

Davidson stepped from his daughter's bedroom and switched off the light. "Good night sweetheart." He turned, and came face to face with the last person he expected to see in the dim hallway. "What are you doing here? How'd you get in?"

"I was… I'm just…" the man stammered in return. "What are you doing at home?" He stepped back into the shadows.

"Wait. What are you hiding? Give that back." Davidson reached out.

The intruder sidestepped and moved toward the door.

Davidson lunged forward. "I said give it back." He emphasized his demand with a strong shove.

The intruder stumbled from the force, then turned and tried to run. Davidson grabbed his shoulder and spun him around. The struggle escalated between the two men. Davidson lunged again, grabbed the barrel of a musket, and jerked hard, pulling the larger man off-balance. Both men fell against the wall. The musket's bayonet pierced Davidson's chest, driving deep.

Davidson slowly collapsed to his knees. "Why?" Blood poured from the wound and pooled on the floor.

The intruder stood as if transfixed over the dying man. Most of Davidson's blood pooled across the hardwood floor.

"Daddy!"

The shrill sound snapped the intruder out of his trance. He whirled and saw Davidson's daughter standing in her bedroom door.

She fainted, crumpling into a small bundle on the floor. Her hand landed on top of the intruder's shoe, causing a soft slap as flesh met leather. He sucked in a breath and jerked his shoe from under her hand.

Slowly and deliberately, he stepped toward Davidson, who was now barely breathing. Blood trickled from his mouth. The intruder stepped wide, but his shoe still landed in blood. He bent and lifted the musket from where it had fallen at Davidson's side. He then turned to stare at the motionless child.

"Such a beautiful little girl." He reached out and gently touched her hair.

ANOTHER BUTT-NUMBING DAY

A watched pot never boils. ~unknown

I hate stakeouts. Ninety-nine percent of the time you sit in a butt-numbing stupor. The mind stupors pretty good, too. When something interesting finally happens, you only have a couple of seconds to react. But here I sat, parked down the street from a Bargain Mart for the fourth day in a row.

This particular BM is the anchor store in a San Antonio strip mall. These knick-knack and gadget stores are great sources for cheap gifts, as long as you don't mind brand names like Panda-sonic and KichinAid. But I wasn't here to shop. I was watching for a woman in a sky-blue Taurus.

Once again, I'd parked Pickle Toy—my red Mustang GT—beneath the sparse shade of a sad-looking Chinaberry tree that poked out of a small dirt square in the sidewalk. Pickle Toy may sound a bit Freudian, but it works for me. I make up acronyms or phrases to help me remember the license plates of important cars. Mine is PKL 20Y.

Today, Pickle Toy felt more like a jalapeño. Even having the windows rolled down didn't provide much help against the mid-

July Texas heat. The sluggish breeze wafting across my face now and then did little more than deliver the unmistakable, acrid smell of melting asphalt.

My makeshift fan—a manila folder still woefully lacking in case-related contents—wasn't much help. A single drop of perspiration slipped from between my breasts and ran with a slight tickle down my stomach and into the damp waistband of my khaki shorts. I shifted my position, causing a noisy *thwuck* as my thighs separated from the leather seat.

Yuppies sped by in their SUVs, sealed tightly against the heat and outside world by their A/Cs and heavily-tinted windows. No one noticed me as I sat, slowly melting. I'd much rather have been on Max, my Yamaha Maxim motorcycle, but it's hard to do a stakeout on a motorcycle.

I glanced in the rearview mirror and uttered an involuntary *hrmph* at my reflection. Tanned, oval face, mousy brown hair, brown eyes. At least my lips were a nice shade of pink, otherwise I'd be monochrome. I sighed. *I don't look too bad for thirty…my thirties.*

I turned my attention to the manila folder, only nominally more interesting than my reflection. Inside were very few pages, so I knew little about the woman—or her Taurus. The most valuable item was a newspaper clipping provided by my client, Stephen Davidson.

The article discussed a ground-breaking for the San Antonio Spurs new HemisFair Arena, but it wasn't the text of the article that drew my attention, it was the accompanying photo. Either Davidson or someone else had circled the face of a woman who stood in the background, just another small, light-colored oval in the crowd. I couldn't tell actual hair color in the black and white photo, but I could see that it was long and dark.

Davidson claimed to know nothing about her, including why she attended the ground breaking. He didn't even know her name. He'd hired me to follow her and submit regular reports about where she went and what she did. He knew she and her Taurus would likely end up across the street from where I now sat. His answers to my questions about how he knew were vague at best. Either he didn't know—or didn't want to tell me—how he came to that conclusion. My money was on the latter.

I normally don't take such obscure cases, but I'd just completed my last big job, a complex insurance fraud investigation, and didn't have anything else going except for some records searches and background checks. Besides, he'd given me a large four-figure advance, much more than my normal retainer—plus a bonus if I was successful. Of course, he'd decide what *successful* meant, but just getting such a fat advance made me take the chance.

I'd given up after hours of waiting on Monday, Tuesday, and Wednesday. Today, I'd already been in my personal sauna for over two hours. It was close to noon, and I was starving. I figured I could last another hour at most before I called the whole plan a bust.

I was debating between Church's Chicken and Taco Bell when my dead butt and glued-down thighs were finally rewarded. I watched as a sky blue Taurus pulled in front of an unmarked, gray door around the corner from the Bargain Mart's entrance.

I presumed the long-haired woman who stepped out was my target. She wore a long-sleeved, red, western-cut shirt and a denim skirt that nearly reached her ankles. *Odd clothing for such a hot summer day*, I thought.

Her black leather shoulder bag looked large enough to hold a small car, and it appeared about as heavy. Her most distinctive feature was her hair, a dark mahogany cascade of wavy curls that hung nearly to her waist. I pushed back a lock of my own damp, shoulder-length hair as she casually brushed a hand through her smooth and shiny mane.

The woman walked quickly to the door, then stopped and glanced back over her shoulder. I hunched down, trying to keep my sweaty thighs from *thwucking* again. She must not have noticed me, as she returned her attention to the door, unlocked it, and slipped through.

I peeled myself off the car seat and hurried across the street. I don't know what made me happier, having my surveillance rewarded or just getting out of that damn Mustang-shaped oven.

The Taurus's license number was H59 VBW—*Hot 5'9" Very Bad Woman*. I had no idea what her real height might be, but she was close enough to 5'9" for me to remember, and in those heavy clothes she *had* to be hot. As for the *Very Bad Woman* part, well, time would tell.

When I reached the gray door, I paused and studied its location on the wall. I assumed, based on simple geography, that it led to the back area of the Bargain Mart, but no Delivery Entrance or other sign identified the door. I gently tried the knob and found it locked. No big surprise. I guess she didn't want to be disturbed.

I walked to the Bargain Mart—*NOTHING OVER $1.00!* the sign above the entrance screamed in large, neon-orange letters. I pushed open the finger-and-noseprint-smudged door and was immediately assaulted by cold, dry, musty air. My skin briefly bristled with a covering of goose bumps, and I couldn't help but shiver.

Little hellions ran wildly up and down the aisles, playing chase or keep-away, while parents browsed the dozens of bins, racks, shelves, and tubs of cheap products. Store clerks in matching Day-Glo orange smocks scurried back and forth like ants, followed closely by herds of customers waving their arms and yelling questions in English and Spanish and TexMex, that odd combination of both languages. I took an involuntary step back, then forced myself forward.

One of the few men in the store, and the only one wearing a suit, quietly picked up items that had been thoughtlessly dropped by the kids—or their parents. I figured he was more likely the manager than a member of that rare breed, a thoughtful customer.

I moved away from him and turned in a slow circle, scanning through the crowded store. Satisfied that my mystery woman hadn't slipped in through a back door, I walked to the first bin and looked in. It held a conglomeration of plastic bagel slicers and potato peelers. Each item was shrink-wrapped securely enough to survive a tornado and was mounted on a little cardboard backing, which looked more durable than the item it protected.

I walked quickly past the remaining displays to the back of the store. In the center of the back wall—a veritable monument to cheap paper products—was a single door clearly labeled *Employees Only*.

Never one to be deterred by a restrictive sign, I pulled the door open and stepped into a small employee's lounge. I assumed the door on the opposite side led to the warehouse area. A young blonde woman sat in a folding metal chair at a battered, puke-yellow linoleum and chrome table. She wore a white knit top, covered entirely with horizontal rows of hot pink flowers, and stretched so tightly across her breasts that one row of flowers was egg-shaped. *If those breasts are real, I'm Harrison Ford's long lost daughter.*

The young woman was painting her nails a bizarre shade of purple and singing an ear-assaulting, off-key rendition of that all-time Tammy Wynette classic *Stand By Your Man*. Thanks to the cheap nail polish, probably courtesy of a Bargain Mart bin, the air was tinged with an odd paint-and-formaldehyde smell I absolutely despise, because it reminds me of junior high, where shop class and biology were next door to one another. My stomach burbled in protest with each breath.

She jumped a foot and looked up guiltily when the door snicked shut behind me. Her sudden movement caused her orange smock, draped over the back of her chair, to slip into a polyester puddle on the floor. She didn't notice. She was too busy staring wide-eyed at me. Her frosted pink lips tried to smile but instead the left side just twitched a little. She either wasn't supposed to be on break or wasn't supposed to be painting her nails at work. Or both. At least she'd stopped singing.

I figured Rosie, my Regular Blue Collar Girl persona, was the right choice, so I pulled it out of my mental costume closet and put it on. I cocked my head and bit my lip. "Hi." I forced a silly grin. "I just started this morning and our boss, Mr. um..."

"Greenwood?" prompted the blonde.

"Yeah, Mr. Greenwood sent me back here for some more bagel slicers. I guess we had a run on 'em or somethin' or other. He acted like I was s'posed to know where they are, and I didn't want to, like, ya know, look stooopid." I smiled crookedly and twirled a lock of hair around my finger.

"Yeah, that sounds like ol' Woody." The blonde smiled and nodded. She held the bottle of nail polish like a baby bird, her fingers splayed wide to avoid touching anything, as she gingerly screwed the cap back on. She tucked it inside one of the small lockers on the wall. "Come on. I'll show you how the warehouse is laid out. By the way, I'm Pam."

"I'm Rosemary, and thanks."

Pam led the way to the warehouse door. When she reached it, she stopped and turned back to me. "The light switch for the warehouse is to the right inside this door." She opened the door just far enough to slip her hand through. I heard a faint click and the crack in the door glowed brightly. "I never go in here until I turn on the light. The dark creeps me out." Pam pulled the door open the rest of the way and we entered.

I felt both disappointed and satisfied. The woman I'd followed was clearly not in here. The warehouse area was much smaller than I expected, it looked to be only about four-hundred square feet. The walls were lined with metal shelves, stacked floor to ceiling with flimsy-looking, corrugated cardboard boxes. All were stamped on the side with the country of origin, most of which didn't even exist when I was in school. None said *Made in USA*. A small folding table, topped with a box opener blade, scissors, packing tape, and marking pens, stood in the middle of the room.

"These boxes are all labeled with whatever is inside them." Pam explained as she gestured at the walls. "That's part of my job when the shipments come in. I check the contents and then write it on the side of the box." Pam lifted her chin, clearly proud of her extra responsibility.

"Cool," I responded. It seemed appropriate. She'd probably had to work hard to earn the added duty. And I'd bet a steak dinner she hadn't earned a raise along with it.

Pam pulled down a box she had neatly labeled BAGGLE SLISERS and opened it. It was about half full. I grabbed a handful. Pam counted the slicers in my hand, picked up a marking pen, mumbled under her breath as she did some quick math, then crossed out the 43 already on the side of the box and wrote 32 beneath it. She closed the box and put it away.

"Thanks," I said as we exited the storage room. Pam turned off the light, pulling her hand back just before the door closed.

"Always remember to turn off the light or Woody gets really pissed."

"Okay."

"Where's your smock?" Pam asked as we crossed the break room.

"Woody said I'd get one in the morning," I ventured. The last thing I needed was to re-enter the store wearing a smock that might as well be imprinted with *customers please surround me and yell questions.*

"I guess the cleaners didn't get them back on time again." Pam shrugged. "Not the first time."

"Yeah, guess so." I nodded vigorously, happy my excuse worked.

Pam remained at my side as we crossed the room, and it became clear she planned to follow me into the store. "You didn't get a chance to finish doing your nails." I pointed to Pam's right hand. "I'll cover for you if you want to do the last two."

"Thanks Rosemary! I promise I won't be long."

"No problem. I'll tell Woody you're organizing boxes."

Pam was circling the table toward her locker as I left the room. I could hear her again mangling Tammy's legacy song as the door closed behind me.

I dropped the bagel slicers into a nearby bin, put my regular personality back on, and left. I'd just rounded the corner of the building when I saw a puff of exhaust from the blue Taurus's tailpipe as Ms. Mystery Woman started it up. *Damn!* I sprinted for my car, dodging a white Cadillac and a rusted out Chevy Nova as I ran diagonally across the street. I knew she probably saw me, but I didn't give a rat's ass. I just didn't want to lose her so soon.

The Mustang's door handle seared my fingertips with the intensity of a barbecue grill. "Ahhhhh," I hissed. You'd think after living in south central Texas for most of my life I'd remember that metal surfaces on a car can get hot enough to fry an egg. I bit my lip against the pain as I jerked the door open and threw myself in. I yelped as the exposed bare skin on my legs encountered the hundred-plus degree leather.

I scooted as far forward in the seat as I could, grasped the key with two fingertips and fired up the ignition, flipped the air conditioner to Arctic Blast, and peeled out. The Taurus had already moved out of site. I reached the first intersection and swiveled my head like a dashboard bobble dog, trying to figure out which direction she'd turned. I caught site of her car to my right, just as she turned right again.

I turned, shifted up as fast as I could, and accelerated toward the next intersection. When I turned again, I saw her ahead of me, with half a dozen cars between us. I moved behind an air conditioning service truck, hoping its bulk would somewhat conceal my bright red Mustang. If I had it to do over again, I'd buy a nice, nondescript color, but I'd had my Mustang for many years, and affection—not to mention finances—meant I'd keep it for a few more.

We drove through town for ten minutes or so. She turned every two to three blocks. I wondered if she was trying to lose me, but she didn't seem in a hurry. She never dodged around any other cars or went faster than the speed limit. Either she wasn't aware I was following her—fat chance, I figured, since I hadn't been exactly subtle—or she didn't give a damn. I tried to catch up several times, but each effort was thwarted by a red light or stupid driver. I could feel my blood pressure rising with every failed attempt.

Finally, the woman turned toward Interstate 35. I followed, but the idiot in front of me came to a complete stop at the end of the highway's entrance ramp. I nearly plowed into his yellow Camaro's butt and only managed to miss breeding our cars by slamming on my brakes and pulling hard onto the shoulder, which was sparkling like a diamond mine from broken glass.

I compulsively glanced at his license plate, K22 HMM. Yeah, I could almost picture him in a *Killer Tutu for Heavy Metal Music*. I grinned at the thought, but that didn't keep me from leaning hard on my horn and throwing a variety of creative hand gestures in his direction.

He never even graced my excellent mime with a half-glance. He just waited until there was a narrow opening in the heavy traffic and pulled out. Brakes squealed and horns chorused as the seventy mile-per-hour traffic bobbed and wove like bumper-cars, trying to dodge around his car as it slowly accelerated from zero.

I hauled ass around him, plunging in among the dozens of weaving cars and trucks. I was too late. I craned my neck, but couldn't see the blue Taurus anywhere ahead of me. Ms. Very Bad Woman might have taken the next exit ramp for all I knew.

"Aargh!" I rocked in my seat, jerking my arms against the steering wheel. "Asshole!" I yelled at my rearview mirror, as if it could reflect my sentiments back to the idiot, who was still choreographing a traffic ballet behind me. *I hope his tutu makes him itch.*

I was so angry I was shaking. No wonder the Texas Highway Department had recently started an entire television campaign titled *Tips for Using Entrance and Exit Ramps.* I took the next exit ramp, *without* stopping at the end, and pulled into a Walmart parking lot. I sat thinking for a minute, chugging hot, plastic-flavored water from an Ozarka bottle.

I sighed and reached for my cell phone. I'd try pinging Larry for yet another favor. Besides, he owed me one. I'd recently replaced the brake pads on his Ford Bronco. I'd known Larry Morrow since we were five, and except for a few years when an experimental marriage on my part and college on both our parts interfered, we'd remained best buds. We'd briefly tried dating, but decided we liked each other too much to take a chance on ruining everything.

Fortunately for me, Larry was an officer in the Austin Police Department. Unfortunately, he wasn't in, so I left a message. "Hi, Larry, its Marianna. Could you run a check on a license plate for me? I'd run it through myself, but I'm nowhere near my office, and I'm too impatient to wait 'til I get there. It's a light blue Taurus, license H59 VBW. I'm fixin' to head back to Austin. I'll talk to you later." I set the phone to vibrate, tucked it between my legs, and floored the Mustang's gas pedal.

BE PREPARED

You can get more with a kind word and a gun than you can with a kind word alone. ~Al Capone (1899-1947)

Stephanie waited until the gray door closed behind her before flipping on the lights and turning the lock. She leaned against the wall and closed her eyes. That bitch was out there again today, sitting in her little red car. Stephanie smirked. *At least Mizzzz Marianna Morgan is having to bake in the heat while she* does her snooping.

Stephanie pushed herself off the wall, spewing forth a stream of expletives that ended in a guttural laugh. "I don't care who she thinks she is, or who she's working for," she spat into the empty room. "I will *not* put up with this shit."

She'd noticed the woman in the red Mustang three days ago. It was hard to miss such a nice car in this neighborhood. Even so, when it first caught her attention, she hadn't thought much about it. Then she'd seen that a woman was sitting inside, and in this goddamned heat. That alone made Stephanie's mental alarm bells go off, so she'd turned the corner and kept going.

When the Mustang was still there yesterday Stephanie got pissed. She'd worked hard to find this out-of-the-way spot. She didn't know who this woman was or what she wanted, but she decided to find out. The woman may have nothing to do with her, but Stephanie didn't take chances anymore.

Good thing Tom had ways to find out things about people, things like where they lived and what they did for a living. All he needed was a license plate and a handful of cash. Tom had called back within a couple of hours—name, address, occupation.

Stephanie huffed in disgust. *Ms. Marianna Morgan, Private Investigator, is going to be one surprised bitch when she gets her mail today or tomorrow.*

Rooting in the depths of her leather shoulder bag—more a portable suitcase than a purse—Stephanie extracted her comb. She ran the comb slowly and lovingly through her waist-length hair, which was already soft and shiny. She closed her eyes and breathed deeply. Her taut muscles unwound and her fever-hot anger cooled—some.

She adjusted the dark brown waves so they framed and partially covered her angular facial features. Stephanie loved how her hair cloaked her face. When she wanted to hide from others, she tipped her head down and her hair cascaded forward, blocking out those around her.

Stephanie moved into the depths of the room, checking her supplies and making sure everything was undisturbed. She nodded with satisfaction and relief. No one else had been there. She checked her answering machine, which sat on a small shelf near the back of the room.

The machine had recorded two messages. Stephanie pressed Play then almost hit the Delete button as soon as she heard Melissa's sweet, sappy voice. The skinny little bitch always sounded like she was talking to a bunch of preschoolers. Stephanie sighed. The message might be important, so she resigned herself to listening to what Melissa had to say.

"Hi Stepheeeee, it's meeeee! I talked to Tommy this morning and he said he'd made another big sale, so he's gonna have a party at his place. I don't know about you, but I sure can use some moola, so I'm gonna hit him up for some of it. I'm broke again, as usual!"

Melissa's voice broke into a series of squeaky-door-hinge giggles. "Anyway, I thought you might like to know. He also said you're looking for an old gun or rifle or something like that. Carlos said he knows of a guy who might know about that icky stuff. He said he'd hook us up. Aneeeewaaaaaay, I'll let you know if I learn anything. And maybe I'll be lucky, and the guy'll be cute and he'll buy me dinner or whatever. Later. Bye-bye!"

Stephanie rolled her eyes and gritted her teeth. *Okay. Fine. Good. Swell. I listened to the whole damn message, which didn't really tell me much of anything, except that I probably need to intervene quickly before Melissa blows a possible lead on the gun.* Stephanie pressed Delete and waited for the second message to play.

"Hey there Stephie ol' gal." Tom snorted. "Gotcher stuff. Don't forget you gotta be here at two. And bring my money. See ya."

Stephanie frowned at Tom's setting the time they'd meet, obviously with no thought as to whether or not it was convenient for her. She deleted the second message and checked her makeup and hair in the dingy, wood-framed mirror crudely duct-taped to the back wall. Her nose and eyes were red again. *Damn allergies. Whoever named this the Allergy Capital of the World had it about right.*

She dug into her bag, pulled out a small white bottle, and squirted a couple of liberal shots up her nose. The nasal spray was the only way she could keep from having to breathe through her mouth like a panting dog. And July was supposed to be one of the months with the lowest pollen count. She sniffed and wiped her nose, then dropped the bottle and comb back into her bag. *I'm probably getting hooked on the spray, but that's just too damn bad.*

The monstrous bag was also her Quick Getaway Kit. Inside was a change of clothes, makeup, toiletries, and several hundred dollars in cash. Soon, it would also include the *stuff* that Tom had for her. She'd lived loose and fast ever since that terrible death, always on the move. *Be Prepared* had become her mantra. The old Girl Scout motto was the only thing she remembered from her brief stint as a Brownie, but it served her well.

She'd only been back a few months and was still getting her bearings. San Antonio hadn't changed much, but Stephanie had remained on the fringe, hooking up with few people. She wasn't ready for some to know her whereabouts, so she maintained several anonymous hideaways.

A couple, like this one, were primarily for storage. She had another where she slept on occasion. And there was Whiskey Smith's, a nondescript bar in Terrell Hills, where she could relax. It was close to her old neighborhood, as close as she was ever going to get toward recovering her lost childhood.

Most of the time she lived by her wits. She managed just fine, but she was tired. She intended to see the ordeal through to whatever might be waiting at the end. She was no longer sure. Maybe she'd never been sure.

She knew Stephen was trying to find her, but she wasn't ready. Too many years had passed since she'd had any contact with her family. It had been stupid to attend those public functions. She should have known better. But she was determined to find that damn rifle, so she made a point of checking into each new ground breaking.

It was a long shot, but she didn't have anything else to go on yet. She'd definitely have to get in touch with Carlos and find out who the hell he was talking about, and why he was setting up that ditz Melissa instead of herself.

To Stephanie, the rifle's value was much bigger than the price a collector would pay, it was a blood debt. Finding the rifle would help put that whole sordid past behind her. Maybe she could finally find some peace.

That was where Tom Darnell came in. She'd run into him at Whiskey Smith's bar the first time she'd gone there. Stephanie'd worked him like a pro, getting him to spill his guts about his shady income methods. He wasn't too bright, but he and his buddies, Carlos and Virgil, definitely had a knack for making extra money buying and selling pretty much anything they could get their hands on, including antiques and collectibles.

Stephanie had known she'd need help finding a gun stolen so many years ago. Tom had been as good a place as any to start, although he was starting to get annoying. She had no tolerance for sex-hungry men.

She glanced at the large, masculine watch buckled on her wrist. It was easier to read and tougher than a delicate woman's watch. Tom had said two o'clock, which was only an hour from now. She couldn't miss this meeting. Another opportunity would be hard to arrange. She grabbed her bag and headed out. Ms. Morgan's car was still there, she noted as she climbed into her Taurus.

She turned the ignition and glanced in the mirror, exploding into laughter at the sight of the poor private investigator running across the street. *This should be fun. You wanna see where I'm going, sweetie? Like hell. But I'll go slow for a bit so you can at least think you're making progress. A little cat and mouse sounds like fun.*

With that, Stephanie pulled gently and smoothly away from the curb. She didn't turn the corner until she saw Ms. Morgan's car heading in her direction.

"You're late." Tom scowled as Stephanie slammed her car door and walked toward his truck.

"Traffic complications." She laughed.

"I gotta clock in at work in forty minutes. Here." He handed her a wrinkled brown grocery bag. "Glock 30. Hand cannon."

Stephanie opened the bag, lifted out the handgun, and hefted it. The weight, a pound or so, she guessed, felt solid and stable. She smiled. "Tell me about it."

"Forty-five caliber, ten rounds to a magazine, semi-automatic."

"Show me."

Tom spent the next few minutes giving her Gun 101 lessons—how to load the magazine with bullets and insert it into the base of the grip, how to rack the slide to load a bullet into the firing chamber, how to hold the gun and squeeze the trigger in one smooth, slow movement so she didn't jerk it the moment it fired.

"Satisfied?" He hacked a large blob of tobacco juice onto the ground and pushed his stringy blond hair off his greasy forehead.

Stephanie made a disgusted face. "No. I want to practice some shots."

"Ah crap, Steph, I don't have time." He kicked the dirt where he'd just spat.

"Yes you do. The Snake Farm is only ten minutes from here."

He heaved a big sigh. "Come on."

He led her around to the back of the decrepit, single-wide trailer to where three large red and white paper bullseye targets were already tacked to a couple of fence posts about twenty yards from where they stood. The red was faded, but the targets were still in usable shape. Tom was obviously a lousy shot. The center of each target was almost whole, only the outer edges of the white paper was peppered with holes.

"Have a ball." Tom pulled up a lawn chair covered in torn, stringy webbing, and sat down.

"You have to spot for me." Stephanie frowned. "These piece-of-shit used targets'll make it hard for me to see where my shots go."

He just nodded and spat dark brown tobacco juice on the dirt between his feet.

After twenty minutes and thirty rounds—ten in each target—Stephanie lowered the gun and smiled. It'd been easy to spot her shots, most had gone through the pristine center circles—which sure weren't pristine anymore.

"Damn girl, that's some shootin'. You must be a natural." Tom stood and kicked the chair out of his way. "Wish I had more time to watch you mangle my targets, but I gotta get going."

"Fine. How much?"

"Six-fifty."

She counted out thirty-two twenties. "Here's six-forty. That'll have to do."

He frowned. "Yeah, okay." He stuffed the cash in his pocket.

Stephanie followed Tom back to the trailer. He went inside and returned shortly, carrying a small Playmate ice chest and a six pack of Bud. He grinned at her raised eyebrow as she watched him shove five cans into the ice-filled cooler.

"Hey." He shrugged. "I like to have somethin' cool to drink when I'm on my breaks." He popped the top on the can he held and took a long, noisy swallow. "This one won't fit. Guess I'll have to go ahead and drink it now."

He sauntered toward her, grabbed her at the waist with his free hand, and pulled her roughly toward him. "I could take a few minutes, though, if you'd like some fun with a *real* man. I bet I could show you a thing or two. I wouldn't mind being late for that."

Stephanie jerked away. "Get away from me. We're strictly business. Don't forget that."

"Whatever you say, Stephie ol' gal." Tom uttered loud, hoarse laugh. "See ya later." He spat again, climbed into his battered truck, and drove off.

She watched with narrowed eyes until he was out of sight, then she got into her car and started the motor. Her hands shook with anger. To calm herself she spent five minutes combing and smoothing her hair before heading back to San Antonio. Her rapid-fire pulse slowed with each brush stroke.

Tom's a problem. I don't need any more problems. Now that she knew Carlos might have a line on the rifle, she didn't even need Tom much at all anymore.

"Yeah, Tom, see ya later," Stephanie said into her rearview mirror as Tom's white-trash trailer receded in the distance.

A FACE FROM THE PAST

Men willingly believe what they wish.
~Julius Caesar (c.102-44 BC)

Stephen Davidson sat by the window in his darkened apartment. He blinked and yawned. He'd spent most of the day sleeping, fighting another dreadful headache. He felt groggy and fuzzy, as if the hours of sleep had been a complete waste of time.

He unconsciously stroked his shiny, premature bald spot. The remains of his sandy blonde hair ringed his head in a fluffy halo. His dark green eyes were thoughtful as he stared in silence at the early evening sights and cheerful sounds of San Antonio's River Walk.

It was only Thursday, but the number of tourists moving along the famous Paseo del Rio was already swelling toward the weekend crowds. In spite of the July heat, he had his living room window slightly open. An odd combination of smells drifted in—Mexican food from the restaurant in the river-level floor of his building, exhaust fumes from cars and buses traveling the adjacent streets, the mossy, organic smell emanating from the river itself. He occasionally heard a snippet of dialogue from a guide on one of the endless parade of sightseer-packed river barges, laughter from a vacationer, the crying of a tired child.

Stephen watched the shadowed tourists walking along the sidewalk five stories below him. In another hour, it would be dark, and most of the tourists would be gone, having dinner in an area restaurant, or watching TV in their hotel rooms. Then he'd take his canvas bag of canned cat food and feed the small army of strays that lived among the weeds south of downtown.

He only had to walk along the river's edge for a mile or so until the concrete sidewalk ended and the 1800s began. It was the northernmost border of the twenty-five-square-block King William Historic Area, originally settled by German merchants and later zoned as the state's first Historic District.

Most of the King William neighborhood was filled with enormous homes with cupolas, two-story white columns, and wrap-around porches. At the far northern edge of the neighborhood, though, only a few homes existed, perched atop the high, sloping banks of the river.

The lower banks were still wild and untamed. Native plants grew in unruly tangles to the very edge of the water. The deep, murky water teemed with thirty pound carp and catfish, and an impressive number of sleek, deadly water moccasins. The cats lived along this part of the river, between Nueva St. and the sprawling, manicured HEB Grocery headquarters.

Stephen had talked about the Howard E. Butt family with Dr. Myer, his psychiatrist, comparing their childhoods to his own. He'd attended school at the same time as several of the Butt sons. Stephen described the abuse he'd regularly endured from the school's meanest bully. He'd often wondered afterward how the Butt kids had made it through school in one piece with a last name like that.

At least the Butts all ended up with the last laugh. They owned one of the largest private grocery chains in the country. Stephen had not been so successful. Dr. Myer listened patiently, then asked Stephen what held him back from attaining his own success.

Stephen hadn't had a good answer for that question. Dr. Myer diagnosed depression and tried to get Stephen to take anti-depressants. Stephen resisted and promised to stop dwelling on the past, to get out of his apartment more, and to try to make some friends. That'd been three months ago.

True to his word, Stephen had started walking almost every evening. He was walking late one evening when he had to stop and wait for two city workers to finish unloading some equipment and unblock the sidewalk and street.

"How-do," replied a gray-haired man in a khaki jumpsuit, printed on the back with City of San Antonio Public Works Department.

"Evening." Stephen nodded.

"You're out late," said the younger maintenance man.

"I don't much like the daytime crowds."

"A local, huh." The gray-haired man grinned. "Me, neither. That's why I work the night shift."

"You should check out the South Town area," The younger man said.

"South Town?" Stephen asked.

"Thata way." He wave of his hand. "Walk south about a mile and all this tourist crap stops."

"Yep." The older man nodded. "Quiet and wild down there. Jus' watch fer snakes."

"I'll do that," Stephen said. "Thanks."

Stephen smiled at the memory. That was how he'd discovered the feral cats. And the maintenance men had been right. Tourists never ventured along the river this far south of the main downtown area. Stephen could walk here to relax and explore far from the noise and crowds.

When he discovered them, Stephen immediately felt sorry for the dozen or so skinny, timid cats. He loved cats. They gave affection only to those they trusted. And the little gypsy cats along the river reminded him of himself as a small boy, afraid of his own shadow and lonely, but still desperate for affection. They were only now starting to trust him a little. They wouldn't yet get within arm's length, but they did at least come out and start eating while he was still there.

Sometimes, after returning from a midnight feeding, Stephen would wander the two and a half miles of stone walkways that ran along both sides of the developed part of the river. He enjoyed it then, when it was empty and quiet, when even the hardiest tourists had retired to bed. The only people he usually ran into were the police foot patrol and maintenance crews.

Once in a while, he still saw the two men who'd directed him toward the quiet part of the river. He'd learned their names were Gil and Enrico. They were probably the people he'd spent the most time talking to in the six months he'd been back in San Antonio. Except for Dr. Myer.

Stephen stared out the window, wondering what Gil and Enrico did before they started their night shifts. As the sky began to soften into dusk, a brightly lit Yanaguana barge cruised by Stephen's building. He waved back to a young girl who'd seen him sitting in his window. She bounced with excitement, causing little ripples to fan out from the water around the barge. Her mother pulled her back down onto the bench seat, but the youngster managed to sneak one last wave before the barge moved out of sight. The little girl reminded Stephen of his sister. Stephanie would've loved the River Walk. She'd have wanted to ride the barges every weekend.

The popular tourist barges, named after the Payaya Indian word for the clear water of the spring-fed river, were almost always full. The narrated tour covered much more of the River Walk than most could manage to walk. Stephen was determined to overcome his shyness and ride one of the barges. He wanted to venture onto the beautiful River Walk when the sun was shining and the area was alive with activity.

He'd promised Dr. Myer he'd stop *lurking about at night like a vampire,* as the doctor put it. So after he'd been living on the River Walk for three months, Stephen began forcing himself to go out during the day.

His first daytime foray was by taxi to the San Antonio Museum of Art, housed in the original Lone Star Brewery building. He'd chosen the museum because of its location. He'd once toured the brewery and Hall of Horns with his fourth grade class. He still remembered the excitement of watching the machines and conveyer belts in action, brewing and bottling the beer.

He and his friends had hoped they'd get to taste the forbidden drink, but at the end of the tour they'd been given frosty mugs of root beer. Although disappointed at their lack of actual alcohol, they'd still had a great time. And touring the Hall of Horns, with its collection of bizarre two-headed calves and deer and bulls with strange and sometimes self-piercing antler and horn configurations, had made the young school kids feel like they were inside a horror movie.

These days, the Hall of Horns collection was a tourist magnet on the River Walk. The museum now occupying the original brewery included more sophisticated exhibits from ancient Greece, Rome, and Latin America.

He next tried visiting the main downtown San Antonio Public Library, which he discovered he could reach on foot via back streets, avoiding the crowded River Walk and other downtown tourist areas. He found he loved the place and began visiting a couple of times a week. There were no screaming children or excited tourists, just the occasional shuffle of pages being flipped and whispers of those seeking assistance.

Stephen felt at peace walking among the maze-like stacks. He spent hours in the Texana area, reading about the history and geography of his home state. The reference librarian was always friendly and helped him locate some of the more obscure historical publications.

After weeks of enjoying his library visits, Stephen tried to join the bustling daytime crowds on the River Walk below his apartment. But his most recent attempt, only the day before, had sent his pulse racing and his heart pounding. He'd made it only one block from the apartment when his anxiety level grew too much to bear. He'd scurried back home, feeling both disappointment and shame. He decided he'd stick with the library and South Town for a while longer.

He wished his life was less complicated, less scattered. On his lap was a recent copy of the *San Antonio News*, folded open to page four. The cheap newsprint paper was already yellowing. He gently patted the photo. He'd probably looked at it several hundred times. He didn't notice that his fingers grew smudged with newsprint ink. He stroked his bald head again, leaving little black skidmarks across his scalp.

The five-by-seven inch photo wasn't very clear, but it had immediately caught his eye. It accompanied the story of the recent ground-breaking for the ten-thousand-plus seat HemisFair Arena, which was to be located on part of what used to be HemisFair Plaza, site of the 1968 World's Fair.

Stephen had mixed memories about that time in his life. He'd been seven when his sister and Dad had died, and ten when HemisFair finally opened. He and his mom spent many hours there during its six-month run, trying to forget, or maybe just move beyond, that tragic night. He shook his head hard, forcing all the painful memories back into the dark corner of his mind where they belonged.

He'd noticed the photo not because of the significance of the sports arena, or the executives and politicians clustered in the foreground, each grinning and holding a shiny, brand new shovel, ready to break ground that had already been carefully softened and prepared for them. It was that one face in the background that grabbed him and wouldn't let go.

She was only a tiny image in the background, but it was definitely the same woman he'd seen twice before. She was tall, with long, dark hair. The first time he'd seen her was two months ago, four months after he moved back to San Antonio. He was watching the evening news, paying only slight attention to a report about an open house at the old Crockett Hotel. But then he'd seen her standing in the hotel's lobby, sipping a glass of wine.

Can it really be Stephanie? After all this time? He'd always believed she'd died years earlier. He'd told Dr. Myer all about his childhood tragedy, but not about the photo or his hope that it was his sister. He was sure the doctor would insist he go on medication, or worse, recommend he spend some time at the San Antonio State Hospital, where crazy people and drug addicts were sent in hopes they'd get better. He was afraid he'd find he'd only been hallucinating or, at the very least, extrapolating beyond reason.

He hoped Ms. Morgan found out soon, because he couldn't bear to wait long to know the truth. He was too embarrassed to tell the private investigator he suspected she was following his returned-from-the-dead sister. He didn't want Ms. Morgan to think he was crazy anymore than he wanted his doctor to reach the same conclusion.

At first, he'd assumed it was just wishful thinking, that his mind was playing tricks on him with a woman who had a similar look. But one month later, he'd seen her again, in a newspaper article about the opening of the annual downtown Fiesta de San Antonio celebration. He'd studied the photo for hours. He still wasn't sure, but he was cautiously hopeful. It was shortly thereafter that the dreams started.

Three weeks ago, he found her face for the third time, in the photo accompanying the newspaper article he now held on his lap.

He'd called the newspaper the following day, and requested a copy of the photo, but they wouldn't let him have one. Instead he ordered a dozen copies of the paper so he wouldn't have to worry about over-handling and smudging his only copy.

Stephen thought at first of trying to find the woman himself, but he wasn't trained in the art of finding people. Besides, he was afraid. If it really was her, why hadn't she ever tried to contact him?

He'd made a few discreet inquiries among his associates and clients in Austin, where he still maintained a CPA business. Two of them, one an insurance company executive and the other an attorney, had recommended Marianna Morgan. He'd decided to give her a try.

They'd met at her small Austin office last Friday. He gave Ms. Morgan a copy of the newspaper article containing the photo and asked her to locate the woman and find out who she was. He also told her about the blue Taurus and the intersection by the Bargain Mart.

He had not, however, told her he'd seen those in a dream. He was convinced Ms. Morgan would simply think he was crazy. Maybe he was. But even though his logical mind balked, he wanted to believe the dreams were real, that they were actually proof Stephanie was back and their old bond was returning. After all, they'd once been so close, almost inseparable.

He'd even known that time Stephanie had badly twisted her arm when she fell off the slide. He rushed home from Brian's house, arriving while Mom was still on the phone with the doctor. Mom had raised her eyebrows when he rushed through the door, then she'd just smiled and nodded.

Stephen set the newspaper aside and closed his eyes. The raging headache was now only a dull thud, but he could feel it like a ball rolling around in his head, trying to return to full strength. He supposed the stress of not knowing the truth was what had caused his headaches to start. He'd just have to be patient.

He opened his eyes as a raucous burst of laughter spilled through his window. He smiled. He wanted to be that happy again. He *would* be that happy again. No matter what. He'd either find his sister alive after all these years, or he'd learn that he'd been mistaken. Either way, he promised himself, he'd move on with his life, even if it meant taking the damn anti-depressants.

His own life had been unravelling slowly for the past year. After several years of caring for his mother, whose body was slowly eaten away by cancer, Stephen suddenly found himself alone. Six months after her death, he sold his large, comfortable home in Austin's affluent West Lake Hills neighborhood and moved to the small apartment in downtown San Antonio.

But even after living here for six months, most of Stephen's face-to-face conversations still took place in Austin. He drove to his office, ninety miles to the north, twice a week. He only continued to maintain his business at all to service his current clients—with whom he'd worked for many years—out of a sense of loyalty. The small income they provided wasn't really necessary.

He'd been very frugal, had inherited what little his mother had, and had made a large profit on the sale of the home. He considered his continued business activities a minor inconvenience, and a small price to pay for being able to live in San Antonio.

If Stephanie really was alive, she was here, so here was where he had to live, too.

A KILLER PICKUP AND A DISAPPEARING TAURUS

Hard to see, the dark side is. ~Yoda,
Star Wars: The Phantom Menace (1980)

I sped up Interstate 35 toward my office in Austin, dodging around the preponderance of what my neighbors Stan and Eddie call *sluckers*—slow fuckers—puttering along in the lanes around me. I blew on my finger, trying to calm the fresh blister's stinging, courtesy of Pickle Toy's door handle.

Traffic was moving briskly along at eighty. *Speed limit? We don't need no stinkin' speed limit.* I wondered if the Entrance Ramp Idiot was still somewhere behind me giving other drivers fits. At least that was one problem I was done with. One down, 492,894 to go.

I was cranky from my unproductive day spent baking in an automotive oven and losing the person I was supposed to be following. To make matters worse, my mind kept floating back to *Stand By Your Man.*

Damn. If I ever see Pam again, I'll give her hell. It was her fault that stupid song was now stuck in my head.

I turned on the oldies rock station. My day instantly got better as the speakers burst forth with the opening strains of *Hotel California,* my all-time favorite song. I sang along, cranking up both the radio's and my volume. I was just belting out the chorus when I noticed a trucker grinning at me from the adjacent lane. I grinned back and shrugged, but continued my singing. *Hey, it's my car, I can turn it into a private concert hall if I like.*

My cell phone vibrated with an incoming call. It's hard to hear the chime over the radio and general road noise, so I always switch it to vibrate and tuck it between my legs. After a brief thrill from the viby-sensation, I scrambled to turn the radio down before the call dumped to voicemail. "Hello, this is Marianna."

"Hello, Luv," a familiar voice sang.

"Hello, Aunt Louise, how are you?" I smiled. Aunt Louise is really my Uncle Louie. He's been cross-dressing for so many years that everyone calls him Aunt Louise, at first behind his back and eventually to his face. He loved the name, although he claimed quite emphatically that he had no desire to *cut off his little johnny*—he simply preferred women's clothes.

Uncle Louie'd loved his silk and lace since before I was born, so to me his choice of dress was as natural for him as his curly black hair. And I'd never called him anything but Aunt Louise. I occasionally wondered how he'd survived childhood, but didn't want my impression of Aunt Louise as a happy and content person to be shattered by painful stories of ridicule or beatings.

"I called to warn you." Aunt Louise interrupted my musings. "My crystal ball has sent me dire news."

"What is it?" I refrained from adding *this time.* Everyone in the family—and all my friends for that matter—knows that Aunt Louise fancies herself as a psychic and spends hours each week staring into her crystal ball or reading tarot cards. We all humor her, because we know she's trying to look out for us in her own way. And often as not, she's actually right, or seems to be. We've never been sure if it's all just coincidence or if she really has some psychic ability. But we love her too much to ever question her—at least to her face.

"You are in danger." Aunt Louise's voice trembled.

"Are you serious?"

"My dear, the spirits do not lie."

I cleared my throat. "Of course. I'm sorry." I was glad Aunt Louise couldn't see my smirk. It'd have hurt her feelings. "What else can you tell me?"

"A pickup truck will put you in serious danger. You must promise you will be extremely careful around suspicious trucks."

Suspicious trucks? "Um, sure, I promise. Did the crystal ball tell you what color the truck was?"

"No, dear, I'm so sorry. All I could tell is that it was a light color."

"That's okay, I'll be sure to be careful. Thank you for the warning."

"It's the least I can do for my favorite niece. How are your babies?"

"They're fine. As well behaved and loving as usual."

"How many cats do you have now? Five?"

"No, six. Boggle, Polly, Cooper, Mayfly, Georgie, and Deke."

"When did you get Deke?"

"Three months ago. I found him in a drainage ditch next to a Dairy Queen. His real name is DQ, but Deke is easier to say."

"You know, you act like such a tough girl, but deep inside you have a gentle soul. I fully expect you to turn into one of those eccentric old ladies who has forty three cats and yells at the neighbors."

"Who says I'm not already eccentric and yelling at neighbors? And I seem to be working on my total cat count."

Aunt Louise laughed a throaty, baritone laugh. "I'll agree that you're a bit eccentric, but I doubt you yell at the neighbors."

I wasn't sure how I felt about someone like Aunt Louise calling *me* eccentric, but I decided not to pursue it.

"Come see me soon?" Aunt Louise asked.

"I'll do my best." I hung up the phone, smiling as I scanned the highway around me for Killer Pickup Trucks.

Not far north of San Antonio, I saw the familiar yellow billboards —*Snake Farm!* they proclaimed in bright red letters. Those signs always make me think of snakes planted tail first, sprouting up in neat, long rows, their heads waving and tongues flicking as they wait for food. A *Motel Hell* for snakes.

Each sign for the roadside attraction proclaims a different amazing fact. *Worlds Biggest Snake!* says one. *Thousands of snakes!* proclaims another. *Stuffed gorilla!* shouts a third. Some day I'm going to stop and check the place out. I especially want to find out what a stuffed gorilla has to do with snakes. The image of a giant gorilla towering over a cage full of snakes makes me laugh. Would the snakes think it was a real gorilla? Would they even have a clue what a gorilla was? Would they give a damn even if they did know?

I'm also curious about the legitimacy of the place. The rumor when I was growing up in San Antonio claimed the Snake Farm was a front for a whorehouse. When I had a lot of spare time—which would probably be never—I'd find out if that was true or only the wishful thinking of horny teenage boys.

I was just approaching the final Snake Farm sign—*Exit Now for Slithering Fun!*—when a beat up, white Chevy pickup truck barreled up on my tail and swerved wildly around me. The heavy-duty grill guard came within inches of clipping my rear bumper. I stomped my brakes and swerved as far onto the shoulder as possible, while simultaneously shooting the finger and yelling a string of expletives that would have made my retired-machinist-father proud.

The driver obliviously shot across the road, the bed of the truck fishtailing twice in response to the Indy 500 maneuvering. I heard the distinct *tink* sound of loose gravel being slung against my car by the truck's off-road tires. The pickup just barely made it onto the Snake Farm exit ramp. I caught a brief glimpse of a bright red and yellow Snake Farm bumper sticker on the rusted rear bumper before the truck disappeared from view.

I took a couple of deep breaths to help return my heart rate and adrenaline levels to normal. *Crap, I didn't even catch the truck's license plate.* At least I'd noticed the Snake Farm bumper sticker, so some part of my PI brain was engaged in more than basic survival. "Well I'll be damned." I shook my head at my own reflection. "I guess Aunt Louise was right!"

I checked for traffic and eased off the shoulder. The driver of that truck was friggin' crazy. It was a damn good thing traffic wasn't bad today. There's almost no margin for error along this section of the Interstate, where ongoing construction means narrowed lanes and heavy concrete barriers instead of safety shoulders. Interstate 35 has been in this perpetual state of *improvement* since I was a girl. Somewhere, I figured, some bureaucrat decided to make a career out of endlessly altering this ninety mile stretch of asphalt.

At least the rolling Texas hills, dotted with their dark green ash junipers and bright green oaks, helped me relax and shake off the near miss. Today was proving to be a multi-faceted frustration. In addition to having an encounter with a pickup truck, I was not happy about losing track of Ms. Mystery Woman and her Amazing Disappearing Blue Taurus. I was going to have to push Davidson for additional information. I was sure he knew more than he was saying—I just didn't know why he wasn't saying it.

My cell phone vibrated again. "Hello, this is Marianna."

"Hey, Cutie, whatcha doin?"

"Larry! Thanks for calling me back. I'm halfway between San Antonio and Austin. Just got off the phone with Aunt Louise."

"What is it this time?" He snorted.

"Killer Pickup Trucks."

"What?"

"Never mind. I'll tell you later. What's up with you?"

"You asked about a light blue Taurus, license H59 VBW." His voice switched into Official Police Officer, although I'd bet he didn't realize it. "It's registered to a Mabel Winston. I went ahead on my lunch hour and called her for you. I knew you'd ask me to anyway. She sold it, for $6500 cash, six months ago. She's a bit elderly and doesn't remember the name of the woman who bought it or what happened to the receipt. The new owner still hasn't filed any registration papers. Sorry I don't know more than that."

"That's okay, Sweetie, why spoil my run of bad luck? Time for dinner or coffee sometime soon? I miss you. You're one of the few pleasant constants in my life these days. I'll buy, as long as it's cheap."

"You sure know how to persuade a guy." He laughed. "How about Tuesday? I can meet you at Donn's Depot for drinks and we can decide where to go from there."

"Sounds like a plan. I'll see you at seven. Oh, and thanks for calling Mabel for me." *Too bad she was a dead end.*

I made it to the Winchester Office Center in record time. The building was a hulking combination of mud-brown brick and white limestone. The somber—actually ugly—facade made the WOC look like an old library or bank. Maybe my luck was improving, though. There was a parking spot under the monstrous three-hundred-year-old oak that grew beside the cramped, eight-space lot behind the building. I whipped into the narrow space, pulling as far forward as possible so my whole Mustang would be in the shade.

I hadn't even made it out of the car before a noisy, black grackle deposited a large bird poop on my hood. I scowled at the bird but shrugged it off. I'd rather have a cool car than a clean one. Besides, maybe the bird was psychic and was merely commenting on my day.

I had to grudgingly admit that this building was a far improvement over my previous location, while still being convenient for most of my regular clients. My old office had been burgled twice in six months, and I'd lost my computer both times. After the second time, my insurance company had strongly suggested I look for a safer location to *ensure continuation of my policy*. I'd taken their advice and moved.

As much as I'd have preferred to entirely give up an office and instead work from home, I couldn't. ERAS—the Electronic Records Archival Service my license as a private investigator allowed me to subscribe to—required a desktop system, which they registered by serial number. They also required approved malware to be installed, and the computer had to be located in a locked, secure office.

So even though I'd purchased a laptop computer, which came and went with me, I still had to have an office for my ERAS computer. I kept an office phone, too, so I didn't have to include my cell phone number on my business cards, and I didn't have to give it to clients if I didn't want to.

I ran up the wide stairs off the main hallway to the second floor, figuring this was probably the only exercise I'd get for a while. I don't generally bother with the lobby elevator anyway, unless I'm lugging files between my office and home.

I do my best to keep in shape. I do most of my own motorcycle maintenance, which usually requires at least an hour or two of heavy wrenching, tugging, pushing, and cursing. I also scuba dive, and years of experience and training have taught me that *out of shape* and *accidental drowning* are pretty synonymous.

The second-floor hall is lined on both sides with identical wooden doors, each with a frosted glass window. The only break in the visual monotony is the tenant's name painted on each door. Some doors also sport a company logo, signs that a big spender, at least big for such a cheap-ass area, lurks inside the office.

I passed the door marked *Jason R. Storga, Attorney at Law*, above a skyline of downtown Austin. Jason occasionally has jobs for me, usually the things he doesn't want to do, like spend hours with a camera waiting to see if a spouse is cheating or an insurance recipient is not as disabled as claimed. In exchange, I sometimes refer clients of my own to him for legal advice and representation, when things don't quite go as well as the client expected.

My door, the third on the left, sported *Marianna Morgan Investigations* in black, block lettering. Not too catchy, but at least clear and to the point. I'm not a big spender, so I felt no motivation to pay the extra bucks for some kitchy logo. I'd even debated abbreviating my name but decided that'd make me look cheap.

I unlocked the door and entered, flipping on all three light switches, which lit up my one hundred and ninety square foot office like an offshore oil platform. I keep the small space tidy and outfitted with expensive-looking furniture I'd bought at the memorably-named POOP—the Pre-Owned Office Products shop.

The first thing I noticed was that the palm plant in the corner looked as tired and droopy as I felt. I vowed to be nicer to it and to give it some water, starting right after I watered myself and checked my messages. My answering machine blinked a bright green 3 in the small Message Count window. I tossed my purse on one of my visitor's chairs, circled to the machine, and pressed the Play button. I glugged some water from the Ozarka cooler into my water glass and sat down.

"Hi Mare, it's Judy. Don't forget we're meeting at the Oasis at seven tonight for drinks and dinner." Judy Franklin had been my best friend since high school. We'd been meeting at the Oasis the third Thursday of every month since I'd moved to Austin five years ago. Judy was as obsessive as I was compulsive, so she always called both my cell phone and my office phone to remind me of our standing plans. As I listened to her message, I watched a sparrow hop across the narrow sill outside my office window. Even he was panting from the heat.

The second message was from Jason. "Marianna, I have a fraud case going to court in three weeks and I still haven't managed to locate several people I'd like to call as witnesses. Stop by my office in the next day or two. I'll give you everything I've got on them, and you can use that as a jumping-off point for a records search."

I'd have to squeeze Jason's job in, but he paid well, since he passed all his expenses onto his clients anyway, so I tried never to turn down his job offers. Besides, Jason often gave my clients a price break when they found themselves in deep water. I wanted to keep a good business relationship with him.

The third message was a hang-up. I pressed the Caller ID button and jotted down the number. The area code was San Antonio. Both out of curiosity and my personal commitment to ATD—Attention To Detail—I called the number. It rang eleven times before someone answered.

"Yeppers!" The voice was male. He sounded young and had a slight southern drawl.

What the....? "I'm sorry, I guess I called the wrong number." I automatically glanced at the number I'd written down. "Can you tell me who I've called please?" Many people won't tell who you actually reached, assuming you're a telemarketer, but Mr. Yeppers might be young enough to still be gullible.

"Hey, darlin'. This here's a pay phone. Who you tryin' ta' reach?"

"Someone was trying to reach me. I thought I was returning their call. Where's this pay phone?"

"Man-o-man, darlin'." He chuckled. "You ain't got NO clue. I'm, like, standing outside Martin's Drug Store."

"Where is—" I started to ask, but Yep-darlin' cut me off.

"Like, I gotta go, darlin'. Later." Just before the line went dead, I heard him yell, "Hey Carlos, wait up!"

I flipped open my laptop and opened a browser. A simple search like this wasn't worth logging into ERAS, which would charge me for a search. I tried *Martin's Drug Store San Antonio.* I didn't get a hit. Odd. I tried again with *Martin's Drug Store Texas.* This time I got seventeen hits. I quickly scrolled down the list and found only one location in the San Antonio area code. The store was in Terrell Hills, a small city completely enclosed inside the city limits of San Antonio.

Could be something. Could be nothing. But I'd learned the hard way to record even casual experiences when working on a case. I never knew when someone or something was going to turn out to be important, helpful, or both.

I glanced at the clock on the wall above my bookcase. It was already past five. I quickly added the little bit of new information I had to the end of the document in Davidson's directory—the license plate of the Taurus, the basic geography inside and outside the Bargain Mart, my conversation with Pam, and the pseudo car chase we had until we reached Interstate 35.

I saved the document and then started a new one—Other Odd Stuff—into which I recorded the Entrance Ramp Idiot and the Killer Pickup Truck episodes. I also added as much as I knew about the weird phone call I'd returned.

Finally, I opened the spreadsheet I'd started for Davidson and recorded my mileage and time, complete with a brief description of how that time had been spent. I'm pretty anal about my invoices, having been stiffed several times early in my career. I want to be sure I can prove to a client that I've earned my entire retainer, as well as any additional money I'm owed.

I exhaled out a long sigh. Davidson's file was still too damned empty. Maybe I'd have better luck tomorrow. I glanced again at the clock and uttered a surprised *eep*. It was almost six-fifteen. I was going to have to hustle in order to make it by my PO Box and then get to the Oasis by seven. I hadn't even left myself time to stop by Jason's office.

I was halfway between the post office and the Oasis before I realized I'd forgotten to water the palm. I vowed to be nice to it tomorrow.

A CHAT WITH CARLOS

In preparing for battle, I have always found that plans are useless, but planning is indispensable.
~Dwight D. Eisenhower (1890-1969)

Stephanie sat on the last stool near one end of Whiskey Smith's U-shaped bar, impatiently tapping her foot. She couldn't wait much longer, but she really needed to talk to Carlos about the rifle. When she'd called him, he said he'd be by in half an hour. That was forty-five minutes ago.

She sipped her tepid beer and casually glanced around. It was Thursday, so the bar wasn't crowded. Half a dozen people chatted at tables, two other people sat on the opposite side of the bar. Two young men in cheap-looking suits and loosened ties played pool at one of the three pool tables in a brightly-lit alcove across the room.

Stephanie was about to give up when the outside door opened, sending a beam of bright sunlight across the room. She automatically tipped her head forward, causing her hair to partially shield her face, but she continued to watch as two figures entered the room. It took her eyes a moment to readjust to the darkness, but then she saw it was Carlos, and his ever-present sidekick Virgil.

They stopped, obviously getting their bearings. She gave them a minute before waving. Carlos immediately headed in her direction. Virgil shuffled lazily along behind.

"Hey Miss Stephanie," Carlos said in his heavy Hispanic accent.

"Howdy." Virgil's southern drawl drew out the word.

"Evening boys." Stephanie nodded. "Join me for a beer. I'll buy," she added when she saw them hesitate. "But let's move to a table."

She ordered a round, then led the way to the empty table farthest from anyone else, abandoning her warm longneck on the bar. She wasted no time once all three were seated and their beers had been served. She turned to face Carlos. "I hear from Melissa you might have information about antique guns or rifles."

If Carlos was surprised she'd already heard about his latest scheme, he didn't show it. Instead he nodded slowly. "Si, si. I met a guy who has a gun to sell. It is supposed to be very old and collectible, but not the kind of thing you want to put on display."

"Where'd you meet this guy?" Stephanie asked.

Carlos shrugged and shook his head. "I don't remember. I talk to so many people, hear so many things."

Virgil piped in, "Hey bud, wasn't it when we were at the Spurs game? That fat old guy who sat next to us?"

Carlos frowned then nodded. "Si, si. I think you are right. We talked at halftime about many things. Sports, dogs, cars…and guns."

"Tell me more about this gun." Stephanie put her elbows on the table and leaned forward.

Carlos took a long pull on his beer and belched. "It is from the battle of the Alamo."

Stephanie snorted. "I'm sure it is. Just like every celebrity who believes in reincarnation was once an Egyptian priestess, never a slave."

"It's true." Virgil nodded. "But it isn't like, ya know, Davy Crockett's coonskin cap or Jim Bowie's knife. Nothin' like that."

"Si, si," Carlos added. "It is Mexican. There were probably thousands of them, but it is still valuable because it was used at the Alamo." He grinned broadly. "And because of my heritage, I can find a wealthy collector easier than an old, fat gringo."

"You find a wealthy collector." Stephanie drained her beer. "But before you agree to sell it to them, let me know. I'll pay you more than they're willing to."

Virgil suddenly sat back. "Gee, Stephanie, why do you want an old Mexican rifle?"

"Let's just say it has meaning to my family."

"Who ends up with the gun does not matter to me." Carlos shrugged. "I only care because it could make me some good money."

Virgil laughed. "I don't think that ol' dude knows how much it's worth. I'll betcha Carlos here can sell it for lots more than he could."

Carlos shook his head. "You are wrong. That man knew much more than he wanted us to believe. He tried to sound laid back, but his eyes shifted as he spoke. I know that look."

Stephanie sat silently for a moment. *This is interesting. Perhaps I'm nearer my quest than I'd thought possible. Especially so quickly.* "Did he tell you his name?"

"I don't recall exactly." Carlos frowned in thought. "But his name was something like Warren."

"Naw, man, that wasn't it," Virgil said. "I think he said it was foreign." Virgil slapped the table. "That's it! It was Walter."

Carlos turned to stare at Virgil. "Walter is a foreign name to you?"

"Well, man." Virgil pouted his lips. "I've never met any Walters before. It *could* be foreign."

"Sometimes your stupidity surprises even me." Carlos rolled his eyes.

Before Virgil could respond, Stephanie hissed, "A while ago you called him an old, fat gringo. Describe him."

"He was *really* old," Virgil said in a sullen tone.

Carlos shook his head. "Mi amigo, he wasn't that old." He turned to face Stephanie. "He was perhaps sixty or sixty-five."

Stephanie knew that Carlos was older than Virgil, although she didn't know by how much. Virgil appeared to be in his early twenties, an age where sixty probably still seemed ancient.

"Whatever." Virgil shrugged. "Anyway, he was kinda bald and fat. Looked like he spent too much time at a desk."

"That's true," Carlos said. "I wonder how he came across the rifle. He didn't strike me as the type to go, what do you call it…"

"Excavating?" Stephanie prompted.

Carlos nodded. "Si, si. Digging, hunting, excavating. He seemed too soft and out of shape for that."

Virgil drained the last of his beer. "Don't matter, dude, it's money in our pockets if we help him sell it."

Carlos stared at Virgil for several beats. "There is no *our* in this, *dude*. This one is mine."

Virgil didn't react. Perhaps he hadn't heard. Stephanie wondered how he'd feel when he learned his pockets were going to remain empty.

A CLIFFHANGING EVENING

A goose quill is more dangerous than a lion's claw.
~English Proverb

Lake Travis, and the Oasis Restaurant, are twenty miles northwest of downtown Austin. Even with forty-five minutes to get there, I was pushing it. Traffic was already thick as I headed out Loop 1, which doesn't loop around anything. Locals call it Mopac, because the Missouri-Pacific Railway runs adjacent to it, but that's not how it's marked on most maps. It must confuse the hell out of tourists. The city had tried to fix the constant congestion by adding a toll lane. The resulting mess was what most commuters had predicted.

I wished I was on Max, my motorcycle. I love the freedom of a two-wheeled vehicle, the rush of wind across my body, the sounds and smells up close and personal. *Well, most smells.* The noxious fumes from the bumper-to-bumper traffic were even seeping into my car. I sighed and moved to the left lane to get around a Lincoln Giganta XL filled with kids and driven by a slucker woman who was simultaneously combing her hair and flapping her gums into a cell phone. I couldn't tell for sure, but considering how busy both her hands were, I wondered if she was steering with her knees.

The Oasis Restaurant is perched along the side of a four-hundred-fifty-foot, nearly-vertical cliff on the east side of Lake Travis. It's built of more than thirty open-air, wooden balconies, each connected to the one above and below by steep stairs, with only a small, rough-wood rail to keep tipsy patrons from *tipsying* right over the side and into the lake. In places, the cliff face juts jaggedly through the restaurant's oak-plank back wall like Robinson Crusoe's dream house.

Besides its unique architecture, the Oasis is also famous for its corny celebration of the daily sunset over the lake. When I pulled into the dusty, caliche-chalk parking lot at six-fifty-nine, the sun was still at least an hour and a half from setting. Most guests wouldn't arrive for another twenty or thirty minutes, so the lot was nearly empty. I noticed that Judy's white Saturn, license B29 GPA—Both Twenty-nine, Gal Pals Always—was parked in the next row.

I took my gun out of my purse, locked it and my laptop in Pickle Toy's trunk, and headed toward the restaurant. Judy was already at our favorite table—against the rail on the third balcony down. She was sipping a margarita and munching tortilla chips and salsa.

"Hey." I sat down on one of the plastic *wicker* chairs.

"Mmmph," Judy responded through a mouthful of chip.

"Same to you, kiddo!" I dipped a chip into the salsa and slid it into my mouth. My eyes briefly teared up in response to the sudden onslaught of Serrano pepper chunks.

I was still chewing when Chuck, or so his plastic nametag proclaimed, approached our table. He was maybe nineteen, with curly blonde hair that glowed like a halo in the evening sun. His upper lip sported a small mustache-wanna-be. His eyes were turquoise and framed by long, thick lashes. His tan arms and legs were muscular. My heart did a little flip and other parts of me gave a short quiver.

I felt a loud sigh coming on, so I quickly stuffed another chip into my mouth. I couldn't help it. Chuck was cute, and I'd been without a man in my life since dating another local PI five months earlier. Considering how strongly Chuck's presence affected me, I decided battery-enhanced play toys weren't a good long-term substitute. If he'd been older, I'd have flirted. Instead, I ordered a margarita for me and another for Judy, hoping Chuck didn't notice the deep shade of red that crept onto my cheeks.

When he'd gone I turned back to Judy. "So tell me, what's up?"

Judy took another sip of her margarita and smiled. "Want to be a dead body this Sunday?"

I sputtered and choked on a chip, then reached for Judy's drink and took a quick swallow. "Geez, don't say shit like that when my mouth is full!"

Judy laughed. "I'm wrapping up my first Wreck Diver class. The in-water session is Sunday morning."

Judy and I'd been scuba diving for years, and she'd gone on to get certified as an instructor. She ran the Bubbles Below Dive Shop not far from the lake.

"Where in the world do you teach wreck diving skills in a place like this?" I gestured toward the murky lake water.

"The SS Deep Ship."

"Come again?"

"Last weekend, a dozen Austin-area instructors built a fake wreck out of PVC pipe and heavy tarp in seventy feet of water up one of the quieter coves."

"You. Built. A. Wreck?" I raised my eyebrows.

"Yep. A real piece of artwork, too. It's divided into two halves, with escape holes on top of each half. We filled the whole thing with dangling fishing line and ropes. We kicked up quite a pea-soup cloud of silt while making it. It should be a nerve-wracking experience for the students."

"Sounds lovely," I laughed. "And what exactly did you have in mind for me?"

"You can be a dead body the students have to recover. You can tangle yourself up nice and tight in the dangling ropes, a perfect chance to prove you can be a bitch even without speaking." Judy smiled sweetly.

"Who's the bitch?" I stuck out my tongue. But then I thought about it. I was in just the mood to torment somebody. And students allowed into a wreck-diving class had to already be experienced enough divers not to easily panic underwater, so I could have some fun without worrying about killing one of them. "Okay, you've got a deal. Since I haven't been in the water for a couple of months, it'll help me keep my skills from getting too rusty."

"Hah, I know better. You just want to harass the students." Judy snorted.

I threw a chip at her and we both laughed. The chip landed on the wooden deck and was immediately snatched up by an enterprising grackle. We both laughed again.

Judy asked, "What's going on with you? How was your day?"

"Aunt Louise called."

"What is it this time?"

Poor Aunt Louise, she'd never know what most people really thought of her dire predictions. I told Judy about the warning and my subsequent close encounter with the Chevy pickup. "That's why I choked when you asked if I wanted to be a dead body."

"That's a helluva coincidence." Judy raised her eyebrows.

"Yeah, looks like she may have actually gotten one right."

"Are you going to tell her?"

"Are you kidding? She'd call me every day with warnings. I love her dearly, but not enough to become her obsession."

"Yeah, you're right. So how's that new case coming along?"

I sighed. "Not as well as I'd like." I described my experience of losing the elusive woman earlier in the day.

"You still don't know who she is? What'd he tell you when he hired you?"

"To answer your questions—nope and not much." I told Judy about the newspaper clipping and Davidson's reluctance to give me any details.

Judy pursed her lips. "Hmmm. This Davidson sounds like one of the weirdest clients you've ever had. You're sure he's legit?"

"Well, I actually did some checking up on *him*. He's a CPA in Austin. His—"

"Austin? Then why's he living in San Antonio?"

"Good question. His mom died a year ago. Cancer'd been eating her bit-by-bit for several years, and he took care of her. About six months after she died, he moved to a small apartment in the Casino Club building on the San Antonio River Walk. But he keeps his CPA practice in Austin, because most of his established clients are here. He drives up several times a week."

"That's a commute and a half. Why'd he move at all?"

"I asked him about it, but all he'd say is that he now prefers the quiet and solitude of San Antonio."

"Yeah," Judy quipped. "The San Antonio River Walk is the place *I'd* pick if I wanted to live in quiet solitude."

I shrugged. "I hear ya. But that was the only answer I could get out of him, and I asked several times in different ways."

Judy grinned and cocked her head. "Not that I doubt your detective abilities, but why you? I mean, this mystery woman is in San Antonio. And now he lives in San Antonio. Why not hire someone there?"

"I asked him that, too. He said I was referred to him, although he wouldn't say by who. Whom. Whatever. I told him I'd have to charge him for driving time, and an occasional overnight stay, but he didn't seem to care. To tell you the truth, I think part of it is that he doesn't know anyone in San Antonio. Maybe he prefers it that way. Maybe he's depressed and isn't as ready to start a new life as he thought when he moved. Maybe he's trying to escape the old one. After all, he could've gotten an apartment here in Austin."

"Maybe he helped his Mom reach her *final destination* quicker and is now guilt-ridden and hiding." Judy said.

"I sincerely doubt that." I shook my head. "He seems too milquetoast for that."

"Maybe, maybe not." Judy shrugged. "Well, at least you grew up in San Antonio, so you know your way around."

We finished our margaritas as the sun sank lower in the sky. We were halfway through another round of drinks when the sun touched the hills on the west side of the lake. The conversation around us quieted down as everyone turned their attention to the horizon.

At exactly eight-thirty-six, just as the last tip of the sun winked out behind the hills, the Oasis erupted in noise. Bells clanged, employees blew noisemakers, and guests cheered, clapped their hands, and stomped their feet. The whole deck vibrated with the commotion, making me momentarily utter a little prayer that the architects of the place had been experts in designing *cliff dwellings*.

The noisy celebration lasted about a minute, then the outside lights came on and the Oasis returned to normal. I signaled Chuck to let him know we were ready for menus.

The rest of the evening flew by in a swirl of conversation and laughter. It was after ten before we walked to our cars.

"See you Sunday morning at eight-thirty." Judy waved and opened her car door. "Meet us on the pier at Volente Beach. We'll take Large Marge to the wreck site. And add extra weights to your weight belt. It'll make you more like a water-logged body."

"No problem there." I patted my belly. "The extra chips I ate tonight will have the same effect. Oh, and I don't have to contribute to the cost of the barge do I, since I'm going to be dead?"

Judy just laughed as she climbed into her car.

I felt light and breezy as I walked to my car. I loved Large Marge the Party Barge. The pontoon boat, made from bright-white-painted wood, securely staked to fifty-five gallon drums, sported a roof that doubled as a sundeck. Marge also included a bathroom, although I never spent time wondering if it involved any actual plumbing other than a straight pipe down.

I headed home to Cedar Park, a dumpy behemoth on the northwest outskirts of Austin. It has to be one of the ugliest towns I've ever seen. There's no downtown in Cedar Park, it's mostly just rows of fast food restaurants, auto parts stores, and pawn shops, sliced in half by Highway 183, which moves way too many cars every day from Austin to expensive *ranchette* neighborhoods in Lago Vista and Jonestown, both a few miles farther northwest.

But the air is cleaner than Austin's, and I really love my house. I used to love the illusion of rural life that Cedar Park provided, although that's mostly gone now, a victim of growth. The most recent victim of the Cedar Park's genericizing was Winkley's, the town's original general store. I'd loved rambling up and down its aisles, which displayed a little bit of everything—hunting and fishing supplies, live baby chicks and ducks, western-style clothing, cast iron cookware, and in a valiant attempt to meet the changing demographics of the area, espresso makers and gourmet food.

I had a copy of Winkley's final almanac—*For Farmers and City Folk*. My favorite story was *Five Slug-Stopping Success Strategies*. Too bad they meant the slimy kind, not the kind that come out of a gun.

When I moved back to Texas, I didn't want to live in another big city, which is how I'd ended up in Cedar Park. I'd spent several years in San Jose, California, where I started as a novice private investigator. I'd been a technical writer for more than a decade, and I'd slowly grown sick of the wham-bam, thank you ma'am feeling I got from my job.

For all my years of sweat and toil, all I had was a couple of boxes full of manuals in my attic. Those manuals were a monument to wasted paper and time. They described, in agonizing detail, products that were no longer available or had never even made it to market. Some of the book covers sported corporate logos for companies that had ceased to exist. It was disheartening, to say the least.

As a favor, I'd started moonlighting for a couple of computer-illiterate lawyer friends, putting my techie skills to work in ways I'd never thought about before. Over the years, I'd become downright crafty at searching the internet on just about any topic, and I quickly found I had a knack for digging up obscure information.

At first, I worked mostly on insurance and workmen's comp fraud investigations. Then I started conducting background checks of potential employees for some of Silicon Valley's biggest corporations. After a couple of years, I gave up my day job, got my private investigator's license, and set up shop.

It wasn't long before my reputation for thoroughness and success started bringing me more interesting—and lucrative—private clients. I made good money, got to set my own hours, and never had to hear a holier-than-thou engineer utter the phrase *you're just a tech writer* again. Life was good.

Homesickness finally caught up with me five years ago, so I returned to Texas. I'd been born and raised in San Antonio, but I chose Austin, ninety miles farther north, as my new home. There's more high-tech business here, and I was able to rely on investigation jobs for some of my California Silicon Valley clients' local Silicon Hills offices while I built my private practice back up again. And, I'd grudgingly admitted, if all else failed, I could always go back to writing pointless manuals for one of Austin's high tech firms.

Nowadays I have a string of regular corporate and legal clients, so I can pretty much count on a minimum monthly income. But those jobs are usually pretty boring and involve hours of poring through online sites and good old-fashioned public record archives. I took jobs like the one for Davidson as much for the change of pace as for the money.

It was after eleven when I pulled into my driveway. I got my gun and computer out of the trunk, and opened my door. Six cats immediately materialized. "Hi guys." I headed for the kitchen. Twenty-four little feet scurried behind and around me. "Yeah, I know, you're all starving to death. It's been at least ten whole hours since I fed you canned food." I glanced down. All three bowls of dry food were untouched—still perfect little pyramids of hard brown pellets. I waved toward the bowls. "You still have all the food you could possibly eat. There are starving cats in China, you know." I got a chorus of hungry meows in response.

Georgie jumped up on the counter to watch as I prepared dinner for him and the rest of the cats. "Hey, sweetie." I gave his ear a scratch and a tweak.

"Mreowr!" he replied with an enthusiastic wobble of his head. I head wobbled back, wondering what silent communication we exchanged when we did this. Larry swore the cats probably laughed behind my back at how Georgie had trained me to wobble my head on cue. I dug two cans of Friskies Buffet out of the cabinet and divided the Chicken Banquet and Ocean Catch onto plastic plates.

"Come on down, boy. You'll miss out on your fair share," I said to Georgie as I placed the plates on the floor at non-squabbling distances. He promptly jumped down and trotted to an unoccupied plate. Polly took a swipe at him as he passed. I shook my head.

As my feline kids chowed down, I returned to my car for the pile of mail I'd found stuffed into my PO Box. The stack included several catalogs and a dozen pieces of junk mail, three of them sporting *You may have already won!* on the outside of their envelopes. I walked back into the house, shuffling through the tree-killer waste of paper. Buried among the junk was a plain white envelope with my address hand-written on it. It had no return address. The postmark was San Antonio.

I dropped the junk mail on the breakfast table and opened the envelope. Inside was a single sheet of paper. In large letters was a short, terse message:

FUCK OFF OR ELSE! LEAVE ME ALONE.

I stared at the words as if they were written in Sanskrit. Which asshole had sent it? I couldn't think of anyone I'd recently pissed off *that* badly. I shook my head, trying to clear my one-too-many margaritas brain. Could this possibly be from the woman I was following?

She may have seen me sprinting away from the Bargain Mart this afternoon, but had she known about me earlier than that? If so, how did she even know it was me doing the following? If the letter wasn't from her, who the hell was it from? Since she was the only case I was currently working, I'd bet money she was the author.

I tossed the note on the table with the rest of the junk mail. I'd worked many cases. Twice before, I'd received threats in my PO Box, although not quite as succinct and graphic. My post office box number was printed on all of my business cards and stationery. They were on my Facebook page, my Linked-In page, and my simple one-page web site. I'd even forked out the money for a yellow pages ad, quaint and archaic as that was these days. So I always dismissed these crank letters as a risk of my chosen profession, but it still pissed me off.

I thought about calling Davidson, but it was nearly midnight. I shrugged and headed for bed. I'd deal with it first thing tomorrow.

THE LOST TIME

Families are about love overcoming emotional torture.
~Matt Groening (1954-)

Stephen woke with a headache that moved through his head like a flock of screaming seagulls. He had no idea what time it was. He wasn't completely sure what day it was. He must have had a lot more to drink than he remembered. He was beginning to worry. He'd never had a drinking problem and didn't want to develop one now.

He sat up slowly and rubbed his eyes. The bedside clock glowed a green 7:30, but was it morning or evening? He eased his legs over the edge of the bed, plodded to the window, and peeked through the curtain, blinking back the brightness that slammed into his eyes like a hammer.

The River Walk was quiet. A Park Police boat motored slowly by, kicking up a miniature wake. Several ducks bobbed about on the small waves. An employee of the restaurant across the river was hosing bird droppings off the sidewalk below the seventy-five foot tall, hundred-year-old cypress trees.

It was morning, then. It must be Friday.

Stephen closed the curtain and massaged his temples as he shuffled to the kitchen. The last thing he remembered was opening a nice bottle of Merlot so he could have a glass with his dinner. He rarely ate out, preferring instead to cook his own meals. Last night he'd made fettuccini tossed with a sun-dried tomato and Kalamata olive pesto, and topped with chopped basil leaves and thin slivers of Parmesan cheese.

He stopped at the kitchen door, surprised and shocked. His hand involuntarily shot to his head and started stroking his bald spot. The wine bottle sat empty on the counter. The pasta pot, now full of rock-hard remnants, sat on the stove. An uncapped olive oil bottle sat next to the pot. The sink was piled with dirty dinner dishes. He didn't understand what was going on. He was fastidiously neat, suffering from a nominal case of OCD. How could he leave such a mess?

Stephen spent the next hour washing dishes and cleaning the kitchen. He tried not to think about the previous night and what he might have done. Had he stayed inside, drinking alone all night? Or had he gone out after dark? If so, what had he done. He had no memory, which sent a shiver down his spine.

He returned to the bedroom and began straightening it, too. He put fresh white cotton sheets on his bed and dusted his already well-polished solid oak furniture. He moved slowly about the room, gathering the previous day's clothes off the floor. They were scattered everywhere, as if he had tossed them wildly about—another sign that something wasn't right. In his distracted state, he wadded the clothes and shoved them into the small wicker laundry basket, which was half filled with dirty clothes, all neatly folded as was his usual habit.

He was closing the lid when something caught his attention. His eyes grew big as he reached in and extracted yesterday's shirt. He'd worn the pale, Oxford blue, button-down with his khakis, which was extremely casual for him. The mark on the collar was faint, but there was no mistaking what it was—lipstick. He dropped the shirt as if it were on fire and slammed the lid of the basket closed.

He turned. The room turned half a beat slower. Time seemed to stretch and warp in his mind. His heart pounded in his chest. Its jungle-drum rhythm pulsed in his ears. His forehead broke out with tiny beads of perspiration. His leg bones seemed to be dissolving. He walked unsteadily back to the kitchen, using the walls for support, and as guides, since his mind seemed to have forgotten how to get there.

He picked up his white enamel tea kettle and filled it with water. It took some doing, most of the water missed, falling instead onto his shaking hand. He put the kettle on the stove, started the burner, and made his way to the dining table, where he sat heavily on the closest chair. He hung his head and slowly stroked the shiny bald circle at the center of his ring of fluffy hair.

Had he been with a woman? He sometimes got terribly lonely, and had debated using an escort service—as they politely called it—but he'd never found the courage to actually call. Even if he'd had enough alcohol to make him brave enough to contact a service, surely he hadn't entertained her in his own apartment.

He shook his head. No, there had only been one set of dirty dinnerware. So he'd either met her somewhere or left with her as soon as she arrived. But who was she? What had they done together? And if he'd taken her to dinner, why had he eaten beforehand? He shuddered at the realization that he could not remember.

The Lost Time, as Dr. Myer had come to call it, was getting worse. Now he was no longer just losing track of time, he was losing track of people, too. He supposed he should finally agree that he needed medication, something he staunchly argued against every time the psychiatrist brought it up.

No! He shook his head fiercely. *I'm still not ready to go that far. Besides, at least for right now, it's more important to find out if what I suspect is true, that my sister really is alive.*

Maybe once he knew the truth the Lost Time would stop happening. Yes, he was sure that finding his sister was the key to his well-being—perhaps even to his sanity.

ROUNDABOUT ROUTES

Anger is one letter short of danger.
~Eleanor Roosevelt (1884-1962)

My head felt like it was full of cat litter, my mouth tasted like old socks, and my eyes were as puffy and burning as if they'd been attacked by the entire population of a fire ant mound. I wished I'd drunk something besides margaritas.

Someday I'll learn that tequila and I don't mix well. Just a couple of tequila-based drinks give me a rip-roaring hangover. Of course, I only remember *after* my date with Judy, because I *really like* margaritas.

I peeked at the clock, which was shining in my eyes like a searchlight. I'd remembered to close the heavy curtains, but I'd forgotten to turn the damn clock to the wall. It displayed 8:30, still early, okay, relatively early. I decided to give myself an extra half hour and rolled over, turning my back on the searchlight. I'd enjoyed maybe ten seconds of bliss when four of my cats decided it was *not* too early for breakfast. A combined weight of fifty-plus pounds landed on various parts of my body.

"Aargh, go away!"

They listened as well as cats ever do. Mayfly listened so well she proceeded to lie across my face. Her long fur tickled my nose, and I inhaled enough cat dander to leave my eyes and nose runny for a week. My allergies do okay most of the time, but this was too much. I sneezed into Mayfly's stomach, which sent her scurrying to the adjacent pillow, where she crouched and glared.

"Okay, okay." Resigned, I slipped out from under the cats and covers and dragged my sorry ass into the bathroom. I glared at the three cats who followed me. "I don't know why I bother putting up with you spoiled, ungrateful little shits."

As if to prove me wrong, Boggle began twining around my legs, purring loud enough to be heard over the running water. Georgie hopped onto the counter and began doing head butts into my stomach. "Yeah, I know, you love me almost as much as my can opener." I scratched Georgie under his chin, stepped carefully around Boggle, and shambled to the kitchen.

I fed my darlings and poured coffee into my *Dogs think WE'RE gods, Cats know THEY'RE gods* mug. Sitting at the breakfast table, I watched the white wing doves mount a morning assault on my hanging bird feeder. It soon looked like a solid feather ball, but at least the feeder was temporarily safe from squirrels.

I took a long gulp of coffee, sighed, and scratched at Polly's ears. She'd oozed onto my lap in slow motion. I stared at the threatening letter, which still lay open where I'd dropped it on the table.

It was as good a reason as any to have another talk with Davidson. He hadn't given me much to go on. The letter seemed mocking proof that the woman I was following knew more about me than I did about her. That is, *if* the letter was from her.

I decided to assume the letter *was* from her. If nothing else, it would make things more interesting. I emptied the coffee dregs into the sink and carried the cordless phone into the living room, where I retrieved Davidson's card from the dark recesses of my purse. The phone rang five times before he answered.

"Hello?" His voice was soft, almost a whisper.

"Mr. Davidson, this is Marianna Morgan. I'm driving down today to speak with you about your case. I'll be at your apartment at noon. Do you have a problem with that?"

There was a long pause before he answered. "Well, um, yes, I mean no, er, I suppose, uh, that's not a problem." His voice sounded sluggish and dull.

My previous conversations with him had been crisp, professional, and polished. He'd always been friendly and polite. But then so had I. I felt my cheeks burn with embarrassment for how rudely I'd just spoken. "I'm sorry, I had a rough night. Are you all right?" I felt sheepish. It was just a stupid letter.

He cleared his throat, coughed, and then said, more firmly and clearly, "Yes, Ms. Morgan, I'm fine. I'm looking forward to seeing you and discussing my case."

I stood in the shower, eyes closed, water pounding on the back of my head and neck, until I'd used up all the hot water. But at least my hangover was better. I stared into my closet for five minutes, debating between dressing for the comfy, cool Pickle Toy or Max. My head would appreciate the car, but my heart needed lightening, so I dressed quickly before my headache changed my mind, pulling on my riding boots, jeans, and denim shirt.

I stopped briefly in the bathroom to down two Excedrin for my headache and two Sudafed for my runny nose, then grabbed my leather jacket and gloves from the coat tree in the foyer, picked up the letter as I passed the breakfast table, and headed to the garage.

"Be good," I called over my shoulder, knowing damn well that cats have no concept of the word *good*, except perhaps when used to describe fresh chicken, tuna, or steak.

The driveway and street already shimmered from the heat. The one downfall of riding in the summer is the dichotomy between protective leather gear and heat. I'd be okay as long as I was moving. Even asphalt-heated summer air was tolerable at eighty miles an hour. I'd melt, however, if I had to spend much time at lights or sitting in traffic.

I decided to take the back route. It would take longer to get there, but I could completely avoid Interstate 35, so I really didn't care. Besides, it would give me more time to think about my approach.

It was after nine-thirty when I pulled out of my driveway. I waved to Sally, who'd moved next door in May. She was a hairdresser and had immediately converted one bedroom into a single-station salon. I'd started using her to trim my mop a couple months ago. She spent every morning before her first appointment working in her flower beds, which responded with more blooms than my neglected beds would produce in a decade.

Most of the morning-rush traffic had subsided, so I was going seventy before I left Williamson County. I love this ride. Except for the stretch through the yuppie-infested Lago Vista and Jonestown, Ranch Road 1431 is still mostly unimproved, which to me means it's still winding and fun. But it's also well-maintained, so I didn't have to worry about sudden potholes or other unpleasant diversions, and the summer heat meant the deer were done chowing on roadside cigarette butts and had already bedded down for the day. The air smelled of hot asphalt, but it also smelled of freshly mowed hay fields.

I stopped briefly in Marble Falls, at a gas station overlooking the Colorado River, to top off Max and to take a drink-and-drain break for myself. My mouth was extra dry, thanks to the Sudafed, but at least my nose was no longer running. I grabbed a Coke slushy and sucked on it as I leaned on Max.

The morning sun shone on the nearby cliffs of the quarry. The solid granite marble hills surrounding the area had been the inspiration for the town's name and the source for every stone in pretty much every county courthouse in Texas. I'd visited the quarry during multiple field trips as a kid. It didn't look like it had shrunk much in size, in spite of continuous blasting and mining. I wondered if the quarry would ever run out or just continue its slow march toward the town.

I figured greed would win out over environmental concerns and eventually this gorgeous part of central Texas would look like a moonscape, but at the current rate of progress I'd hopefully be long dead before then. Cooled off from the slushy, I again headed south on Highway 281, a four-lane but still beautiful route that would take me straight to downtown San Antonio.

Two and a half hours after leaving home, I pulled into the Rivercenter Parking Garage, more expensive than street-lot parking, but Max wouldn't bake in the sun. Denim jeans aren't thick enough to protect the butt from a hot, black leather seat.

The Casino Club building where Davidson lives is only one block from the garage, so I barely had time to shake out my damp and mashed hair. I reached for the door to the lobby, but then stepped back and looked up. Davidson clearly had taste—and money—to live in such a beautiful and historic building overlooking the River Walk.

The triangular-shaped, art-deco building, erected in 1925, was one of the original locations of the Casino Club, a prominent social club started in 1857 by a group of German men. It was *the* club to belong to until as recently as the early sixties. I'd attended a couple of parties there with my parents as a little girl. It was showing its age by then, but I still loved the curved ceilings and elaborate glass and brass fixtures.

In recent years, the building had been divided into small apartments and condos. The outside stone had been cleaned, and the four-tiered dome that still topped the building was painted in pastel purple, blue, and aqua. I grinned at the thought of how the hard-edged German club members would respond to such sissy colors. They'd probably have been happier had artist Gene Elder gotten his way by painting the dome red and renaming the building The Big Tomato.

After a couple minutes in the lobby, I was somewhat cooler. I picked up the lobby phone and dialed 513. He answered on the first ring. "Mr. Davidson, it's Marianna Morgan. I'm downstairs."

He buzzed me through without saying a word and opened his door after I completed only the first knock in my knock-knock-knock. I had to react quickly to keep the second and third knocks from bonking Davidson in the nose. He stepped aside quickly and extended his arm, waving me in.

I'd never been in his apartment, so I took the opportunity to look around. The rectangular room was divided into a dining area and a living area through the clever arrangement of furniture. The dining area included an antique drop leaf table, pushed against one wall, an efficient way to leave the space open.

The living area had two swivel rockers and a sofa, all upholstered in a subdued abstract pattern of wine, gray, and navy. Three occasional tables were scattered about, each topped with a collection of hand blown glass object d'art and a heavy brass lamp. Three short oak bookcases, filled with classic and contemporary novels—all hardbacks—lined the wall behind the rockers. An impressive collection of signed, limited-edition prints and oils hung on the wall above the sofa.

My initial impression was of someone who was detail-oriented, meticulous, and thorough, but who also had good taste and an eye for style. Everything was color-coordinated, pleasingly arranged, and immaculately clean. It looked artistic but masculine, and it upped my impression of Davidson's sensibilities.

Davidson was clearly not doing bad financially, even if he was only working part-time for a select few clients these days. It looked like the kind of place a professional CPA would live. If he kept books as conscientiously as he furnished his apartment, I'd trust him with my finances. Someday, when I had enough finances to justify paying someone to help me keep an eye on them, maybe I'd talk to him about it. I sat on one of the rockers and placed my jacket and helmet on the floor beside me.

Davidson sat on the sofa opposite me. "May I offer you some tea or coffee?"

It wasn't lost on me that he waited until after he was seated to make the offer. Even though my throat felt bone dry, I wanted to keep things strictly business, so I swallowed with effort. "No, thanks. I don't want to take up too much of your time."

"What can I do for you today?" He offered a polite smile. His voice had that slightly throaty, spongy sound of someone who suffers from one or more of the dozens of local allergy-inducing pollens.

"I have something to show you." I pulled the letter from my jacket pocket and handed it to him. "I received this in yesterday's mail. It was postmarked from San Antonio."

Davidson slowly unfolded the letter, a look of simple curiosity on his face. When he saw the short message scrawled across the page, however, his eyes grew large. "Who sent this?"

"I'm hoping you can tell me. I believe this letter relates to your case."

"I'm sorry, Ms. Morgan, I have no idea who sent this crude threat." His voice was firm, but he avoided looking directly into my eyes.

"Excuse me?"

Davidson straightened his shoulders and looked directly at me. "I'm afraid I've no idea what you're talking about. Perhaps a former client, someone who was dissatisfied, sent it."

"That's bullshit." I gritted my teeth hard to keep from uttering the string of expletives bouncing around in my mouth. I could feel my hangover-induced edginess fluttering at the back of my tongue.

"Really, Ms. Morgan, just because I'm your current client, you cannot assume the letter relates to me."

Davidson continued to look at me, but his eyes were a little too wide, and I could see a small tic at the corner of his left eye. I leaned forward and said in a crisp, controlled voice, "I can tell by the look on your face you know something. What is it?"

His incredulous look made me want to scream, but I sat perfectly still and stared hard at his eyes. After nearly a minute of silence, his shoulders slumped. His whole body looked deflated and hollow. "No, not really," he whispered. "It's just that..."

His voice faded. I waited a heartbeat for him to continue then yanked the letter from his fingers. "Just what?"

"The handwriting. It, um, looks vaguely familiar, but I can't tell you more than that. It may only look similar to someone completely unrelated. Or maybe....maybe it's just wishful thinking."

"Wishful thinking? Someone else is already yanking me around. Don't you start with me, too. Just what is this case really about? Who is this woman you have me following?"

"I'm not... I really... I can't be sure..." he stammered.

I stood up so quickly he jerked back against the sofa as if afraid I might strike him, not that the thought of slapping him silly hadn't crossed my mind. I spoke in as steady a voice as I could muster through clenched teeth. "Look, someone sent me a threatening letter. I believe it's connected with your case. That sort of thing pisses me off big time." I didn't move a muscle, I tried not to blink, although the effort was making my tired eyes burn. I intended to wait him out, no matter how long it took. I was through with all his vague crap.

He looked around, ran his hand in slow circles around his bald head, and, after a minute, let go with a large sigh. He sagged even deeper into the sofa, his shoulders slumped lower, his chin dropped almost to his chest. "Please, sit down. I'll tell you all I can."

A HISTORICAL REVELATION

Character building begins in infancy and continues until death. ~Eleanor Roosevelt (1884-1962)

"It all started in nineteen-sixty-five, when I was seven," he began.

I raised my eyebrows and inadvertently uttered a small *hrmph.*

"I'm quite serious." His forehead knotted. "Please bear with me."

I nodded.

Davidson ran his hand over his balding head several times as if checking for hair. "When I was seven, my father was an assistant professor of Archeology at Trinity University. He was working on excavating ruins that had been unearthed during the construction of HemisFair, which was scheduled to open in nineteen-sixty-eight."

I smiled at Davidson's mention of HemisFair. "I wasn't born when HemisFair took place, but my parents told me many stories, and I've see their photos dozens of times. It's never before occurred to me that it was an archeological site."

"Very much so. The construction effort was massive and encompassed most of the southeastern part of downtown San Antonio. The crews regularly uncovered ruins and relics from the city's early days, when Indians still lived in the area and the Alamo was an active mission and fort."

"What exactly did your father do?"

"He was senior assistant at that time, so spent most of his time overseeing and supervising the archeological digs. He was responsible for ensuring that all relics were properly cataloged and transported to the university for further study."

"What happened to the relics they found?"

"The archeology department's research group first cleaned and photographed each item. Then they were given to the Alamo Historical Society for storage or display. Anyway, Dad came home one evening with a rifle they'd unearthed just two blocks south of the Alamo, the site of one of the Mexican army's batteries around the time of the battle. The rifle was still whole, and the wooden stock was barely deteriorated. Dad showed us an engraving on the lockplate—a Mexican eagle with a snake in its claws. He said it proved the rifle's age and authenticity. I was so impressed. I still remember how my hands shook when he let me hold it."

"You said everything went to the archeology department. What was he doing bringing it home?"

"He said he wanted to show us a real Alamo relic before taking it to Trinity." Davidson frowned. "But he never took it back. I know, because I overheard him talking about it on the phone several days later. He was trying to sell it. It wasn't until years later that I learned just how deeply in debt he was at the time. He had massive school loans, and he and Mom had just bought our house in Terrell Hills."

"Terrell Hills?" I raised my eyebrows. "That was a pretty exclusive area back then. You just said your family was in deep debt. How could you afford to live there?"

"Parts of Terrell Hills were definitely up-scale, but we lived *across the tracks* as it were. Our neighborhood was mostly filled with university faculty and the domestic staff for the homes in the wealthier sections of the city." He made a crooked smile.

"I'd forgotten about that. Those of us who grew up in San Antonio always pictured the separate little cities, like Terrell Hills and Alamo Heights, as being havens for the rich."

"I'm sure the city leaders and realtors worked hard to maintain that impression." He compulsively ran his hand over the top of his head again. "Anyway…the family debt wasn't helped by the fact that Mom was a housewife, to use that period's terminology. An assistant professor's salary is pitiful, at best. I didn't understand as a young boy that my father was just trying to find a way to get by, and an Alamo-era rifle would bring a large sum from a private collector."

"Why didn't your mom work?"

Davidson just stared at me.

I blushed. "Of course. Good mothers didn't work back then, no matter how badly the extra income would have helped."

Davidson frowned and nodded. "Especially wives of university staff. It would have been unseemly and made Dad look bourgeois."

"So your dad resorted to selling stolen goods instead." I smirked.

"Ironic isn't it. Better to take a chance on getting caught as a thief than admit you weren't man enough to take care of your wife and kids on your own."

"Excuse me…" I cocked my head. "You said *kids*—you have siblings?"

"Yes," he said, his voice almost a whisper. "I had a twin sister."

"Had?"

"She was murdered."

"Murdered! When? How?" The concept ricocheted around in my brain like a bullet. This wasn't even on the long list of possible responses I'd expected. If he was trying to jerk me around, he was doing a good job.

"Please, Ms. Morgan, I'll get to that, if you'll let me."

I coughed back the words that were on the tip of my tongue. "Okay. I'm listening."

"About two weeks after my father showed us the rifle, we were scheduled to attend a symphony performance at the Municipal Auditorium. My sister and I didn't particularly enjoy these outings. We were, after all, only seven. But my mother insisted they'd build character."

I leaned forward. Wherever this story was going, he had my full attention.

"The evening of the performance, my sister came down with a fever. Dad stayed home with her, and I went with Mom. She figured two wasted tickets was better than four." He shrugged, then after a brief pause continued. "We got home around ten-thirty. The house was dark, including the front porch light. I remember Mom grumbling about *that man's forgetfulness*. She was always after him for forgetting things. But when she put her key in the lock, the door just kind of slipped open. I can still hear the squeaking hinges sometimes in nightmares. That was one of the things Dad kept forgetting to do—oil the door hinges." Davidson sighed and shook his head. "But after that night...." He sighed again and stared blankly at the wall behind me.

"What happened?" I prompted softly, my previous anger slipped away on a cloud of curiosity and concern.

He started, as if he'd forgotten I was there. "I tried to push past Mom into the house, but she grabbed my arm. She called to Dad from the porch. He didn't answer. The house was silent. No TV, no radio, no voices. Mom dragged me off the porch and over to the next door neighbor's. Mr. Johnson returned to the house with us. I remember he had a flashlight and a pistol. He made us wait outside while he went into the house. He hadn't been inside more than a few seconds when we heard him holler. Mom told me to stay put and rushed inside. I didn't listen. I followed right on her heels."

"Brave move for a little kid. You must have been scared to death."

Davidson nodded. "Rightly so. Dad was on the floor outside my sister's bedroom. There was so much blood," Davidson's voice trailed off to almost a whisper. "The hall floor was covered with blood. Dad's blood. It'd even soaked into the hardwood. For as long as I lived there, I never again stepped on that part of the floor, even though Mom had it sanded and refinished."

"What had happened to your father?"

He cleared his throat and sighed. "He'd been stabbed through the heart. He'd bled to death."

"That's awful." I sat back, hand on my chest. "Had they stabbed your sister too?"

"No. Well… I'm not sure. My sister was missing."

I could feel my skin chill, as I paled from his words. I had only one sibling, too, an older brother. We got along okay as kids, but there was a six year difference in our ages. Still, I shuddered at the thought of his just vanishing. "But you said your sister was murdered."

"That was the ultimate conclusion, but no one knew much that night."

I frowned. I was trying to make sense of what he was saying. "Please go on. You said you and your mom got home and found your father. What happened next?"

"Mom just stood there screaming. I was rooted to the spot beside her. Mr. Johnson called the operator—nine-one-one didn't exist yet—and then got us both into the living room and onto the sofa. Two Terrell Hills police officers arrived within minutes. An ambulance was there shortly after. And a couple of officers from the San Antonio Police Department came, too."

"SAPD? In Terrell Hills? How'd they get involved?"

Davidson shrugged. "Terrell Hills didn't have their own dispatcher, they used the SAPD's channel. A couple of patrol officers were only a few blocks away. They heard the call and came to see if they could help. I still remember how nice they were to us and the other cops. One of them brought me a glass of milk, although I didn't drink it. Anyway, the two men from the ambulance and one Terrell Hills police officer went into the hall. The SAPD officers and the other local officer started organizing a search. They went from house to house, and soon all the neighbors were out in force."

"But they didn't find her, did they?" My own voice was now barely a whisper.

Davidson closed his eyes and sighed. "No. There were only four men in the Terrell Hills Police Department back then. They filled out a missing person's report that night, and they organized a search of the area, but only for three weeks. They said that was all they could do, especially with no other leads to follow, but that they'd keep her on the daily Hot Sheet for another couple of months." Davidson turned and stared out his window. The frown on his face was bitter. "Three weeks."

"Why didn't they look longer?" I asked, my full volume, and then some, returning. "Couldn't they have asked for help from the Texas Rangers or the Bexar County Sheriff's Department? My god, she was a little girl."

"You grew up here. You know what it was like. I remember Mr. Johnson saying he was surprised that the SAPD officers came at all." Davidson's voice was harsh.

I nodded. Anyone who'd spent time in San Antonio, especially back then, knew there was a running feud between the different law enforcement groups, especially between San Antonio and Terrell Hills. San Antonio had tried more than once to annex the small burg. After well-publicized, bitter fights, they'd failed each time. So San Antonio had grown up around the smaller city, swallowing it like an antibody surrounds a bacteria. In a typical fit of spite, San Antonio politicians refused basic support services to any city that had escaped the bigger city's snare, including Terrell Hills.

Davidson turned back to me. His eyes flashed with anger. "Can you imagine how I felt?" As he continued to speak his voice rose an octave and his lower lip stuck out petulantly. I could see the little boy he'd been at the time. "They all gave up. They quit trying. It was like they didn't really care. But I did. SHE WAS MY SISTER!"

His shoulders shook and his voice hitched. He reached for a throw pillow and hugged it tightly. "They gave up so soon. The police, my mother, Mr. Johnson. All of them. I felt so helpless. There was nothing I could do." A single tear tracked down his cheek.

"I'm so sorry." I truly felt for the poor man. I could only imagine how he'd felt as a child, watching everyone he counted on let him down. As I watched, he sat up straight, wiped his cheek, and carefully returned the pillow to its corner of the sofa, smoothing it to remove the hand imprints he's squashed into it only moments before. When he spoke again, his voice was normal, the tormented inner child relegated once again to the dark corner of his mind where he'd buried it.

"Such arrogance," he spat. "The power-mongering police wouldn't even ask for outside help."

"I'm sure that must have been painful. But what's it have to do with now? Why are you putting yourself through it all again by telling me about it?"

"Because it's time you knew the truth." He sighed deeply and stroked the top of his head for several seconds. "I still remember the funeral as if it were yesterday. We sat in the front pew of the Trinity United Methodist Church. My mother wore a black hat and thick veil. I was in a brand new suit. Even in her grief, Mom insisted on blue instead of black, because it would be more practical for wearing at other times. But I never wore that suit again. I just couldn't. I sat like a statue through the service, staring at Dad's casket. I can still hear the preacher droning on and on about salvation and God's will. I think that's the day I lost my faith. I never attended church again until my mother's funeral last year. We never had a funeral for my sister. She just slowly disappeared from our lives."

His voice faded and then stopped, as if he'd run out of enough air to push words from his mouth. He looked directly at me, and I could see fresh wet streaks on his cheeks.

"The police never determined who broke in, or why?" I asked.

"Apparently, someone who'd heard about the rifle decided to steal it. It was missing. I remember overhearing Mom telling the officers about the rifle, and that Dad had borrowed it to show us. They kept asking her about property passes and permits. She finally started crying and they stopped. They were walking away when she called them back and told them the truth, that Dad planned to sell the rifle. She didn't mention their deep debt."

"Did your mother or the police have any idea who may have stolen the rifle?"

"The police assumed a potential buyer or middleman my father had spoken to. Whoever stole it must have found a private collector, because the rifle never surfaced."

"Was anything else stolen?"

Davidson nodded, his lips pursed in a thin line. "My sister's bedspread."

An icy trail ran down my spine. "Oh," was the best I could manage.

"And Dad's yellow rain slicker," Davidson said.

"Was it raining that night?"

"No." Davidson frowned. "I remember the night was very warm for September, even by Texas standards."

"But even if it was raining it would be odd to think of the murd...intruder worrying about getting wet. So why take a raincoat?"

"I don't know," Davidson said. His face distorted for a moment, probably from morbid thoughts similar to my own. "As for my Dad's murder, the police believed it was accidental—part of a burglary gone wrong. No one was supposed to be at home that night. It was only at the last minute that my parents decided my sister was too ill to attend."

"Who knew you weren't supposed to be home?"

"I have no idea. Mom might have told friends, Dad might have told others at the university. My sister and I complained to schoolmates about having to go to the symphony, not that that matters."

Great. So the list of possible suspects is pretty much anyone and everyone the family knew. "What about the murder weapon?"

"I know there wasn't anything at the scene. But I don't know what the conclusion was, what my Dad was actually murdered with." Davidson's voice hitched as he spoke.

"Why did the police think your sister was taken?"

"I don't know. No one talked to me about it, and I only overheard bits and pieces of conversations."

"Maybe the burglar panicked and took your sister rather than take a chance she could identify him."

Davidson uttered a long, shaky sigh. "I've tried not to think too graphically about it. About what might have happened to her afterward..." He turned toward me, the haunted, pained look in his eyes made me shudder. "We never received any ransom calls or notes, and no one ever claimed to have seen her. I know the police told Mom they believed my sister was later killed and her body was, well..." Davidson looked away and began rubbing his head again.

For his sister's sake I hoped the police were right. The alternative could definitely have been far worse. I was confused, though, about the point of the story, as revealing as it was about Davidson's character. "But how does this fit in with the woman I'm following, and with the letter I received?"

"Because I believe the woman you are following may be my sister."

"Excuse me?" I blinked several times, as if that could make things clearer. "So you think the cops were wrong?"

BOND, TWIN BOND

No matter where you live, brothers are brothers and sisters are sisters. The bonds that keep family close are the same no matter where you are.
~Takayuki Ikkaku, Arisa Hosaka and Toshihiro Kawabata, Animal Crossing: Wild World, 2005

Davidson nodded. "Yes. I've spent many years *knowing* she was dead, and suffered through thousands of nightmares of what happened to her after she was taken from our house. Believe me, Ms. Morgan, this possibility is as hard for me to accept as it is for you."

I doubted that. Wishful thinking can be a powerful thing, but I didn't say anything.

Davidson sighed and rubbed the top of his head. "Since I've moved back to San Antonio, my confidence in that old *truth* has been seriously shaken. Three times now, I've seen a woman I'm convinced may be her. Twice in the background of a television news story, and once in the paper, in the photo I gave you."

I thought about what he was suggesting. There were certainly records of adults who'd dropped out of society to start life over with a new identity. But most missing children, especially young children, turn out to be the victims of others' foul intentions. So the possibility that his kidnapped sister was now the mysterious woman I'd been hired to follow was pretty remote. "I'm sorry, but that's a pretty big leap of faith. Are you sure it isn't just wishful thinking?"

"I don't know." Davidson put his hand on his chest as if to calm himself and then lifted his hand to polish his bald spot some more. I was beginning to think he'd gone bald from the excessive rubbing.

"The photo you gave me, and the woman I saw at the Bargain Mart, is dark haired. Your hair is fair. Yet you think she's your twin sister. Why? From what I saw, admittedly briefly, she doesn't look much like you."

"I don't know," Davidson said again. "But every bit of me believes I'm right. Maybe it's because we're twins. They've done lots of studies about the so-called twin bond. Maybe I recognize her in more ways than just physical appearance. And she could have died her hair. "

"Okay, let's pursue the twin bond thing for a minute. Shouldn't she feel some pull to you as well? Don't you think she'd have tried to contact you, if she really was alive? After all, you've stayed in this area for your entire life. She could certainly track you down fairly easily."

"I don't know." Davidson was getting awfully repetitive. He also wasn't being very helpful.

"If you're so sure she's alive, why don't you go to her yourself? You're the one who directed me to the Bargain Mart. You could just as easily have sat there as I did, and for a lot less money."

He stood and paced from one end of his small apartment to the other. "No matter how much I want to *believe* it's her, I'm not sure it *is* her, and I don't want to confront a total stranger and come off as some sort of lunatic—or stalker."

I nodded, but couldn't help wondering if he *was* a bit of a lunatic. He'd made *me* the stalker.

He paused his pacing and turned to face me. "And if it *is* her, why has she never tried to find me after all these years? Why would she have chosen to remain isolated? I don't want to just show up. I might frighten her, or anger her in some way I can't fathom. She may have been brainwashed. She may not even remember she has a twin brother. Who knows what she was told, or what was done to her."

He has me there.

Davidson again sat on the sofa. "If she *did* live, there's no way of knowing her mental and emotional condition. What if she's now completely hateful? Or evil? Or even psychotic or sociopathic? What if she wouldn't recognize me, no matter how much we still look alike? I'm afraid to face a reality that may be very different from the one I want."

"Well…Well…" I was definitely at a loss for words. I didn't know if he honestly believed everything he'd just said, or if he was trying to convince us both. I shook my head, stood, and looked down at Davidson. I studied him, looking for any sign that he was yanking me around. What I saw was a combination of fear and hope etched on his drawn, pale skin and in his eyes. As far as I could tell, he really believed what he'd told me.

For the moment, at least, I'd give him the benefit of the doubt, but I was definitely going to reserve final judgment until more facts were in. "Okay. I see now why you were reluctant to tell me who you thought I was following. But how would she know about me? How could she have sent the letter?"

"I don't know, unless there's someone else involved." He told me about the previous night's apparent liaison with a woman.

"You're sure you don't remember anything? Just how drunk did you get?" I couldn't help the incredulous tone that crept into my voice.

"I don't know." He buried his face in his hands. "Even if I drank the whole bottle, I shouldn't have lost the entire night. Perhaps she drugged me."

"That's a pretty big stretch." I smirked. But I could see his shoulders were shuddering from withheld tears. *Dammit. I'm not trying to be a bitch.* I just found his story difficult to accept. I softened my tone, sat beside him, and gingerly patted his arm, even though it was hard for me to do. "Is this the first time this has happened?"

"No," he admitted quietly. "I've started calling it the Lost Time, because I've recently lost quite a few bits and pieces of time, but never a whole night before. I've started seeing a psychiatrist, but I still want to believe it's just the stress of wondering if my sister is alive after all these years, and that it'll pass when we learn the truth."

"That's possible." I tried to sound sincere. "Why don't you at least cut the booze out completely for a while. Perhaps your *lost times* will stop."

"Yes, yes, I will." He lifted his eyes to mine. "Thank you for not assuming I'm crazy." He tried to smile, but his mouth didn't seem up to the task.

I figured it wasn't a good idea to say what I really thought at the moment. Instead, I changed the subject. "Let me think about this."

"May I call you tomorrow?" Davidson asked. "Perhaps you'll have come up with a more solid plan, or at least some additional ideas, to find out who this woman is."

"I won't be around tomorrow. I'll be out riding."

"Riding?" Davidson asked with raised eyebrows.

I shrugged. "I belong to a motorcycle club called the Hill Country Cruisers."

"Please tell me about it."

I could tell by Davidson's tone of voice that he was asking for a change of topic. I figured a change of topic would help my mood, too. "Every Saturday morning at nine the group meets for breakfast at the Blue Bonnet Cafe in Marble Falls. From there we head out for a ride through the hill country."

"That sounds like a nice way to spend a weekend day." Davidson smiled. "How many riders go along?"

"Around seventy-five or so. Most of the Austin riders meet at eight on the southwest side of town, and ride to Marble Falls together. But that's out of the way for me. Instead, I take 1431 from Cedar Park and join up with them at the cafe. I kind of like it that way. It gives me some time to ride alone as well as the pleasure of a large group ride." I realized I'd been babbling a bit and gave Davidson a sheepish grin. "Sorry. I've probably bored you with my long-winded answer to your question."

"Not a bit," Davidson said with a warm smile. "I remember the Blue Bonnet Cafe. I've eaten there many times in the past, although not for several years. Is it still as good as ever? Do they still bake those wonderful pies?"

"They sure do." I laughed. "And they were just voted best place to eat breakfast in Texas. Maybe you should drive out there soon. Maybe it'll help you feel a bit less lost and isolated."

"That's a good idea. I could use a break from the slump I've been in."

"I'll be off." I gathered my helmet and jacket off the floor. "Keep me posted if you think of anything else. And thanks for finally telling me what this case is really about."

"You're welcome, and I'm sorry I withheld the information before now. I let my pride and fear overrule my logic."

"That's okay." I nodded and shrugged. "I might've done the same thing. By the way, what's your sister's name?"

"Stephanie."

Of course. Stephen/Stephanie. He and his sister had been born in the bad-joke days when even boy/girl twins were named alike and dressed alike.

I mulled over what Davidson told me as I walked back to the parking garage. I could see why he was a bit wiggy. If his *dead* sister had suddenly started popping up around town, he was probably a lot wiggier than he acted. His story had enough holes in it to make a nice hamster habitrail, not the least of which was where had she been all this time, and with whom. But I'd go with what I had for now, because I liked him. He was like a lost puppy, kind and friendly but also desperate for love and attention. I just hoped he wasn't going to bite me down the road.

The sidewalk radiated heat and was packed with strange-looking tourists. From the looks of the outfits, makeup, and hair, the Intergalactic Travel Consortium was in town. I saw hairdos—on women *and men* in every shape and color imaginable—spiky gold solar flares, silver spiral galaxies, swooping white spaceship wings, and some that were so bizarre they defied description.

I reached the garage without incident or abduction by aliens. I was so happy to be away from the oddballs on the street that I gave Max an affectionate pat on his leather seat before climbing on. As I rode past the large Henry B. Gonzales Convention Center, I glanced over. The center's marquee proudly announced in multi-bulb lettering:

WELCOME NATIONAL HAIR STYLIST
COMPETITION FINALISTS

3:07 PM *** 103°

So, my suspicions about aliens were confirmed. Well, almost. It wasn't intergalactic delegates, but close enough.

I could feel every one of those hundred and three degrees sitting at the Market and Alamo Street light. When I moved my foot, my boot pulled from the melting asphalt with a sucking sound. The ride back wasn't going to be nearly as pleasant as the ride down, no matter which route I took. I decided to go back the way I'd come. Talking about the Blue Bonnet Cafe made me realize how hungry I was. I could almost smell the chicken fried steak and chocolate cream pie from here, or maybe it was just the frying fat and sugar smell of the Mexican buñuelos pastry stand on the nearby corner.

I eased up the Highway 281 entrance ramp and revved Max to sixty almost immediately. I was halfway to the city limits before it struck me—Davidson revealed more than before, but how did he know Stephanie drove a sky blue Taurus and hung out behind a gray door next to the Bargain Mart?

Angry at myself for not having thought of it before, I whipped past an aging hippie in a rusted vintage VW Beetle, leaned into the wind, and rocketed my ass out of town.

MUSING AND SCHEMING

The greatest obstacle to discovery is not ignorance—
it is the illusion of knowledge. ~Daniel J. Boorstin (1914-)

Stephanie sat at the Jim's Coffee Shop on Broadway, staring out at the late evening traffic. On the table in front of her sat a mostly untouched chicken salad and heavy white mug of coffee. Her fingers drummed softly on the table.

She mulled over what she'd learned from Carlos and Virgil. Could it really be the same rifle? If so, she *must* get her hands on it, no matter how much more she'd have to pay than any buyer Carlos might find. But then what? She couldn't sell it. She lived too transient a life to keep it anywhere safe.

She decided not to worry about what to do if, no *when,* she got her hands on that rifle. Instead, she turned her full mulling to the *how.*

Carlos had said he didn't care who got the rifle, that for him it was all about getting the most money he could out of the deal. But was that true? When push came to shove, would he let her have it? Perhaps he'd think a Mexican buyer would pay more because it was part of their heritage. Or maybe he'd grow reluctant to sell right away, thinking he could find a better deal from someone who wasn't a friend.

Stephanie snorted aloud at that last thought. She most certainly didn't consider Carlos and Virgil friends, but she knew their definition of friend was more lax than hers. In fact, Stephanie didn't consider anyone to be a friend. She had no use for other people, people who snuck behind your back while lying to your face, people who let you down when you most needed them, people who hurt you, people who—

"Aw, crap," Stephanie said with a frown. She didn't need to dwell on past relationships or the disappointments they had wrought. She took a large gulp of the now lukewarm coffee then forced herself to eat a couple of bites of salad, mostly because she didn't know when she'd be eating again.

After a few minutes, she felt her spirits lifting. She decided her sullen mood was at least partly due to blood sugar. It could also, of course, be because as she ate, a plan came to her.

Yes, that's exactly what I need to do. Why get into a bidding war with Carlos? I'm smarter than him. I'm more cautious than him. And I'm definitely more devious than him.

Stephanie's mouth twisted into a tight-lipped sneer as she ran over the idea again and again, looking for gotchas and tightening up details. It would take some more play-acting on her part, cozying up to Carlos and acting like a real bud, but she could do it if it meant she'd get her hands on the rifle, maybe even with *no* exchange of money.

She nodded with satisfaction as she rose and tossed a handful of dollars on the table. Carlos would never know what hit him, figuratively speaking. Virgil was always clueless, so there'd be no change there. And Stephanie would have the rifle.

Yes, she was sure that finding the rifle was the key to her well-being. Perhaps even to her sanity.

HILL COUNTRY CRUISE

Danger, Will Robinson, danger. ~Robot, Lost in Space (1969)

Saturday morning brought a promise of beautiful weather, especially by July standards. Puffy, popcorn-shaped clouds dotted the sky, enough to hint at a chance of afternoon rain. I'd definitely sacrifice the sun in exchange for lower temperatures. I finished my morning chores—feeding cats and scooping litter boxes—then dressed and put on a bit of makeup, hoping it would offset the helmet hair look I knew I'd be suffering before long.

A day of motorcycle riding, friendship, and good food beckoned. I grabbed my bright yellow rain gear and stuffed it into Max's right saddle bag, shoved my purse and cell phone into the left one, and headed to Ranch Road 1431 for the second day in a row.

More and more winding country roads are falling victim to the highway department's determination to widen and straighten everything in sight. This is all well and good for the harried commuter, but it sucks for weekend rides. Thank goodness, though, once you left Cedar Park, 1431 narrows to two lanes full of fun and challenging twists and curves.

A few miles west of Lago Vista, where the northernmost fingers of Lake Travis reach, I crossed the first of two cattle guards. I love the idea that a main thoroughfare still requires cattle guards to keep loose livestock from wandering away from home. The brup-brup sound the motorcycle tires made as they crossed the heavy iron pipes of the cattle guard also reminded me that ranches in this area span the road, and cows roam freely back and forth. I kept a watchful eye, because any encounter between a cow and a motorcycle is a losing proposition for the motorcycle. I guess it wouldn't do the cow any good, either.

The ride to Marble Falls was more relaxing than yesterday's, thanks to having a more pleasant destination. When I wheeled into the Blue Bonnet Cafe's parking lot at least thirty other bikes were already there. Eric, Bill, and Christine pulled in behind me. We waved and exchanged a flurry of *g'mornins* as we pulled off helmets and rocked bikes onto center stands in the steeply angled lot.

We entered the crowded restaurant and were quickly greeted by a graying *blonde* waitress sporting one of the biggest Texas Big Hair looks I'd ever seen. We followed her as she wound between closely-packed tables with the skill of a slalom skier. Friends hollered our names and waved as we passed. I felt lighter and happier than I had for days.

After the Rancher's Special breakfast of three eggs, bacon, sausage patty, biscuits smothered in country gravy, and pan-fried hash browns, I waddled to the parking lot with the other riders. We had a loud debate about the day's ride before we settled on heading west from Marble Falls to Lake Buchanan, another destination along the Colorado River, and the reason this area is sometimes called the Chain of Lakes. Seven lakes span the Colorado, ending in downtown Austin with Lady Bird Lake, named after former President Lyndon Johnson's wife and champion of the environment. Lake Buchanan is the northernmost, and largest of the bunch.

As a kid, I proudly announced one Monday morning at Show and Tell that I'd visited all seven lakes the day before. Mom didn't tell me for years, but the teacher actually called to tell her I was *telling fibs* at school. I'd love to have seen Miss Sprouse's expression when Mom confirmed my story with the terse question, "Would you like me to name them?" That Sunday jaunt had taken all day. Today's ride would only take a couple of hours, including a midpoint stop for a beer. But even these short jaunts reminded me of the fun we'd had on those Sunday rides so many years ago. Thoughts of Davidson's troubled childhood arose, but I shook my head hard, determined to forget work at least for the day.

I straddled Max, revved the engine, and followed the pack. Fifty or sixty motorcycles look and sound pretty impressive, and several small boys shouted and waved at us as we sat at the light. We tooted our horns—Bill's eighteen-wheeler ah-ooga airhorn got special cheers—and then waved as we headed out of town.

It's almost impossible to talk over the roar of motorcycle engines. We tooted horns, waved hand signals, and even waggled our heads to communicate interesting scenery and the need for a gasoline or potty pitstop. The farther we rode, the more I felt my tense muscles relax. I was especially grateful today for the diversion. I also love the sense of belonging I get from these rides. My parents live in Seattle these days, and my older brother moves around a lot as a high tech consultant. Growing up, we were a close family, and I've stayed in touch via emails, texting, and phone calls, but it isn't the same. Riding through the country like this, surrounded by others like me, makes me feel less lonely and isolated.

In spite of myself, I again thought about what Davidson told me. Was I really following his sister? They were fraternal twins, not identical ones, but I should still be able to tell once I got her face to face. A drive down to Terrell Hills was definitely in order. Maybe I could learn something worthwhile from the neighbors, if any of the Davidson's neighbors still lived nearby.

Around two, the Hill Country Cruisers stopped for lunch at Lake Buchanan. The Dam View restaurant overlooks the lake's two and a half mile long, S-shaped dam, the longest multiple-arch dam in the

U.S. I'd always intended to walk its entire length, but never made it past halfway. I always get distracted by the four-foot catfish that hang out where the lake meets the dam. Years of visitors tossing them dog food and French fries have turned the fish into fat, friendly, fresh-water monstrosities.

From my chair, I watched several of the dam's thirty-seven flood gates. Water seeped from the gates, leaving mossy green stripes down the concrete. I wondered how many years the downstreamers had before the 1937 dam failed and billions of gallons of water headed their way in a torrent.

We spent a good hour hanging out at Dam View, trading riding adventures and other lies. It started to sprinkle as we paid our bills, so we decided to bag more scenic riding and head straight home. It would be an easy ride for me—all the way back 1431 to my neighborhood turn-off.

Once we reached Marble Falls, we went our separate ways. A few brave souls stopped at the Blue Bonnet again for pie. Most of the others headed south toward home. I decided I'd abused my cholesterol count enough for one day and headed home, too.

I swung east toward Cedar Park, happy to be alone again, with the sounds of birds and cicadas adding a nice background chorus to the quiet thrum of Max's engine. Twenty miles east of Marble Falls, a beat-up, rust-bucket of a white Chevy pickup truck with an enormous grill guard roared up from behind. I figured the truck's motor must be in better shape than its body to catch up with me. I wasn't exactly creeping along, although I was going slower than normal thanks to the light rain. I moved as far to the right as possible—trying to stay out of the jumble of rocks and assorted crap on the shoulder—to let the asshole pass me. He was obviously in more of a hurry than I was.

He pulled up even and matched my speed. I glanced left, and our eyes briefly locked. He grinned, his lips curled back, exposing his teeth. I caught a glimpse of long, stringy blond hair and a scruffy mustache before I whipped my head back to the road. Then, without warning, he cut sharply to the right.

"Hey fuckhead!" I yelled. "What the hell are you doing?"

I swerved onto the shoulder. The wheels spun through rocks and slick caliche mud. Max's front wheel caught a large rock and shuddered violently. Then came the tankslappers. *Oh shit.* The handlebars whipped back and forth, slapping my hands against the gas tank. I tried desperately to hold on. It was too late.

The right handlebars pulled free from my hand. The front tire, now almost completely sideways, suddenly grabbed traction. The bike flipped. I sailed through the air—rising in slow motion. Then I hurtled down, a stretch of dirty pavement loomed large in my vision.

In the split second before I landed, my brain screamed *TUCK*! I tried, but almost instantly felt the searing pain of body parts meeting ground. The world spun as I rolled like a rag doll. I slid and bounced through rocks, gravel, and dirt. Max flipped end over end six or seven feet in the air, then disappeared in a cloud of brown dust. I could hear the sound of Max smashing apart. It was quickly replaced with the sound of my own voice screaming from the pain of my skin being torn off by the gravel tearing through my jeans.

After what felt like forever, I slid to a stop. I took a couple of ragged breaths. Max had also come to a stop, his engine dead. Silence surrounded me. I lay there, stunned. *At least I'm still alive.* I wiggled my fingers and my toes. At least everything still worked. I sat up slowly and pulled off my gloves and helmet. The center of the tinted visor was scraped from top to bottom. The helmet was scraped flat on one side and had cracked down the other.

I tossed the ruined helmet aside and looked myself over. I wasn't in any better shape than my helmet. My jeans hung on me in tatters—the loose, ragged edges dark with blood. My exposed parts were no longer covered with skin, just raw hamburger flesh, stickily coated with dirt and gravel.

Except for lots of shredded skin and one fairly deep gash extending from my upper thigh almost to my knee, I seemed fine. I tried standing, but the searing pain in my left ankle made me sway and told me that it was definitely *not* fine. It was broken or badly sprained. I grunted and gritted my teeth.

I hobbled to what was left of Max, who'd come to rest about twenty-five feet past me. I'd recover, but Max was a goner. *Goddamit. I loved that bike.*

"Shit," I mumbled, and then yelled, "SHIT! SHIT! SHIT!"

I heard an engine rev and looked up at the road. The white pickup truck was stopped about fifty feet away. The driver looked at me for a long moment, and then opened his mouth in a full-toothed grin. After a few more seconds, the truck accelerated down the road, rear tires squealing. I just caught a glimpse of a yellow and red bumper sticker on a rusty bumper as the truck disappeared.

"You goddammed fucking Killer Pickup Truck!" I screamed. I cursed through gritted teeth that I hadn't had a chance to catch the truck's license number.

I rooted around in Max's torn and scraped saddle bag, extracting my cell phone, which was thankfully intact. There was only one signal bar, so I said a silent prayer and dialed 911. It seemed to take forever for the cell phone to make the connection, but finally a bored-sounding woman answered, "Nine-one-one, what is your emergency?" I explained as calmly as possible that I'd been in a hit-and-run accident and that I was injured.

She asked for specific directions, and I did the best I could. "I'm off the south shoulder of 1431 about halfway between Marble Falls and Cedar Park."

She asked for an exact address.

"You've got to be kidding." Even though my cell phone had survived the accident, I decided investing in a new GPS-enabled phone was probably a good idea.

The operator finally accepted that I could give her no additional details, and she said the police and ambulance were on their way. "Stay put," she said.

Like I could get anywhere in my current situation.

I sat on the remain's of Max's left saddle bag and tried to remove my left riding boot. I winced in pain. The ankle was already too swollen. So I waited, amusing myself by picking the larger bits of gravel out of my skin and tapping my good foot in time with the pounding of my injured ankle. I lost track of time after about twenty minutes.

"Ma'am, are you all right?"

I felt a warm, steadying hand on my shoulder and looked up. My eyes didn't want to focus. My head felt heavy.

"I'm cold." I giggled at the thought of being cold in the middle of a Texas July, even if it was raining.

Giggling must have been the wrong response, because the kneeling officer suddenly stood and hollered, "Hey, Kaminski, bring a blanket down here RIGHT NOW!"

A second officer, Kaminski I assumed through my fog, came trotting up, carrying an ugly green plaid blanket. She and the officer who'd first spoken wrapped the blanket around my shoulders. Kaminski handed me a styrofoam cup filled with something dark and hot—it tasted like tea.

"The ambulance is on its way," the male officer said gently. "I'm Deputy Patrick O'Meara. This is Deputy Kathy Kaminski. We'll both stay right here. Are you warmer now, ma'am?"

"Yes." I looked up into eyes that were the blue of the Caribbean Sea. "Thanks. Shock, I guess. And please call me Marianna. I feel old enough right now without being called ma'am."

Deputy O'Meara smiled and reached out to push back a lock of hair that was hanging in my eye. "Sure. Marianna's a nice name. I'm not surprised you're in shock. You're pretty beat up. Can you tell us what happened?"

I told them about the accident and gave them as detailed a description as I could remember of the white Chevy and its piece-of-shit driver.

"We'll see what we can do to track him down." Deputy O'Meara frowned. "But it's a long shot, with no license plate number."

I sighed. "I know."

The ambulance arrived. Two paramedics trotted down the embankment toward us, slipping and sliding on the loose gravel.

"Hey, watch it!" I called. "That's my skin on those rocks."

Deputy O'Meara laughed and patted my shoulder. "You're going to be just fine."

The paramedics fussed over my ankle, carefully cutting away the tattered remains of my jeans. I fainted while they were forcing the boot off my left foot, now even more swollen than when I'd made the attempt.

I snapped awake when one paramedic poured some kind of antiseptic that stung like hell over the open wounds. The other wrapped everything in white gauze, which didn't stay white very long. They slipped a self-inflating bootie over my ankle and pulled its ring. It puffed up, enclosing my ankle and foot like a burrito. I grunted from the pressure pushing against swollen, raw skin.

Once my ankle was stabilized, they turned their attention to the gash on my right thigh. One paramedic cut the tatters off my jeans, exposing the oozing wound in all its glory—or gory. The other poured more antiseptic on it. I flinched and winced from pain.

"Looks like you need stitches," the paramedic wielding scissors said.

"Can you do it here?" I asked.

Both paramedics and both cops just stared at me.

"Okay. I just hate hospitals." I sighed, resigned to my fate.

"Understandable," Deputy Kaminski said, "but even I can tell that cut needs more than side-of-the-road tending. Looks pretty nasty."

"Let's get you up and into the ambulance so we can take you to the hospital," the paramedic with the antiseptic said.

"My pride wants to insist I'm fine, just take me home, the cut's not that bad, and my ankle will be fine, but my primitive brain is yelling *I want drugs and I want them now!* so let's go. But no stretcher. I feel safer trying to walk than having you carry me flat on my back through this slippery caliche mud."

We made slow progress to the edge of the road. It took all four of my rescuers to help me up the final embankment and into the back of the ambulance.

"Wait! What about Max?"

"Max?" Deputy O'Meara glanced down the hill. "I thought you were alone."

"My motorcycle."

"Oh. I'll call a wrecker to come get it. Where do you want it taken? Doesn't look like there's much left."

"No, I'm afraid not. Could they take him to Zabor's Motorcycles in Austin? It's on Braker."

"Sure. You go on. We'll be in touch if we have other questions."

"Deputy O'Meara, Deputy Kaminski, thanks for all your help. If I had to be in an accident, at least I was cared for by two pretty nice folks." I smiled at both of them, wondering if Deputy O'Meara noticed I lingered just a bit on him.

"You're more than welcome." Deputy O'Meara leaned toward me, making a pretense of ensuring my leg was out of the way of the ambulance door. "And please call me Patrick." When he stepped back, I saw Deputy Kaminski was grinning from ear to ear.

I figured three things—Patrick had noticed my extended gaze, so had Deputy Kaminski, and Patrick was going to get a bit of a ribbing during their ride back to headquarters.

As one of the paramedics closed the ambulance door, Patrick smiled again and waved. His smile was warm and friendly, his eyes caring and concerned. I couldn't help but trust him to take care of Max—and me. I smiled back.

As we drove off, I looked back toward Max and mouthed a silent goodbye to my old friend.

WEEKEND ACTIVITIES

Don't get mad, get even. ~Robert F. Kennedy (1925-1968)

Stephanie slammed the gray door with the full force of her frustration and twisted the lock. She hadn't had nearly as much free time today as she'd wanted. There were too damn many irons in the fire. She dug through her purse and extracted her comb, which she ran slowly through her hair. She relaxed with each stroke, as if the repetitive movement unwound a spring deep inside her.

Her eyes adjusted to the dim room, and she noticed the blinking message light on the answering machine. She'd considered a cell phone, but preferred not to be that reachable—or traceable. Sometimes old tech was best.

The answering machine showed only one call. *It'd better be Darnell. He said he'd take care of that bitch on Saturday, and Saturday's quickly drawing to a close.* She moved to the back of the room, and pressed the Play button.

Darnell's voice sounded haughty. "It's done. She'll be laid up for a few days, at least. I'd like the rest of my money. Call me." He laughed, then the message ended.

She picked up the phone and dialed his number. She heard him hack on the phlegm in his throat and then spit what she knew was a large blob of tobacco juice before he spoke. "Yeah?"

Stephanie frowned in disgust. Her voice was subdued, but had a throaty, hard edge. "Tell me."

"Sure thing, Stephie ol' girl." Tom uttered a wheezy laugh. "Ran 'er off the road east of Marble Falls. She's hurt, and I'm pretty sure her motorcycle's trashed. Last I saw of her she'd hobbled over to the bike and was cussin' up a blue streak."

"I told you to get her out of my hair," Stephanie said through gritted teeth. She stopped combing. Her internal spring spiraled back into full tension.

"And I did. She'll be out of commission for a while. I can kill her if ya like, but it'll cost ya a *lot* more dough."

"You said you watched her walk to her bike. I hardly call that out of commission."

"I *said* she *hobbled*. Jeez, Steph, give me a break. I sat in my friggin' truck for four hours waitin' for her ass to get back to Marble Falls so I could follow her."

"Yes, I'm sure that was hard work."

"Fuck you. I had better things to do. The piss-ant amount you're paying me doesn't count for much when you figger how much time I wasted. Look, I gotta get going. You have the rest of my money or not?"

"Yes-I've-got-the-rest-of-your-money." Her teeth were clenched. One small vein in her forehead pulsed rapidly.

"Gonna bring it to me?"

"Like hell. You can come get it."

"Aw, Steph, you love the Snake Farm. I'll be here 'til eleven. Besides, I'll let you stroke my favorite snake!" He hooted with raw, coarse laughter.

Her teeth clenched even tighter. "I'm not driving that far, and anyway, I've got to be somewhere else for a while. You can meet me in San Antonio at midnight."

Tom emitted an over-exaggerated sigh. "Fine. Sure. How about Whisky Smith's? I got some business in that part of town."

She resumed the long, slow stroke with the comb through her hair. "That'll do just fine." She hung up the phone, closed her eyes, and pulled her lips into a pale, pencil-thin smile. *You want a break you bastard? I'll give you a break.*

MY OWN LOST TIME

Sleep tight, don't let the bedbugs bite. ~unknown

Judy answered the phone with a terse, "Yes."

"What the hell's wrong with you?" I asked.

"Oh, it's just you. Sorry. I've gotten about a dozen damn telemarketing calls today, and I figured it was another one. What's up? Ready to go diving in the morning?"

"Can you come get me?"

"Tomorrow? Is something wrong with your car?"

"Now."

"I'm supposed to meet Richard for dinner in forty-five minutes. We're trying that new sushi restaurant on Lamar."

"Please."

Judy must have finally heard the strain in my voice. "Marianna, what's wrong? Where are you?"

"I'm in the Seton Northwest emergency room with a wicked sprained ankle and a Frankenstein slash on my leg and there's blood all over what's left of my jeans and I think I left at least half of my leg skin on the rocks along 1431 and I left my helmet in the dirt where I landed because it was cracked open and Max isn't rideable anymore but that's okay because I'm not in any shape to ride him anyway and—"

"Whoa! Slow down. What happened?"

I took a long, deep breath. "I was in an accident."

"My God. I'll be right there."

"I can't dive with you tomorrow."

"Shut up, kiddo."

Thank God the cats stayed off the bed. Even the weight of the sheet hurt. And thanks to some pretty kickass painkillers, I slept through the night, but it wasn't a restful sleep. I awoke Sunday morning feeling like I'd been a featured guest contestant on the World Wrestling Federation show.

I raised up on one elbow—a task that took a while to accomplish—and squinted at the clock. It was just after eight. I was amazed that none of the hoard had demanded breakfast. Maybe they could be understanding after all. I pushed myself up the rest of the way and gently slid my legs over the side of the bed.

As soon as I moved my left leg, my sprained ankle loudly protested. The hard plastic and velcro brace helped, but there was no way to keep everything perfectly still. Even the slightest movement felt like the searing jolt of a cattle prod, which I had felt—once—but that wasn't an experience I like to remember very often. I sat, panting, for a full minute, trying to quiet the various throbs and stings that snaked across my body.

The cats had obviously been watching, because as soon as I sat up, all six of them jumped onto the bed. They still kept their distance, though, choosing instead to form a furry semi-circle around me. I wondered if Judy fed them the night before or if they were sizing me up as a breakfast option.

I stood and tried to balance on my good foot. That wasn't going to work. I leaned my other leg against the bed for stability, and carefully unbuttoned the cotton shorty robe Judy had dressed me in. Bless her heart, she'd found the one thing I could sleep in that didn't require me to raise my arms over my head. I grabbed the crutch Judy'd leaned against the nightstand and lurched my way into the bathroom.

Glimpsing myself in the mirror was a mistake, but I had to know. I pivoted, looking over my shoulder as much as my stiff neck would allow. "You look like hell," I groused to the black, purple, and blue hag staring back at me.

My normally monochromatic skin now looked like a technicolor painting. At least my helmet had protected my face. I had only one dark purple bruise along the base of my right jaw. Below the neck, however, I was a wreck. Probably almost as bad as Max. I still had most of my skin from the waist up—my leather jacket had sustained the damage instead—but large purple and black bruises were already blooming on both forearms, my left shoulder, and my right shoulder blade.

Waist-down was the worst. I was almost solid bruise. My swollen legs looked like they'd been removed and replaced by giant alien's legs from the planet Plum. I was surprised I still had blood in my veins, so much seemed to be stuck in freeze-frame beneath my skin.

In high-relief contrast to the purple were the large, white gauze bandages patchworked on my lower landscape. Both kneecaps, the front and side of my right thigh, and my right hip were heavily swathed. The skin below them stung every time I moved. I peeled back the largest bandage, the one on my right thigh. Beneath it was the long gash, neatly stitched but still oozing. Surrounding it was puss-and-blood colored road rash.

My stomach did a little flop. "You sonofabitch," I mumbled. "What the hell did I do to you?" I pressed the tape back in place. No need to look under the other bandages. I knew I'd find more of the same.

I will find the asshole who ran me off the road. I hadn't recognized him, at least not in the brief glimpse I got. His truck wasn't familiar, either, although something tickled deep in my memory. I tried to think about it, but there was no way my brain was going to engage today. Latent shock, pain, and narcotics had seized control.

I sighed, then popped another couple of pain pills in my mouth. I couldn't stand the thought of any more fabric against my skin, at least not for a little while, so I wobbled naked back through the bedroom toward the kitchen. I fed the kitties, grunting with effort as I bent over to place their plates on the floor, and started extra strong coffee for me. Sitting on a rattan-covered dining chair while naked and raw didn't seem like a good idea, so I leaned on my crutch while waiting for the coffee to brew.

Balancing my steaming mug, I made slow, awkward progress back to the bedroom. I needed a shower, but the emergency room doctor had been very clear that I couldn't get my skin wet for at least twenty-four hours, to give the fragile, thin scabs time to toughen up a bit. The long slice down my thigh would have to stay dry even longer—until the stitches came out. I sighed, set my coffee on the night stand, dropped the damn crutch on the floor, and crawled gingerly back into bed. By then the pain pills had kicked in. I fell asleep without taking another sip of coffee.

I woke to the ringing of my cell phone. The voicemail greeting kicked in by the time I found it on the floor, probably knocked off the nightstand by a cat. I glanced at the caller ID. It was Larry, the only person other than Judy I'd willingly talk to in my current state. I pressed the Call Back option and waited.

"I should come whup your butt." In spite of his choice of words, Larry's voice sounded worried.

"You're too late."

"So I hear. Judy tells me you were run off the road yesterday."

"What time is it?"

"Nine-thirty. Don't change the subject."

"Bring me some breakfast?"

"It's nine-thirty at night."

"Oh. I guess I slept all day." I stroked my fingers through my hair. It felt like straw. "Well, maybe not. I seem to remember the phone ringing, and I think I peed once or twice, and I'm pretty sure I took more of those great pain pills."

Larry's voice softened. "Cutie, I'll be happy to come over and bring you some food. Give me thirty minutes."

I crawled out of bed, still stiff and sore but better than I was in the morning. I ran a comb through my dirt and gravel-dulled hair. It didn't do much to improve it. The most prominent result was a hailstorm of gravel bits all over my bathroom floor. I couldn't very well meet Larry naked, so I managed to pull cotton shorts and a T-shirt on, although it took awhile. I'd barely finished when the doorbell rang.

Larry kissed me on the forehead and stepped back. His eyes moved down and then back up my entire body. He whistled. "You look like one of those impersonist paintings—*Stormy sunset over raging seas* or something."

"Impressionist," I corrected automatically.

"Whatever. Come on into the kitchen. Have you fed the cats tonight? They looked at me like I was tuna."

"No." I grabbed a throw pillow off the sofa and carried it with me. I put it on top of the rattan chair seat and slowly and gently lowered my butt onto it. Larry took two brisket and scrambled egg breakfast tacos out of a paper bag and put them on a plate. He opened each flour tortilla and added a generous stripe of bright red salsa. He placed the plate, a fork, and a glass of orange juice in front of me and sat down.

"Tell me what happened." His forehead furrowed with worry.

"Can I eat first?"

"You have ten minutes."

"What a guy." I downed both tacos in less than five. I hadn't realized how hungry I was until the food was in front of me. And Larry, bless his heart, knew that my favorite dinner was breakfast.

He placed our plates in the sink and sat back down. "Okay, start talkin'."

I filled Larry in on my previous day's fun. "When did Judy call you?"

"After she got you home last night. I called the Williamson County Sheriff's Office and they connected me with Deputy O'Meara. He faxed me a copy of the police report."

"If you saw the police report, why'd you need me to tell you what happened?"

Larry gave me a patronizing look. "Come on, now, Marianna, you've seen police reports. *Just the facts, ma'am* is a pretty good description. I wanted to hear the finer points directly from you."

"Sure." I tried to nod but it hurt too much.

"By the way, he says *hi*." Larry displayed an evil grin.

I blushed. Dammit. I took a large swallow of juice. "Who?"

"I'm not gonna fall for that innocent game. You don't play innocent well enough to fool your friends."

I tossed my head. "Ouch. Shit. Says you. I happen to be an excellent personality impersonator. And Innocent Girl is one of my best impersonations."

"Okay, fine, little Miss Shirley Temple, but you still know very well who."

I smiled and shrugged. "Do you know Patrick?"

"My, my. First name basis already?"

"Shut up and answer the question."

He raised his eyebrows. "A challenging suggestion, but I'll do my best."

I responded in a manner worthy of any mature but mangled biker chick—I stuck my tongue out at him.

"We both worked South Austin when we were rookies," Larry said. "After about a year in the APD, he moved to Georgetown and transferred to the Williamson County Sheriff's Office. We've met a couple of times here and there over the years. He's a nice guy. You could do worse."

"Yeah, I could've gotten stuck with you."

Larry's expression turned serious. "Was this just an accident?"

I shook my head. "Don't think so. He seemed deliberate in his actions."

"You think this is related to your current case?"

I shrugged. "Could be any case, former or current. I wouldn't have thought this case was so inflammatory to the parties involved, but I'm beginning to change my mind."

"What now?"

"I don't know. Probably not much for a day or two. Between my sore body and drugged brain, I'm not much good to anyone, including myself."

"Anything I can do to help?" Larry reached over and patted my arm.

"I wish, but I honestly don't know what you could do. I'll think of something. I have to. If not to solve the case, for my own peace of mind."

DIGGING THROUGH HISTORY

A library is a repository of medicine for the mind.
~Greek Proverb

Stephen awakened Sunday morning with the remnants of a splitting headache. He was growing worried at the frequency and intensity of his headaches. Thanks to this latest one, he'd spent most of Saturday sleeping. He remembered starting awake once, shaking and sweaty, at around three in the afternoon, from the middle of a nightmare.

He was seven again, standing in the hallway, staring at his dad's body, at all the blood on the floor. His sister's bed, stripped of its pink-flowered bedspread, dominated the background. Someone was talking gently in his ear, telling him to come on, come in the other room. He was screaming his sister's name over and over. He sat up for a long time after that dream. He'd stroked his head until the skin stung, and he'd self-consciously yanked his hand away.

Oh, God, Stephanie, what happened to you after that night? He shook his head to dispel the memory of the dream and return himself to the present. He refused to let Sunday be as wasted as Saturday.

Besides, he hadn't fed his cats since Friday. He took two aspirin and forced himself to shower and dress.

Telling Ms. Morgan about his father's murder and sister's disappearance had brought all the painful memories back from the dark corner where he thought he'd permanently buried them. He knew it wouldn't be easy to bury them again. Maybe it was time to face them down for good. He decided on something he'd never before had the courage to do, he needed to see what had been written about the incident after it happened.

He grabbed a notepad and pen, in addition to his sack of cat food. He avoided the River Walk—already busy with foot traffic—and walked the backstreets to the northern edge of the King William district, where his clutter of cats lived. He'd laughed when he discovered the word for a bunch of cats was *clutter*. When he'd mentioned it to a client who also loved cats, she'd grinned and said, "One cat can be a clutter!"

He started opening food as soon as he arrived at the dense growth along the river's edge, knowing that the *skrink* sound of the can's pull top would act like a kitty magnet. Sure enough, he had only plopped the congealed contents of two cans onto the ground when the youngest and bravest of the cats slinked out from the bushes and hurried to the food.

Stephen opened five more cans of the strong-smelling mush and then backed away. He stood in the shade of a large oak and watched for fifteen minutes. When he saw that all but the shyest of the cats were eating, he nodded and walked quietly away.

He always felt good after his forays to his cats, and he headed for the main library with a smile on his face.

Stephen loved the view of the library as he approached. In the early 1990s the city built the building as an art deco wonder of angles and pillars. The imaginative structure included walls whose tops were cut into uneven zig-zags, still-life piles of six-foot concrete balls, and tiny peek-a-boo windows in unexpected places.

The main bulk of the building was painted in a riotous color now known, thanks to a city-wide name-the-color contest, as Enchilada Red. Here and there were highlights and accents of sunshine yellow, lavender purple, and cobalt blue. All in all, Stephen thought it was a block-sized, eye-popping thing of beauty and wonder. Just looking at the architecture of the building lifted his spirits.

Stephen caught the elevator to the sixth floor, walked through the familiar stacks of the historical and non-fiction Texana area, and stopped. To his left was the long information counter where the nice librarian worked.

The rest of the room to his right was filled with rows of white-oak reading tables, currently occupied by three men and two women, each silently perusing large hardback books. He'd sat at those tables many times himself, reading the Texas history books that were too valuable or rare to check out.

Today, though, Stephen planned to venture beyond the tables. He'd never made a conscious decision to avoid the archives in the back room, but he realized that until now it was as if the room hadn't even existed.

Stephen turned toward the petite brunette behind the counter. She was busily typing on a computer keyboard. She looked up and smiled when he approached.

"Good morning." Her soft but clear voice was the mark of a well-trained librarian. "Welcome back. How may I help you today?"

"Good morning." Stephen gave her a warm smile. "I'd like to review some old newspaper editions. Do your archives go back as far as the mid sixties?"

She nodded. "They most certainly do. We have newspaper archives that go back as far as eighteen-sixty-seven. They aren't indexed, though, so you'll have to provide me with the dates in which you're interested."

"I'd like copies of the *San Antonio Express News* for Sunday, September twelfth, ninety-sixty-five, through perhaps a month after that date."

"I'm afraid that newspaper wasn't published back then. At the time, the city had three newspapers, the *San Antonio Express*, the *San Antonio News*, and the *San Antonio Light*."

"Three newspapers." Stephen shook his head. "And the city was so much smaller."

"Remember, though, there was no internet." The librarian smiled. "I find it sad that newspapers seem to be a dying breed. The *Express* and the *News* merged in nineteen-ninety, and the *Light* ceased publication in nineteen-ninety-three."

"I'm not much into online news," Stephen said. "I prefer real newspapers. I wish we still had more than one. Competition is healthy."

"I agree with you. I like the snap of the paper as I turn and fold each page. The news seems more real to me when I'm holding it in black and white between my hands." The librarian laughed. "I guess I'm a relic. In any case, follow me, and I'll show you where you'll find the microfilm reels." She circled the counter and headed past the reading tables.

Stephen caught a faint whiff of her floral perfume as she walked by. She always wore the same scent. *Gardenia, I think.* They entered the Genealogy room, passed a bank of small microfilm viewing stations, and stopped at a row of cabinets. The librarian pulled open a shallow drawer, which was full of small cardboard boxes.

"As you can see by the labels, each of these boxes covers either a two week or one month period for a single newspaper." She gestured toward the cabinets. "You can go through the drawers for each newspaper and pull the boxes covering the dates you want. Have you used our thirty-five millimeter viewers before?"

"No, I haven't." He shook his head.

"Come on, let's take one of your rolls and I'll show you how they work." She extracted a roll from the drawer of *San Antonio Light* archives. She gently touched his arm as she walked to an empty viewer.

Stephen silently followed, feeling as bashful and awkward as a junior high kid at a prom. *Am I reading too much into her touch?* She was always friendly, but today was the first time she'd touched him. Had it been so long since he'd been attracted to a woman that a simple touch caused such a strong reaction? He uttered a small *hrumph* at the thought.

The librarian paused and turned. "Did you say something?"

Stephen felt his face grow warm. "Um, ah, no. Just clearing my throat."

She moved on and stopped at one of the vintage viewers. She spent the next few minutes showing Stephen how to operate the unit. Once the one-inch film was wound onto the spindles, turning the crank-style handle positioned each frame over the lens, which displayed the image in its original newspaper-page size on the frosted white viewing screen. He could zoom in and print any part of a page with the touch of a button—and a dime.

"Do you have any questions?" She lightly placed her hand on his shoulder.

Stephen again found himself flustered. "No, no thank you. I think I'm all set."

"Okay, I'll leave you be. Have fun." She laughed softly and patted his shoulder.

Stephen felt a warm tingle flow across his skin from the point of her touch. "Thank you for your help." He gave her a shy smile, then watched until she rounded the corner.

Time to get to work. He turned his attention to the viewer and ran his hand around the top of his head as he scanned quickly through the pages of the first spool.

BLACK AND WHITE

Once a newspaper touches a story, the facts
are lost forever, even to the protagonists.
~Norman Mailer (1923-2007), Esquire, June 1960

Stephen found the archives a fascinating look back in time, and he repeatedly paused as first one headline then another caught his eye.

He found an ad for Space Age Housing in the newly opened Village North part of Terrell Hills. The most expensive was $19,000. Of course, that'd been a fortune back in 1965. His family could never have afforded to live in the exclusive Village North area. If they'd had that kind of money, maybe his dad…

Stephen rapidly cranked the spool forward to stop the pointless thoughts. He stopped again, though, at the front page for the September 12, 1965 edition. The main headline leapt out at him—*Betsy's Death Toll May Climb to 200.*

He'd completely forgotten about Hurricane Betsy. It had plowed through the Gulf of Mexico, ravaging island communities and putting a large part of the Texas coast on alert. Stephen and his sister had participated in regular hurricane drills at school. When the school bell emitted three shrill rings, students were marched into the long central hallway where they sat, backs against the wall and heads between their knees.

Stephen shook his head and smiled sadly. He and his sister had performed this practice drill less than a week before she disappeared, sitting side by side and holding hands. Who would ever have guessed that the least of their fears was Betsy?

Stephen glanced over the front page, pausing at an article titled *Effect of Viet Nam - S.A. Airport Begins to Hum*. The article provoked another memory. It was late summer of 1965, and his family had driven to the airport to meet his grandparents, who were going to visit until school started.

Stephanie had become frightened when a formation of at least a hundred fatigue-dressed troops marched by. She'd clung to Stephen and whispered, "What's going on? Who are they?" All he could do at the time was hug her back. He'd been too young to realize that the Viet Nam war was raging, or that San Antonio was one of the primary staging grounds for troops. He closed his eyes and could still feel her trembling against his side. Stephanie had never seen her grandparents again after that trip. She was gone less than a month later.

Stephen wound the spool forward until another article caught his eye—*The Word in Math These Days is Sets*. He laughed loud enough to draw a glare from a man who sat several viewing stations away. "Sorry," Stephen whispered as he felt his face grow warm with embarrassment.

He chuckled softly as he read through the article, which was trying to explain to parents the new concept of math sets by using analogies like dinner parties and china cabinets. There was even a half-page spread of hieroglyphic-looking cartoons showing different types of sets. The author of the article actually referred to the concept of sets as the *emancipation proclamation of math*.

New math certainly hadn't emancipated Stephanie. She'd struggled with it in first grade. Stephen had picked it up right away, and had used Stephanie's dolls and toys to try explaining it to her. It'd helped, but in second grade Stephanie wasn't there to learn anymore.

Stephen's math grades had suffered terribly for a while. His enthusiasm for his favorite subject disappeared along with his sister. He'd eventually thrown himself wholeheartedly into math again, though, because it was a great way to escape the vagaries of the real world. He supposed that was why he'd ended up as a CPA, where everything was black and white.

He quickly scanned other articles that made him realize how much time had passed, and how much things had changed. One was about the first computerized clocks installed at Randolph Air Force Base, complete with a painstaking explanation of the binary numbering system. Stephen smiled at the idea of computers being a novelty.

Today his cell phone was more powerful than all of those early computers combined. And he certainly couldn't do his job without the computer in his office. It was too bad such devices hadn't been around when he was trying to teach Stephanie about sets. It would've been much easier.

An article by William F. Buckley Jr. about the new Liberal Establishment, in which he called them suckers and claimed they were suffering from moral lesions, brought back a memory Stephen had of overhearing a conversation between his Dad and Professor Wagner, a fellow Assistant Professor at Trinity.

Stephen had been tucked behind the sofa, playing hide and seek with Stephanie, when his Dad and Professor Wagner entered the room. The conversation made almost no sense to him at the time, but he'd always remembered it because of the angry tone in the two men's voices.

His dad was complaining about the men who ran the university. He'd said they were afraid of the younger, more capable Assistant Professors, that those in charge referred to their underlings as part of the Liberal Establishment. Professor Wagner had agreed that advancement was about politics and backstabbing.

His dad said the old fogies kept him as an Assistant Professor and that other, less qualified men were being made full Professors, while he was stuck in the lower ranks. He'd blamed the university's administration for keeping him poor.

Even when Professor Wagner had countered that it was those same old fogies who'd put Stephen's dad in charge of the dig, his dad had just cursed and said it was only because they wanted him out of their hair for a while.

Stephen sat back and stared at the viewer, his eyes wide. *Maybe Dad felt justified in stealing the rifle.* In an odd way, the thought made Stephen feel better. He knew it must've taken a lot to push his dad that far. Feeling trapped, unappreciated, and backstabbed would certainly have helped.

Stephen stopped his scrolling again to briefly scan an article about how politicians in the south, who used to hide at the mention of Hubert H. Humphrey's name, now publicly embraced the Vice President, in spite of his championing of civil rights.

Racism was rampant in the south, even as late as 1965, but a very nice black family had moved in down the street from the Stephen about a year after his dad was murdered. He'd become good friends with Andy, probably his only real friend through those difficult first years alone.

Stephen had been beaten up several times by Tommy-something —the school bully—for playing with *that nigger,* but Stephen and Andy had stayed friends until they moved to opposite coasts to attend college. Stephen thought maybe he'd try to look Andy up, just to say hi and see how things were going.

After scrolling through a few more pages, he found the article that was his primary motivation for visiting the library. It was on the front page of the September 12 *Local News* section. He read the black and white summary of that horrible night.

Local Man Murdered, Daughter Missing

A Terrell Hills man was brutally stabbed to death in his home Saturday. The victim was Trinity University Assistant Professor Chester E. Davidson, 33.

Nora Davidson found her husband's lifeless body lying in a large pool of blood around 11 pm when she and their son returned home to 566 Cragmont. A second child, a daughter, was missing.

Terrell Hills Detective Garland Everett said evidence indicated the murder occurred during a burglary. He also said it was the first murder in over five years for the quiet community.

Stephen felt a stab of anger in his stomach. He'd forgotten about the media's sensationalism and yellow journalism back then, before public outrage forced them to straighten up. The article didn't even mention the search for his sister. It did, however, print their home address, so gawkers would know where to go for their latest thrill. He quickly glanced through several other stories on the Police Blotter page. They were all just as sensationalistic, and they all included home addresses. Stephen grunted with disgust.

He sat back, closed his eyes, and stroked the top of his head. He thought about the brief official search conducted for Stephanie. He still couldn't believe his sister's disappearance had warranted so little of the police department's time. At least the neighbors continued after the police moved on to more immediate things.

The images were still seared into his mind with hot white intensity and detail. The volunteers—friends, neighbors, and strangers—crowding onto the family's front lawn. Mr. Johnson calling out instructions through a makeshift megaphone, quickly made from an old posterboard, the remnants of some school project still showing around the outside of the cone. The flyers with Stephanie's school photo on it, enlarged until it was grainy and blurred, plastered throughout the neighborhood. The faded and torn flyers, still up weeks after the police cancelled their search and concluded that Stephanie must have also been murdered, after the neighbors had slowly returned to their own worries and schedules. The pitying stares, nervous smiles, and sad eyes of the teachers and classmates at school when he'd finally returned—alone.

He'd been so happy and innocent, sitting in his plush velour seat high in the balcony of the Municipal Auditorium, his Mom on his right, his sister's unoccupied seat on his left. He'd actually had a good time that night, but he'd still been jealous of Stephanie, because she got to stay home and watch *The Patty Duke Show*.

They loved watching it together. It was the only show on television about twins. They didn't even care that Patty and Cathy Lane weren't really twins, just Patty Duke playing both parts.

He'd made Stephanie promise to tell fill him in on the show. He sat back in the library chair, remembering how quickly his priorities had changed. He'd never even watched Patty and Cathy's weekly escapade again, let alone worry about that night's episode.

Sitting in the library so many years later, Stephen was surprised he could still hear bits and pieces from the symphony's performance of *Peter and the Wolf*. He could still picture the conductor, his bushy gray hair bouncing, as he animatedly told everyone to listen to the characters in the music, which were hidden there to discover. He'd explained how the French horns were the wolf, and the violins were Peter. How the music could paint pictures in your mind if you let it. Stephen shook his head hard and sighed loudly, which generated an annoyed *sssshhhh* from someone sitting at a nearby viewer.

Stephen rewound the roll the librarian had pulled and returned to the cabinets for more, absentmindedly rubbing his head as he scanned the boxes for the right date.

There were articles in the *San Antonio Express* and the *San Antonio News* the day of his father's murder, almost identical to the one he'd already read in the *San Antonio Light*. On Monday, September 13th, he found his father's obituary notice. It was one small paragraph buried among notices for the other dead, all under the single, bleak heading *S.A. Obituaries*:

> **Chester Eric Davidson,** 33, of 566 Cragmont; services 2 pm this Saturday, at the Trinity United Methodist Church; interment to follow at Atchison Cemetery.

That's it? One badly punctuated sentence is all there is to show for my dad? No mention of Mom or himself. No mention of his dad's life or career. Nothing. Just the facts, ma'am. He uttered a ragged sigh.

Stephen scanned the rest of that edition, as well as several others, looking for anything on the search for his sister. He found nothing until October 2, just a couple of short paragraphs in the *San Antonio Light*.

> **Search Discontinued for Missing Girl**
>
> Neighbors have given up on their search for a missing girl who disappeared from her home at 566 Cragmont on September 11, the night her father was brutally murdered and left in a large puddle of blood on the floor outside the girl's bedroom.
>
> Stephanie Davidson was the daughter of Trinity University Assistant Professor Chester E. Davidson and his wife Nora. Flyers will remain posted in local businesses and Terrell Hills Police Detective Garland Everett says the case will remain open.

...was the daughter...WAS the daughter...not IS the daughter...

The article pierced his heart. The few sounds in the library became muffled, as if he were hearing them from under water. His heartbeat pounded in his ears. His forehead felt cold. It was hard to breath. The room swayed. Everything turned to shades of gray. Stephen suddenly felt a steadying, warm hand on his shoulder.

"Are you all right?"

He took a deep breath, quickly wiped his eyes, and looked up into the concerned face of the librarian. He cleared his throat. "Yes, I'm okay. Thanks."

She smiled and patted his shoulder. As she walked slowly away, she glanced back once with concern etched on her face.

Stephen sat for a few minutes, breathing slowly and evenly. When he thought his legs could once again be counted on to support his weight, he rewound the last roll of microfilm, placed all of the boxes on top of the cabinets, and walked to the information desk.

"Thank you again. You were very helpful." He found it was easy to smile at the librarian, in spite of his recent emotional incident.

"You're quite welcome." Her intense green eyes seemed to peer deep into him. Her smile was warm and sincere. "Please feel free to let me know if I may be of more help."

"I will." Stephen turned to leave and then turned back. "Excuse me, what's your name?"

"Patricia Graves. Patty."

"Thank you again, Patty. I'm Stephen. Stephen Davidson."

"Stephen," Patty repeated. "It's nice to finally know your name. I've seen you here so often I've been meaning to ask, but something always interrupted."

As Stephen left the library he found a spring in his step that he'd not experienced in many months. *Patty. What a nice name.*

UPS AND DOWNS

The art of living lies in a fine mingling of holding on and letting go. ~Havelock Ellis (1859-1939)

I woke up bright and early Monday morning feeling pretty good, at least for someone whose body was in a state of rebellion. I fed the cats and drank an entire pot of coffee. I used duct tape and a garbage bag to cover the stitches on my thigh, then showered for the first time since the accident. Even the gentle setting on my Shower Massage felt like an industrial power washer against my scabs and bruises, but just getting clean was a luxurious and decadent feeling.

I put the remainder of the Vicodin in the medicine cabinet and downed a couple of Tylenol. They'd let me stay verbally coherent, at least as much as usual. Being off the heavy meds also meant I could drive, so I could get over to Zabor's to see about Max. And I also wanted to do some follow up on Stephanie Davidson. First, though I'd have to find a car that didn't include a clutch pedal.

I dressed in loose, navy, cotton slacks and an oversized Hawaiian shirt. The combination made me feel frumpy and fat, but at least they didn't bind or rub. It took a while to work my good foot into a sock and shoe—bending over was an Olympic effort. I combed out my wet hair and fluffed it with my fingers. I decided to bypass the hair dryer. It sounded too heavy.

It finally occurred to me to check my answering machine. Judy'd called at noon. Aunt Louise had called at three-thirty. I decided to wait a day or two on Aunt Louise. I needed to figure out how honest to be with her about my accident.

I called Judy. "Hey, kiddo, how was the dive?"

"Marianna! How're you feeling? I got worried when I didn't hear back from you, but Larry called to say he'd fed you and that you'd slept through the day."

"I'm okay, just sore and stiff. My ankle will take some time to heal, but at least it isn't broken, and I didn't tear any ligaments. Plus it's my left one, so I can drive. Look, I don't want to dwell on my aches and pains. Give me a diversion. Tell me about the dive. I'm really sorry I had to miss it. I was looking forward to getting wet. Getting rained on while sitting in the dirt's just not the same."

"We had a good time. Rhonda, one of our *dead bodies*, wound herself up good among the dangling rope and fishing line. Poor Diana got stuck recovering her. She was the fourth student to do a rescue, so the water inside the Deep Ship was so silted up it might as well have been chocolate milk. You couldn't see six inches, even with a flashlight. It took Diana so long to untangle Rhonda that they both had to spend some decompression time before resurfacing."

"I've been diving with Rhonda. She's…um, a good-sized woman. She'd be hard to get out of a wreck even without the bondage."

Judy laughed. "You're right, and it was even worse because Diana is maybe four-ten and ninety pounds dripping wet. But she did good. I think it gave her a big confidence boost, too, which is half the battle."

We chatted for a while longer, avoiding the topic that was foremost on both of our minds. Finally, Judy asked *that* question. "Did someone deliberately run you off the road?"

"I've been thinking about that. I'd like to believe it was an accident, since the truck never actually touched me, and it was trying to pass on a curvy stretch of road. It could've been bad driving. But I don't think so. After I went off the road, the other driver pulled over, but he just sat there. When I'd stopped sliding I looked up at him. I was about to call for his help, but the friggin' asshole looked directly at me, grinned, and sped off."

"What do you think he did it for?"

"Probably related to a case, but whether it's the current one or an old one is anybody's guess at this point. I ride that route almost every Saturday, so it wouldn't be hard for someone to set me up."

"True. Any idea who it might be?"

"No, except the truck somehow seems familiar. But I've been so doped up, I can't place why or where yet. And it may be my imagination. There's a buttload of white trucks out there. I'm not giving up, but I'll have to chew on it for a bit."

"Let me know if there's any way I can help."

"Actually there is one way. I really want to get to Zabor's to check on Max. I doubt there's anything Bob can do, but I need to go there anyway. I can't drive Pickle Toy—my clutch foot is out of commission. Can we swap cars for a few days?"

"Yeah, sure. I can pop over in about an hour."

"I guess I can try to keep busy. But get here as soon as you can. I'm going stir-crazy."

"Yes ma'am." Judy laughed and hung up.

I puttered around the house for a while, cleaning and straightening as best I could. I wasn't ready to deal with Davidson just yet, but at least I had to let him know I wasn't going to be very productive for a couple of days.

Luck was on my side, I caught his answering machine. I left a message that I was *ill* and would be taking it easy for a bit. I promised to call soon.

Getting in and out of Judy's Saturn was a challenge. I had to be a bit of a contortionist to get into the car with a crutch and a brace-enclosed left ankle, but the rest of me was still pretty stiff and sore, especially my right thigh, so my contortability was somewhat limited. Once in, though, driving wasn't too bad.

I pulled into the small lot at Zabor's Motorcycles and contorted myself back out of the car. Bob Zabor was the best motorcycle repairman around, but I didn't think even he could help Max now.

Charlie looked up as soon as I walked through the door. "Hey, Marianna. Man o' man, what happened to you?"

"Close encounter with a truck and a road. Where's Bob?"

"In the back, changing the oil in his Hawg." Charlie pressed the intercom button and summoned Bob from the back bay area. Bob walked through the swinging doors, wiping his hands with a shop rag that was already black with grease.

"Looks like you've already got enough grease on your hands, without adding more," I said as he approached.

Bob grinned broadly, but it quickly faded away. "Geez, Marianna, ya look like hell. No wonder Max looks like he does. What happened?"

I gave Bob a quick rundown of the accident. "What's the story on Max? I don't expect good news."

"Good, 'cuz I ain't got none for ya. Come on. He's out back."

We moved together through the bay—Bob walking and me lurching—and out to the weed-choked scrap area. Max was a sad site. I bit my lip and shook my head. I wasn't about to let Bob or anyone else see me cry over a motorcycle.

The forks were twisted and bent so badly the front wheel was completely sideways and pushed back until it was touching the engine. The handlebars were cocked at a wild angle, the fiberglass fairing was shattered, and most of the windshield was gone. The right saddlebag was scraped and gouged from end to end. The seat vinyl was ripped wide open, spilling out its cotton-batting guts. The punctured crank case was slowly dripping oil onto a dandelion, which didn't look too healthy as a result. Surprisingly, except for a generous coating of dirt, the gas tank was in perfect shape.

"Not much left, is there?" I sighed.

"Nope." He waved the rag toward the bike. "That tank's still lookin' okay. I'll give ya twenty bucks for it. I'm afraid all I can offer on the rest is to take care of the disposal."

I knew that even pre-accident Max wouldn't have been worth more than nine hundred dollars. But he'd been a good ride for a long time. I reached down and pried the dangling plastic Yamaha Maxim logo from the side cover. "I'll take this as a souvenir of better times. And I'll take you up on the twenty dollars. I'll use it as part of my down payment on a new bike."

I left Zabor's determined to avenge Max by figuring out who was behind what happened.

MURDER SUSPECT?

Never apologize before you are accused.
~Charles I of Great Britain (1600-1649)

My next destination was my office. I hadn't checked messages in a few days, and I also wanted to see what I could find out about Stephanie Davidson. If she was alive, and still using that name, there'd be a records trail somewhere. I figured I'd start the easy way, with electronic searches. I could always go to the Bexar County courthouse later.

I swung into a handicapped spot without batting an eye. Sticker or no sticker, I wasn't crutching my ass across a hundred feet of hot asphalt parking lot. I rode the creaky, slow elevator to the second floor and was clunking down the hall when I heard my name.

"Marianna!"

I turned to see Jason Storga's head poking out his office door. "Got a minute?"

"Jason, I'm sorry" I pivoted on my crutch to face him. "I forgot all about the message you left me last week."

"Holy moly." Jason's eyes grew big as saucers. "Looks like you had a reason to forget. What happened?"

"Motorcycle accident." I noticed my answer was getting less specific each time someone asked.

He stepped back so I could enter his office space. His assistant Rebecca's desk was empty. Guess she was at lunch or on an errand. Jason and I proceeded to his private office.

I eased onto one of his guest chairs. "Tell me what you need."

"I need you to track down as many of these people as you can find." Jason handed me two sheets of paper. Down the left side of the first sheet were three names. Down the right side were the bits and pieces of information Jason had for each person. Two included San Antonio as a possible location, the other was likely in San Marcos, around an hour up the road. None included a complete address or phone number, or other useful information like social security number. The second sheet was a list of case-related factoids I could use to verify that the person I found was the one Jason needed, and not just a nobody with the same name.

"Challenging." I raised my eyebrows. "When did you say you needed them?"

"The court date is less than three weeks. I know I'm not giving you much to go on. But," he added with a big grin, "I have complete faith in your abilities."

"Oh great." I laughed. "No pressure there."

Jason waved away my comment. "Find whoever you can. Even one additional witness will help my case."

"I'll do my best." I stood. "Give me a couple of days."

Jason was about to speak when his phone rang. He signaled okay to me as he lifted the receiver.

I was shocked when I opened my office door. "Oh, God, I'm sorry. I forgot all about you." The palm in the corner of my office was now so droopy that the tallest stalk was bent in half, its leaves touched the floor. I filled my water pitcher in the restroom and poured the entire contents on the powder-dry potting soil.

"Sorry," I said again to the plant as I carefully straightened the bent stalk and leaned it toward the wall for support. I stapled a couple of leaves to the wall, hoping that would help hold the poor thing upright until it recovered.

After completing my paramedic duties, I settled in at my desk. I glanced at my answering machine. I was happy to see only one waiting message. I wasn't in a mood to spend the afternoon returning a bunch of calls—or even *one* call—so before punching Play I decided to get my digital paperwork out of the way.

I flipped open my laptop and updated Davidson's file first, adding everything that had happened since Thursday. I had to struggle to pull all the memories out of my post-accident brain, which was probably still flushing the last remnants of Vicodin out of its synapses.

I don't normally wait so long between updates, but I hadn't exactly been at my best the last few days. I could've done the updates at home, but I'd decided long ago to work on case files in my office. It's too easy for me to blur the line between office and home. In the past I'd ended up with one never-ending work day. I only faithfully carted my laptop back and forth because I used it for personal things like Facebook and watching cheesy videos on Youtube.

I'd also learned the hard way that computers crash, and sometimes paper backups are all you have, so as soon as I entered the last update, I printed out a copy and stowed it in the file cabinet. I next created a detailed invoice for Davidson. I carry insurance, but the deductible is high and the coverage is crappy. I'd need all of the advance Davidson had given me just to pay the damn medical bills, so I was going to be sure he knew I was earning it.

Secretarial duties finished, I logged onto ERAS. My subscription to it costs more per month than I like to pay, and they charge an additional fee for each search, but it's the only way to access information not usually available to non-law enforcement folks like me.

Unfortunately, a private investigator has no more power or authority than an average citizen, so we have to use other means, such as a database brokerage service, for digging up facts. Legally, a database broker is only supposed to provide information for specific, legitimate reasons, but there are almost always ways around that minor technicality.

I get better results from ERAS when I search with a social security number or birthdate, but that wasn't an option in this case, so I typed Stephanie Davidson's name into the search field. I briefly debated where to start, but skeptic that I am, I selected Death Records and sat back. It would take ERAS a few minutes to complete a search through its millions of records. Of course, if Stephanie had been killed by her abductor, there would be no official record of her death. But like I said, skeptic that I am…

Beep.

94 records found

The message blinked on my screen. *Damn.* I didn't want to wade through all those records. I repeated the search, narrowing its scope to Texas.

13 records found

Well shit. I felt like an idiot when I realized I *did* have Stephanie's birthdate. It'd be the same as Davidson's. I pulled up his account and jotted down the date—January 16, 1958.

I repeated the search for the third time.

0 records found

I continued searching through ERAS's available databases—property, marriage, divorce, name change, assumed name, telephone (listed and unlisted), voter registration, driver's license, and license plate (in case she'd owned other cars before the Taurus), loans, liens, credit reports. Nothing. Nada. Zip. I wasn't surprised.

Whoever this mystery woman was, she'd managed to stay out of the public's eye, not to mention the government's files, for fifty-plus years. It's possible she had no permanent address and she lived on a cash-only basis. It's been done before, usually by survivalist, militia wackos, but it isn't easy. Of course, if she'd been raised by whoever'd abducted her, it was highly unlikely she'd remained Stephanie Davidson. She might not even remember she'd ever had that name, so there might be nothing subversive going on, at least in her mind.

I was frustrated. I hadn't really expected this case to be easy, given Davidson's close-mouthed nature, but I hated the feeling of being trapped inside a blank room with no windows or doors.

Hoping to calm my frustration, I spent time searching ERAS for the names on Jason's list. I got various hits on each of them and printed the results. I wouldn't know until I called if the hits were really for the people Jason needed.

I could feel my energy level dropping fast, so I decided I'd call them later, although I'd probably still have to search the Bexar County Courthouse records archives in San Antonio. As powerful as ERAS is, it's only as powerful as the data that gets uploaded to it, and that can take a long time. So I rarely use it as my only resource, but it's a heckuva good place to start.

I logged out of ERAS, and pressed Play to retrieve the solitary message on my answering machine. "Ms. Morgan, this is Detective Joe Fincher from the San Antonio Police Department. Please give me a call when you receive this message."

Nice. Friendly. Polite. Terse as hell. *Oh, well.*

I played the message again and jotted down Fincher's number. I couldn't wait to find out what *this* was all about. I was lucky—he was in the squad room filling out paperwork. "Ms. Morgan, thank you for returning my call. I'd like to ask you a few questions."

"How can I help you?"

"Do you know a Tom Darnell? Is he perhaps a client of yours?"

"Nope, sorry. The name doesn't ring any bells at all. Why do you think I should know him?"

"We found your business card in his pocket."

"Oh? What did he say about it?"

"I'm afraid he didn't have much to say. He's dead."

Well. That shut me up. At least for a a few seconds. "Look, detective, I really wish I could help you. But I honestly don't recognize the name. What happened to him?"

"He was found early Sunday morning outside of Whiskey Smith's bar. He'd been shot twice in the head. The bartender noticed the victim's white truck when he closed up at three."

"White truck? What kind of white truck?"

"A nineteen-seventy-two, white, Chevy pickup. Is that important?"

"I was run off the road near Marble Falls on Saturday afternoon by a guy with long, stringy hair and a cheesy mustache. He was driving a beat-up, older model, white Chevy truck with a heavy-duty grill guard on the front."

Silence from the other end. Then, "Ms. Morgan can you verify your whereabouts around midnight Saturday?"

I couldn't stop myself. I laughed loud and long.

"Ms. Morgan?"

"I'm sorry. I was on my motorcycle when I was run off the road. I spent a good part of Saturday evening in the emergency room. A friend picked me up and took me home around eight. I spent the rest of the night in a Vicodin coma. I've got badly strained ligaments in my left ankle and I'm on a crutch. I sure didn't drive to San Antonio to kill anyone. Besides—and you can verify this with Deputy Patrick O'Meara at the Williamson County Sheriff's Office —I had no idea who ran me off the road, or why."

"I'll contact Deputy O'Meara for a copy of his report. We may need to call you again, if we have additional questions."

"That's fine. Can I ask you a question?"

"Yes, ma'am, although I'm not sure I can answer it."

"Where is Whiskey Smith's bar?"

"Broadway and Thacker Street."

"Isn't that Terrell Hills? Why is the SAPD involved?"

"Whiskey Smith's borders Terrell Hills—it's just inside the San Antonio city limits. Why?"

"Just curious," I replied. "That's a long way from Marble Falls." I wasn't about to tell him my current case involved Terrell Hills. But at least maybe my *blank room* had just developed a tiny window. Now all I had to do was figure out what I could see when I looked out.

MY LUCK O' THE IRISH

Two people shorten the road. ~Irish proverb

I woke up Tuesday morning to find all six of my babies ringed tightly around me, which made me feel snug and safe for a change instead of stapled to the bed. I laid there for a good half hour enjoying the peace and quiet—at least until the phone rang. Mayfly bolted off the bed like a rocket, using my hip as a launch pad.

Wiggling my way between the cats like a snake slithering in grass, I fumbled for the phone. "Who the hell is calling at the crack of dawn?" I grumbled to Cooper. Then I glanced at the clock, which displayed 9:30. "Okay, never mind." Cooper yawned, stretched, and rolled half his body over. He looked as if he'd been caught in a taffy-twister.

"Hello." My voice sounded dry and brittle.

"Marianna. Ms. Morgan. This is Officer Patrick O'Meara. Are you all right?"

"Patrick." I sat up, suddenly much more alert. Four cats went tumbling, and they all let me have it through a chorus of growls and hisses. "Yes, I'm fine. I pushed it a bit yesterday, so I allowed myself the luxury of sleeping in."

"Geez, I'm sorry, I sure didn't mean to wake you up. I can call back later."

I cleared my throat. "No, no, that's fine. I'm normally an early bird, so it's high time I get up. What's up?"

"I got a call from Detective Fincher."

"Oh, him." I laughed. "I'm on his short list of potential suspects. I hope you told him I was in no shape to drive to San Antonio to off this Darnell person. He didn't sound like he believed me."

Patrick's laugh was hearty and rich. "Don't worry, you're cleared. I wanted to let you know I'd talked with him and to also tell you I took care of your motorcycle, um Max. And, well, I guess I also wanted to find out how you're feeling."

I was touched. And a little tickled. It'd been a long time since anyone but Larry, Judy, and Aunt Louise had cared about me. Maybe today was my lucky day. "I'm okay. Sore and stiff, but no permanent damage. I made it by Zabor's yesterday. There sure isn't much left of Max. I guess when I'm healed up, I'll be looking for a new bike. Maybe a Suzuki this time."

I stroked Boggle's sleek orange fur. "Look, it may be a long shot, but I have to see Darnell's truck. I need to know if it's the same one that ran me off the road. Can you tell me where it's impounded?"

Patrick cleared his throat. "The police won't let you into the impound yard to look at a vehicle involved in a homicide." He paused. A long pause. I was about to break the awkward silence when he continued, "Um, look, I'd…well, would it be all right if I drove you down there? I can certainly get into the impound. Besides, I might actually be able to close a pretty obscure hit and run. That'd look real good to the sheriff."

"Of course I wouldn't mind! I'd appreciate it." My heart did a little flutter. I was glad he couldn't see the stupid grin on my face.

Thirty minutes later, I was still damp from the shower as I stood and stared into my closet. No way in hell I'd wear baggy clothes again today. I managed a pull-over soft knit top and khaki slacks. I grunted as the fitted waistband bit into tender skin, but I figured a couple of Tylenol would help me get used to it.

I'd barely gotten my shoes on when Patrick arrived. I opened the door and caught my breath. I'd forgotten how blue his eyes were. They shone like sapphires, surrounded by a mass of rust-red curls that still managed to look unruly in spite of Patrick's short haircut.

I wanted to wind my fingers through those curls, pull him toward me, and… I shook my head to put an instant end to a *very* premature fantasy. I'd been out of circulation too long. I make friends slowly and intimate friends even slower. Too much exposure to the seamy side of life, I guess.

"Are you okay?" His eyes clouded with concern.

"Yes," I squeaked. I swallowed and then, in a more normal voice, said, "Yes. Sorry. Just dizzy for a second. Probably thanks to the drugs I took all weekend. Come on in." Turning, I hobbled toward my living room. Patrick closed the door and followed close behind.

"You seem to have a few cats." Patrick laughed. He moved from sofa to chair to loveseat to hearth, giving each available cat a friendly stroke and chin tickle. I judge people by how many of my cats remain in the open—or come out of hiding—to allow a lowly human the honor of showering them with affection. Behind his back I nodded my approval. Patrick scored a five on my Cat-o-Meter.

When he turned to face me, I could again see concern in his eyes. "Are you sure you're up to this? You look pretty banged up."

"You should see the parts of me that are covered by clothes." My cheeks grew warm as I blushed. "Well, um, I mean, my legs have the most bruises, and…" *Oh, hell.*

Patrick grinned. "Don't worry. I knew what you meant."

Good thing, because *I* wasn't completely sure what I meant. "Ready to go?"

We drove toward San Antonio at the pace of a snail. It was really the legal speed limit, but I don't think Pickle Toy—or Max—had ever actually gone that speed, except when a radar detector was nearby. I chuckled.

"Something strike your funny bone?" Patrick asked.

"I was just thinking, *so this is what the speed limit feels like?*"

Patrick laughed. "Sorry. The last thing I need is to get a speeding ticket while on pseudo-official business in a county-owned car and with a civilian along for the ride."

"That's okay, I'm in no particular hurry."

"Oh, before I forget, I brought you a present." Patrick gestured toward the back seat. "In that envelope. Can you reach it?"

It took some squirming, but I managed. I panted from the effort such a trivial action put on my battered body. Inside the envelope was a copy of the police report on Tom Darnell.

"Thanks!" I read through the sparse information on the form. "Where the hell is Route 3, Box 14, New Braunfels?"

"I don't know. I'm sure the San Antonio cops are on it."

We chatted about all the things a non-couple casually discuss. We compared the pros and cons of where we grew up—me in San Antonio and him in Cleveland. We learned we both prefer hot weather. We both love sports—although he's into basketball, and my choice is road racing. We both scuba dive. We both have the same favorite food—Mexican—although we disagreed on the best restaurant. Our only clash was over music. He loves country and western, which I can just barely tolerate. But we both love oldies.

I couldn't help weighing relationship possibilities. By my calculations, we had at least a workable potential, but I wondered what he thought. I glanced toward him and saw a faint smile, and there were crinkles at the corners of his eyes. A good sign.

The San Antonio Police Department impound yard is on the far southwest side of town, a stone's throw from the Lackland/Kelly

Air Force Base runway. The runway is used infrequently these days, but was once continuously active.

When I was a kid, the base was the Air Force's main flight training center, future pilots spent hours doing touch-and-go flights in everything from monstrous C5 transports to supersonic fighters. Our house was twenty miles away, but directly under the flight path. Planes regularly broke the sound barrier, shaking our windows and scaring our cats, until it became illegal to *go boom* over populated areas.

The impound yard was surrounded by an eight-foot, wood privacy fence, gray with age and warped into a series of waves and bulges. The battered electronic gate was securely closed against a metal pole rusted into Swiss cheese. Patrick pulled up to the intercom and pressed the button. A crackly voice blared into the car.

After exchanging Official Secret Cop Passwords, the com grew quiet and the gate swung open with an ear-piercing metallic squeal. We drove through and parked between two immaculately clean double-axle *dually* tow trucks, the two rear wheels on each side bulged from the sides of the trucks like a weight-lifter's biceps.

I followed Patrick into the portable building that served as the office. An ancient air conditioner stuck precariously from the one window, gurgling and burping out tepid air. The little red strips tied to the unit's front plastic grill waved weakly. I've always wondered why people put those strips on their air conditioners. If the damn thing is so crappy you can't actually tell it's working without visual cues, isn't it time to replace it?

Three large, sweaty men filled the small, stuffy room. Two sat at antique computers, slowly one-fingering out reports about vehicles they were adding to the yard. The third leaned on a makeshift counter, exhaling cigarette smoke toward a *Thank you for not smoking* sign, probably posted thanks to a city ordinance that was unwelcome at places like this. I couldn't help it. I coughed. He glared, but dropped the butt on the dirty concrete floor and squashed it out under his greasy Red Wing boot heel.

I sat on a battered folding metal chair to give my underarm a break from the crutch's rock-hard rubber top while Patrick asked about the location of the truck. My eyes burned from the combination of cigarette smoke and old sweat that permeated the room. After two minutes Patrick caught my eye and jerked his head once toward the door. I got up and followed in silence.

He looked up into the clear, blue sky and took a long, deep breath. "I didn't mean to be rude, but I was doing my best to inhale as little of that air as possible."

"No problem. I was trying to see how long I could hold my breath, too."

The impound yard itself looked about like I expected, with its rows of cars, trucks, vans, and other odd vehicles lined up side by side like multi-colored metal corpses in a disaster movie. There appeared to be several hundred vehicles in the lot. Some were new, likely the booty from a drug raid. Others looked as if they'd already had one ride through a car crusher. I tried not to think about what the drivers of those ended up looking like.

I lurched along through the gravel yard, my crutch tip slipping on the loose rocks.

"Here, let me help." Patrick hurried to my side and put a firm, strong arm around my waist. With all the grace of two kids in a sack race, we made our way to the third row of vehicles. I stopped abruptly ten feet from the truck and stared. Patrick did a little two-step trying to stop with no advance warning.

"That's it." I tried—unsuccessfully—to keep my eyes from tearing up as I stared at the heavy-duty grill guard. "That's the same goddammed truck."

"Are you sure? Accidents happen so fast, and there are lots of white pickups in this area."

"Will you check the rear bumper for a Snake Farm sticker?"

"Sure." Patrick moved down the side of the truck. "Bright yellow and red one," he called from the back of the truck.

"Then I'm sure," I called back. "So, the son-of-a-bitch who tried to run me off the road is good and dead," I said more softly, as Patrick returned to my side. "I hope I don't sound like a flaming bitch when I say I'm glad he is. Of course, now I'll likely never know *why*. I figure it's case-related, but then again, maybe I was just the unlucky winner of his Bad Mood Award."

"You're right, you'll probably never know." Patrick shook his head. "But at least you weren't hurt too bad. And no, I don't think you sound like a flaming bitch, as you so colorfully put it. I understand." He put his arm around me and squeezed my waist.

Tingles rippled through neglected parts of my body, and I couldn't help but blush. To divert his attention from my crimson cheeks, I pointed toward the truck. "Can you help me get a closer look?"

We squeezed together between the truck and a mangled Lincoln Navigator parked beside it. "What the hell could do this to a Navigator?" I mused.

"Train. The impound manager said the truck was *next to a big friggin Navigator whose driver didn't feel like waiting behind the crossing gate at a train track*. I guess the train won."

"Guess so." I returned my attention to the truck. There were blood splatters on the dashboard. The driver's window was a mosaic of broken glass chunks, still clinging to each other by a generous spray of dried blood and some gooey gunk that was probably bits of brain. My stomach hitched as I reached for the door handle, but Patrick grabbed my arm.

"Sorry," he said. "I promised the yard gorilla we wouldn't mess with it, since it's evidence in a murder. There's probably nothing important inside anyway. The local cops would've gone over it pretty thoroughly."

"Okay." I shrugged, but still felt a little disappointed. I hadn't expected to find anything in the cab. I'd just wanted a closer look at the final resting place of the jerk who'd hurt me and killed Max.

"Well, I guess I'm done," I said. *At least with the truck, but not with The Late Mister Tom Darnell.* I had to know more about this guy and why the hell he'd decided I should become roadside debris. But I kept my thoughts to myself. No matter what my hopes for the future, I currently didn't know Patrick very well. I smiled brightly at him, hoping I didn't look guilty. "Anything you need here?"

"Nope, I've got what I need." His voice took on the cadence of a news reporter. "The victim of the hit-and-run positively identified the vehicle. Case closed." He laughed and continued in his normal voice, "Who knows, maybe I'll get a bonus, or at least an atta boy. Hit-and-run accidents are rarely solved. So, thank you, ma'am, your cooperation is greatly appreciated." He smiled and bowed.

I laughed so hard I almost fell off my crutch. "It's the least a little ol' southern belle like me can do for such a kindly gentleman." I used my best southern drawl. I didn't dare attempt a curtsy, so I batted my eyes in perfect Scarlet O'Hara fashion.

"How about a late lunch?" Patrick asked as he helped me back across the lot.

"Sounds good to me. I know just the place."

We circled back to the north side of the city and pulled in at La Fogata. The waiter brought us iced tea in pitcher-sized glasses, as well as our own little personal baskets of hot, crispy tortilla chips and bowls of fresh tomato, onion, and serrano pepper salsa. I ordered the aguacate relleno, a poblano pepper stuffed with crab and shrimp and deep fried. At my urging, Patrick ordered the carne adobada plate, a La Fogata specialty of pork marinated with bay leaves, cinnamon, and red peppers. When the waitress set our plates down, the smells rising from their mix of spices made us both moan with anticipation.

"This is wonderful." Patrick sighed after his first bite. "I never knew Mexican food could be this good. You win. My apologies for disagreeing with you earlier about the best restaurant. I better follow your suggestions from now on."

"Apology accepted." I winked. "I grew up on Mexican food. It was a weekly ritual at every school cafeteria in the city, from elementary through college. And I understand that you Yankees sometimes need educating about what constitutes real Mexican food. I've eaten Yankee chili in New York—it looked and tasted like beef stew, complete with bell peppers. Bleah."

"But remember, I said I'm from Cleveland."

"That's still north of Dallas. You're a Yankee. Sorry."

In a greatly exaggerated British accent, quite a stretch for an Irish Ohioan, Patrick said, "I humbly ask your forgiveness for the unfortunate location of my birth. I moved here as fast as I could."

I laughed and held up my iced tea. "I officially welcome you to Texas, greatest country on earth."

"Thank you kindly, ma'am." He tapped his plastic tea glass against mine.

The drive back to Austin felt relaxed and comfortable. I leaned back and watched the scenery as Patrick maneuvered smoothly through the heavy traffic. I noticed he inched the speedo a touch over the speed limit once in a while. I smiled at his daring.

"What's that for?" he asked.

"Just enjoying the ride. I rarely get to relax on this drive, because I'm usually the one behind the wheel."

"Then enjoy yourself." He flashed a wide, warm smile and reached over and patted my knee. "I'll take care of you and get you home safe."

"I know." I returned his smile.

For the remainder of the drive, we took turns talking about our life's passions. I told Patrick about some of my scuba diving adventures, and how diving made me feel weightless and free, like a mermaid. "If they ever figure out how to do gill implants, I'll be first in line."

Patrick told me about hang gliding, and how it gave him the same feelings of freedom, but he felt like an eagle or hawk. "I'll bypass the feather implants, though."

We both laughed.

When we pulled into my driveway, I turned to face him. "Would you like to come in for a glass of iced tea? I'm meeting an old friend for dinner, but I've got a couple of hours or so before I need to get ready."

"I'd really like to, but I promised the sheriff I wouldn't be gone the whole day, and I'm dangerously close to having broken that promise. I'd like to see you again, though. How about dinner, say Saturday at seven-thirty?"

"Sounds good."

I smiled for the rest of the afternoon—while I made a gimpy attempt to putter around the backyard, as I showered and dressed for my date with Larry, even while I scooped the litter box.

My smile managed to stay put in spite of Larry's taunts and teases as we had drinks in the old Southern Pacific boxcar at Donn's Depot, through our dinner at the fifties's style Hut's Hamburgers, and while I was changing clothes for bed.

I probably smiled in my sleep, too, although the cats won't say. My life took me down some pretty scary paths, so I was looking forward to where this more-promising path might lead.

THE SEARCH BEGINS

Be careful what you wish for. ~unknown

Stephen hadn't previously considered trying to locate the rifle stolen the night of his father's murder. It had never been important. But he finally accepted it as the cause of his father's murder and became determined to track it down. What started as a casual thought was quickly mushrooming into an obsession.

He decided to take Tuesday off and dedicate the day to his newfound mission. He spent Monday in his office in Austin, updating the books for several of his clients and sending out their monthly reports. Now he'd have a day or two before they received them and called with questions or comments.

Although he felt bad about her accident, he was glad that Ms. Morgan was off the case for a few days. He wanted to start the search on his own, *needed* to start this part on his own. He knew he'd still need Ms. Morgan's help at some point, but wanted to contribute to solving his problems in some way. He'd share whatever he discovered when they met again.

Scanning his notes from the newspaper archive articles, Stephen nodded. He knew just where to start. He flipped through the telephone directory and dialed.

"Terrell Hills Police Department." The woman who answered was businesslike but friendly.

"I'd like to speak with Detective Garland Everett about a very old case." He rubbed his bald spot absentmindedly.

"I'm sorry, but Detective Everett passed away five years ago."

"Oh." Stephen paused, unsure how to proceed. "Well—"

"I believe Detective Crawford Boone was Detective Everett's partner back then. Would you like to speak to him?"

Stephen sighed with relief. "Yes, please."

"Hold on and I'll connect you."

Stephen jotted down the name while he waited.

"Boone." The detective's voice sounded gravelly and well-worn.

"Detective Boone, my name is Stephen Davidson. I'm hoping to follow up on an old case from nineteen-sixty-five, when you were partners with Detective Garland Everett. He was the chief investigating officer when my father was murdered in our home the evening of September eleventh of that year."

"Geez, that *is* an old case. I was a young rookie back then. Garland was my first partner. Case doesn't ring a bell offhand. Tell me more about it."

"Well, my father and sister were home alone the night our home was broken into. I was with my mother at the symphony. My father was killed and my sister was abducted. An Alamo-era rifle was stolen."

"Whoa! I remember now, that was one of my first cases. I'll sure tell ya whatever I can. So you're that kid from back then? All grown up. What do you do these days?"

"I'm a CPA."

"That's a good way to make a livin'. Guess you've turned out okay. A damn shame about your sister, though. How old was she?"

"Yes, sir, a real shame. My sister was seven, so was I. We were… are…were…twins." Stephen paused and took a couple of deep breaths, to slow his heart and calm his nerves before continuing. "I know very little about the rifle that was stolen, but I've decided to see if there's any way to determine whatever happened to it. If I can find the rifle, at least I'll have some closure."

"You don't want much, do you." Detective Boone snorted. "I'll have to dig up the old case report. Gimme the address where you lived."

"566 Cragmont."

"And do you remember the date?"

Like it was yesterday. "September 11, 1965."

"Got it. Damn. That date again. With a body still missing the case'll be in the Open files down in records. It's pretty quiet today, so's it'll give me somethin' ta do. I'll call you back in a coupla hours."

Stephen answered the phone before the first ring finished, his heart beating wildly. He vigorously rubbed his head, anticipation and hope escalating the rate of his nervous habit.

"You sittin' on toppa that thang?" Detective Boone laughed. "I never even heard it ring on my end! Anyways, I found the file. See'n as you're family, I can give you a copy of the case if you like, but you gotta get it in person. I can't mail it. Can you come out?"

"I'll be there in thirty minutes." Although he hadn't consciously avoided the area, as he drove north, Stephen realized he hadn't been in Terrell Hills since he'd gone away to college.

Stephen thought Detective Boone's looks were a perfect match for his coarse, gruff voice—salt and pepper military haircut and wiry mustache, deeply hooded brown eyes topped with bushy eyebrows, and prominent, hairy-edged ears. His features were all just slightly off mark on a head that seemed to sit directly on his shoulders, with no evidence the man even had a neck.

The men exchanged firm handshakes and Detective Boone signaled for Stephen to sit on the stained and threadbare chair beside the detective's scratched, gray metal desk.

"Here ya go." Detective Boone slapped a thick pile of paper down on the edge of the desk next to Stephen. "Lots of paper, not much fact, but you're welcome to get whatever ya can out of it. There's copies of the original photos in there, though, so be prepared for seein' some stuff that might upset ya a bit."

"Thank you." Stephen briefly closed his eyes and laid his hand on top of the papers. "Can you tell me about that night? I was young, and everything was so traumatic, my memory's pretty fuzzy. I really don't know anything about the investigation."

"Sure, though my memory's fuzzy, too. But I scanned through the file before ya got here ta refresh myself. Garland was a bulldog with that case, and it frustrated the hell outta him that he never could close it, 'specially with a missing little girl. And having a rookie like me followin' him around only made it worse. I believed he was the best detective who'd ever lived—still do—and he didn't like havin' his new partner's first case just fade away like it did." Detective Boone shook his head. "Too bad his heart hadda give out a few years ago."

"I remember meeting him once." Stephen smiled. "He came by the house a few days after that night. He was very nice. He even brought me a Junior Officer badge. I kept it for years."

"Yep, a helluva guy. Anyway, we started the search for your sister right after we got there and realized she was missin'.

Neighbors came from all over ta help, even some nearby San Antonio cops who heard the dispatch showed up."

"I remember that." Stephen nodded. "I also remember Mr. Johnson saying something about it. He was surprised the SAPD came at all."

Detective Boone shrugged. "We didn't have our own dispatch channel, we used the SAPD's, so the SA cops in the nearby neighborhoods sometimes came in to help. Screw the politics, cops help cops. But even the extra help didn't do no good. I'm still sorry about that. It's gotta be tough, never bein' able to put someone to rest, ta always wonder what mighta happened."

Stephen felt his stomach quiver with emotion. He took a deep breath and willed himself to focus on the technical details of that night. "The articles I found in the newspaper archives said the search was only conducted for three weeks. Why such a short time?"

"Ya gotta understand..." Detective Boone shook his head. "We were pretty small back then, only four officers. We just didn't have the resources. And the San Antonio cops hadda get back ta their own beats. The neighbors and family kept on lookin'. We didn't have no choice 'cept to put the case on the back burner."

Stephen nodded, but didn't try to speak over the lump in his throat. Getting angry with Detective Boone now would do nothing but hamper his chances of getting the information he needed.

"Anyways, we questioned your momma about what was missin' from the house. She said that the rifle, yer sister's bedspread, and a old yella rain slicker was gone. She knew a little bit about the rifle, called it a Brown Bess, and said it had a bent-tipped bayonet. Shoulda made it easy to identify. She said Chester's crew'd dug it up off South Alamo, where the Fairmount Hotel sits these days. You livin' here when they moved that thing?"

"The Fairmount? No, I wasn't," Stephen barely had time to say before Detective Boone continued.

"Damndest thing I ever seen. They hoisted the whole friggin hotel up on these giant pneumatic tires and drove it four city blocks from where Rivercenter Mall is now to where they set it down on South Alamo Street. They even drove it across the river. Had to take down power lines, street lights, parking meters, pretty much anything that hung down or stuck out. But they didn't so much as crack a window in that hotel. Betcha didn't know it's listed in the Guinness Book of World Records as the heaviest building ever moved like that."

"No, I didn't know that." Stephen returned to the subject at hand. "I'm sure my mother didn't know too much detail about the rifle. She was never very interested in historical artifacts. She tended to refer to them as *old bones and stuff.* Can you tell me what you found out about the rifle?"

"Oh, yeah, sorry. Sure, and it's all in the files there. We talked to the other guys on your dad's archeology team. None of them said they'd seen the rifle when it was dug up, but they was able to show us others like what your momma described. We visited a coupla antique stores, hoping someone might point us to private collectors, but they weren't no help. We never followed up after that, had to move on to other cases. If you really want to find that rifle, I'd start with the local antique dealers." Detective Boone shrugged. "Trail's probably pretty cold, but it's as gooda place to start as any. Maybe you'll have better luck than we did."

"Okay. May I call you again with more questions?"

"Sure. And for what it's worth, I hope you find that rifle. Who knows, maybe it'll even lead you to your sister."

HITS AND MISSES

Research is the process of going up alleys to see if they are blind. ~Marston Bates (1906-1974)

Wednesday morning, my body was almost back to normal, except for my still-gimpy ankle, so I figured I'd best get back on the case. Jason Storga had given me a small job, but Davidson was currently my primary source of income, and I couldn't very well bill for time if I wasn't actually doing anything.

I called Davidson's apartment. Not there. I tried his cell phone, but it went straight to voicemail. Maybe he'd actually gotten his own ass back to work, too. I scrolled to his third number in my address book and dialed, my brain taking a split second derail to ponder how ludicrous it was to still refer to calling a person's number with *dial*.

"Stephen Davidson, CPA."

"Good morning, Mr. Davidson, this is Marianna Morgan. How are you today?"

"Ms. Morgan. Glad to hear from you. I'm fine. Are you over your illness?"

"Yes, but I wasn't ill. I was in a motorcycle accident. Someone ran me off the road."

"Oh my God, are you all right? What happened?"

"Some jerk in a white truck ran me off the road. I'm okay, just a bit battered and bruised, and I've got a badly sprained ankle, so I'm still using a crutch. But no permanent damage, except for my motorcycle. I'm afraid he's totaled."

"I'm so sorry. Are you sure you're ready to work again?"

"Yep. I'm going to the Bexar County Courthouse to search their archives for any records on Stephanie, unless you have any new ideas or information." I still wasn't convinced it was his sister, but I figured I'd go along for now, since he seemed to believe it.

"Well, actually, I've done a bit of sleuthing on my own. Could you come by my office here in Austin before you head south? I'd like to give you copies of some files."

"I'll be there in an hour."

Davidson's office was in the Littleton Towers, a glass high-rise just off Congress Street, only a few blocks from the state capitol building. At night, like most of the buildings in the downtown district, the Littleton Towers is outlined from sidewalk to roof with glowing neon lighting, making the nighttime skyline a mass of rainbow-hued lines and angles. The Littleton Towers was outlined in hot pink. I wonder how the local NRA office, housed in the same building, feels about that. I parked Judy's Saturn in a parking garage that charged way too much money per hour and made my way to Davidson's office.

"Please come in, Ms. Morgan. Goodness gracious, here sit down. Let me move your crutch out of the way. May I get you some coffee?"

"Yes, thanks, if it's not too much trouble. Black, please." I wondered briefly if Davidson had fussed over his mom the same way. Maybe he missed having someone to care for.

The coffee was on a small counter tucked in the corner of Davidson's spacious office, which was furnished in a masculine combination of dark mahogany and maroon leather. He handed me a ceramic mug full of thick-looking coffee and a manila folder packed with an inch of paper.

"What's this?" I set the coffee down and opened the file.

"That's the complete case file from nineteen-sixty-five." Davidson's voice expressed an odd mix of pride and sadness. "I've decided I want to try locating the rifle that was stolen." His hand slipped to the top of his head, and he began to stroke his bald spot.

"Yourself, or did you want me to work on it?" I tried not to stare at his hand. I remembered his nervous dome-polishing habit from the last time I'd seen him. I shifted nervously, wondering if he was noting any unconscious habits I might have.

"Is something wrong?"

"No, no, just restless today, I guess. Anyway, did you want me to look for the rifle?

"I'd like you to continue focusing on my sister, at least for now. I'm happy to start following up on the old case information. It'll make me feel useful."

"Sure." *Oh great. The hardest cases to solve are the ones where the clients want to feel useful.*

Davidson told me about his conversation with Detective Boone. I described my accident—he sat and stared at me with raised eyebrows and a mouth frozen in a horrified O.

After an hour I stood. "I'd best head for San Antonio. Thanks for the copy of the report. I'll read it and we can talk again after."

Two hours later I was tromping through the basement of the Bexar County Courthouse on my way to the Record Archives room. As I passed the Licenses and Permits room, a young Hispanic couple emerged. He was wearing a brown polyester suit. She was in a simple white satin dress, visibly bulging at the tummy, and carrying a purple bouquet. They were surrounded by several adults and younger children, no doubt parents and siblings present to witness the quickie wedding. At least everyone was smiling.

I entered the archives room, signed in, and moved to the back, where twenty or so ancient mainframe terminals were lined up on two rows of long tables. Half a dozen people were scattered among them. I had a choice of crappy yellow or brown screens, each displaying a cryptic and unfriendly menu of abbreviations and acronyms. Seems the County Records Department was still in the dark ages of computer technology.

Hoping it'd be easier on my eyes than the harsh green, I chose brown. These government systems were the bane of my investigative work, with screens so old the menus were burned into the phosphor, and interfaces that'd been designed by surly programmers who hated the idea of *outsiders* being allowed to use their masterpieces.

After a few minutes of squinting, I'd figured out most of the menu. I started with AN, which stood for Assumed Name. I painstakingly moved through CI—Criminal Inquiry, PD—Phone Directory, DR—Deed Records, and even BT—Bond Tracking.

I expected to find nothing on Stephanie, and I wasn't disappointed. The best success I had was in locking up three terminals while attempting to back out of one search process or another. Trying to reset the system proved a waste of time, so I just kept moving to different terminals.

After completing my search on Stephanie, I spent some time working on Jason's list of witnesses. I managed to find more information than I'd gained a few days ago from ERAS. I also managed to lock up two more terminals.

As I was leaving, I noticed a county employee staring at the terminals I'd used. She had her hands on her ample hips and was shaking her head. She looked up and scowled. I couldn't help but blush. Before she could yell at me, I scooted around the corner and made my escape.

I stopped in the courthouse coffee shop, where I sat and flipped through the contents of the case folder Davidson had given me. It included the original police report, gruesomely detailed photos of the bloody murder scene, statements from Mrs. Davidson, the neighbor Mr. Johnson, and even Stephen, although the latter was understandably short and simple, given that he'd only been seven.

A good portion of the file consisted of names, addresses, and brief statements of all those the police had questioned with respect to Stephanie and the missing rifle. Most of those questioned about Stephanie were what I'd expect—neighbors, her teacher, other school staff, and relatives.

None had any idea what might've happened. Everyone had the same opinion that no one seemed to be angry at the Davidson family. There were no rumors or reports of child molesters in the are. No strangers had been hanging around the school. No one knew anything. Or at least no one admitted to knowing anything.

The list of those questioned about the rifle included all of Chester Davidson's university associates, men working on the construction of HemisFair, the antique dealers in San Antonio, and even a few Alamo-era historical experts. They weren't much help to the detectives, either. Apparently no one had seen the rifle before Davidson's dad borrowed—okay, stole—it.

I found that hard to believe. There would've been archeologists all over the dig site. Construction crews hate to be held up while academics crawl around on hands and knees with toothbrushes and dental picks. The university'd have sent all available hands to recover as many artifacts in as short a time as possible.

If I were Davidson, I'd start with the father's former associates. Maybe someone had seen something. Maybe they were working with Chester Davidson all along and had been afraid to talk to the police. It seemed logical that Chester hadn't thought he could penetrate the shadowy world of private collectors by himself. Then again, he was deeply in debt, so he may have been too selfish to share with someone else.

If the police had explored these possibilities, they'd come up with nothing, or at least nothing worth noting in their case files. Maybe I was extrapolating too much due to boredom. Maybe Chester Davidson had managed to sneak the rifle into his goody bag or toolbox or whatever archeologists carried their tools in.

I realized as I sat sipping my tepid, bitter coffee that I really knew very little about the world of archeology. Maybe I could take a University of Texas extension class in my spare time. I snorted at the idea of that much spare time, eliciting a raised-eyebrow stare from a man at the next table. I shrugged and returned to my reading.

My mind was wandering more than usual, so I shook my head to clear it. I was going to have to find a more productive way to track this mystery woman down. Hoping to pick up more details, I decided to go to the library and look at the newspaper stories from the time of the break-in and murder.

The main downtown library looks nothing like it did when I was a kid. The old library was in a small limestone building not far from Davidson's apartment. Most recently that historical building housed the Hertzberg Circus Collection and Museum, with its twenty-thousand items of Big Top memorabilia, including Tom Thumb's carriage. I'm not big on circuses, so I never bothered to go. I guess not enough other people had, either, seeing as the place had closed down. I still picture the inside of that building with its tall stacks, dim lighting, and narrow aisles. The new Technicolor, art deco library is a polar opposite to the old. I wondered if it too would be considered historical in fifty years.

After a bit of assistance from a nice archival librarian, I sat at a viewing station with a stack of thirty-five millimeter film spools and a pile of dimes. I spent two hours scrolling through newspaper editions. Okay, I admit it took so long because I kept stopping to read old articles and ads.

It was the little things that struck me most, and made me feel old —ads for big department stores that had since gone bankrupt, grocery ads listing T-bone steak for forty-nine cents a pound, movie listings for new movies like *Dr. Strangelove, The Sound of Music*, and *The Saboteur*. All the best movies were showing at theaters that had since been torn down or converted to other uses.

It took my entire stash of dimes to print out the articles I found about the Davidson case. Unfortunately, even the ones I found didn't include much meat. I sighed, realizing my day had proved to be pretty damn unproductive. I decided an ice cold beer was in order, and I knew just the place to go.

Whiskey Smith's is a typical neighborhood bar—clean parking lot scattered with sedans and expensive pickups, a small number of round tables and chairs in a dimly lit room, a large u-shaped bar surrounded by thickly padded barstools with backrests, and three pool tables in a well-lit area beyond the bar.

Considering it was only four in the afternoon, the bar was already crowded with imbibers, all chatting in a friendly, familiar way with a thirty-ish, female bartender I'd describe as attractively normal—normal-sized breasts, minimal makeup, dark brown hair tied back in a ponytail instead of being teased into a Texas-sized tangle. She was wearing a San Antonio Spurs T-shirt and jeans. I slipped onto one of the few unoccupied barstools.

I watched her move up and down the bar, refilling and serving customers. She seemed to know most everyone's name and drink preference.

"What can I get you?" She smiled as she approached me.

"How about a Shiner Bock, if you have it on tap."

"Coming right up." She deftly pulled a frosted mug from a deep freezer, filled it with foamy, gold beer, and plopped it onto a paper coaster in front of me. "I'm Tammy. What's your name?"

She's certainly a perky little thing. "Marianna." I gave her my most friendly smile.

"Welcome to Whiskey Smith's. I haven't seen you in here before."

"No, I don't get onto this side of town too often." I glanced around. "You seem to know most everyone in here."

She nodded. "I like to get to know my regulars. Excuse me." She moved to serve another customer. I sipped my beer and felt its icy trace slide down my throat. Most Texas beer drinkers think Shiner Bock's the best beer there is. I'm not a beer connoisseur, but I figured I could at least support the local guys, and the aptly-named Shiner Bock is brewed at the little Spoetzel Brewery in Shiner, Texas.

I took a bigger swallow and again looked around the room. The clientele was distinctly white-collar class, probably slipped away from the office early to have a quick one or two before heading home. Although most patrons were men, there were four other women at the bar, dressed in business-casual blouses and skirts or slacks. One older woman, still clinging to the *Women's Dress for Success* idiocy of the eighties, wore a floppy bow tie.

When Tammy wandered my direction again I said, "Mind if I ask you a few questions?"

"Why? You aren't a cop." She wasn't asking—she spoke with the confidence of one who reads people for a living.

"My motorcycle and I had a recent encounter with Tom Darnell, the guy that was found dead out front in his pickup. I guess I was just curious what kind of guy he was."

"Then I don't mind your questions. At least as long as I can space my answers between customers."

"No problem. Were you here last Saturday when Tom was murdered?"

"Nah, Henry Soto works weekends. I'm glad it wasn't me who found him." She shook her head. "This is a quiet neighborhood, shit like that just isn't supposed to happen around here."

There were murmurs of agreement around the bar.

"Did Henry know Tom?" I asked Tammy.

"Yeah, Tom was a regular on the weekends. But Henry didn't like him. More than once he called Tom a lowlife skank."

"I knew him, too," said a middle-aged man in a polo shirt and khaki pants. "He grew up in this neighborhood, lived about three houses from us. He was no good back then, always in trouble at school. Eventually got sent off to reform school or juvie camp or someplace like that. If he was murdered here Saturday night, I guess he was still no good." He shook his head and took a large swig of beer. "Bad eggs never change. Terrill Hills was much better when he got sent away."

I whipped around so fast on my bar stool that my wrist knocked against my beer. I scrambled for it with both hands. "He grew up in Terrell Hills?"

"Yeah, his parents moved here when he was around eight or nine," the man responded. "The whole lot of them were a pretty poor example of humanity, but a real good example of a dysfunctional family. We didn't call it that back then. They were just known as the Trash Family.

He shook his head and paused, apparently deep in thought, before continuing.

"Tom's dad worked for the civil service at Kelly Air Force Base, or at least they paid him—I don't think he did much actual work. His mom was a housewife, but she sure didn't seem to dedicate herself to raising her son. My parents swore the mom was a drunk and the dad regularly beat everyone in the family. Tom was wild from the start, but I guess I can sort of understand, if his home really was as bad as it sounded." He swallowed the last of his beer and slid the empty mug across the bar. "There you go, Tammy. Thanks again. I guess I'd best get home."

"See you Bernie." She waved.

I turned my attention back to Tammy. "Do you know anything about who Darnell was with on Saturday night?"

"Henry told the police that Tom was with a woman. She was really tall with long brown hair and a giant purse, but that was all he remembered." She shrugged. "Saturday was crowded and we lower the lights more on weekends."

I figured customers would be moving around by Braille if they lowered the lights more than they were now, but I didn't comment. Instead, I tossed a five on the bar and slid off my stool. "Thanks, Tammy, I appreciate your help."

I sat in my car for a few minutes in Whiskey Smith's parking lot. What the hell was going on here? The description of Tom's female friend sure did sound like the brief glimpse I'd had of Stephanie last Thursday behind the Bargain Mart. If that was true, then she was possibly involved in his running me off the road. And that made things much more complicated.

It was time to make another call to Davidson. I tried his office, cell phone, and home. Naturally, he answered none of them. I left the same message at each number. "Mr. Davidson, this is Marianna Morgan. I'd like to talk to you about Tom Darnell, to see if you recognize the name, and if you've seen him lately. I understand he grew up in the same neighborhood you did, so you may have known him at school. I have reason to believe he may somehow be connected with your case. Please call me back as soon as you get a chance."

THEN AND NOW

Things are never quite as scary when you've got a best friend. ~Calvin, Calvin & Hobbes

Stephen checked for messages as soon as he got home from work Wednesday evening. There were five. It'd been a long day, and he was tired, but he pressed Play anyway. One was an offer for life insurance, two were from clients, one was a hang-up, and one was a disturbing message from Ms. Morgan.

He sat down, lowered his head, and slowly rubbed his hand across his bald spot. Tom Darnell. Just hearing the name again bubbled up painful memories from his childhood. Tom's family, well *Tommy* back then, had moved to the neighborhood two years after Stephanie's disappearance. Darnell instantly became the new school bully, beating up kids, stealing, grabbing at the girls. He was finally caught vandalizing neighborhood cars. Soon after that, he got shipped off to a ranch for troubled kids.

Stephen thought about those scary and abusive times. He was small for his age, and he'd had a hard time getting over Stephanie. Even two years later, he'd still felt like only half a person. He'd grown introverted, quiet, an easy target for a bully. Darnell had directed a fair share of his abuse onto Stephen.

Looking back, he was sure he'd been suffering from depression. His mother had definitely fallen into an emotional hole, barely able to deal with her own issues, certainly not able to help him deal with his. So he'd suffered the abuse in silence. Ms. Morgan's phone call brought it all back.

Sitting in his small apartment, Stephen suddenly felt choked and crowded, and his heart pounded in his ears. He desperately needed air. He grabbed his bag of cat food and headed out, then paused on the sidewalk below his apartment. Overhead, thousands of grackles swooped down to light on the tall cypress trees lining the river, preparing to roost for the night. He watched their precision flying as they dodged and darted around tree limbs and each other.

Stephen couldn't help but smile. He'd spent many mornings watching the city's maintenance crews hosing a fresh, thick layer of bird droppings off the sidewalks and park benches. Even the city's attempt to scare the birds away at night with air rifles had proved fruitless.

The heat of the day had subsided, and a light breeze wafted around the surrounding buildings and along the water. He started to walk south to feed his cats, but then changed his mind and instead turned north at the corner. The library was a mile long walk from his apartment, but the exercise and fresh air revived him and lifted his spirits. He wasn't sure what he was going to do when he got there, but his heart beat in anticipation.

He reached the library less than fifteen minutes before it was to close for the night. Feeling conspicuous carrying a canvas bag of cat food, he took the elevator to the sixth floor and hurried to the Texana information desk. His heart did a happy little flutter when he saw that Patty was there. He approached quickly, trying to keep the canvas bag below her eye level over the counter.

She smiled when she saw his approach. "Well hello there Stephen. It's good to see you again. I'm sorry we're about to close, and I can't let you use a viewing station."

"That's all right." Stephen returned her smile. "I didn't really come to view more archives. I, um, was hoping to, well, to see you again. Do you have plans after the library closes? May I buy you a cup of coffee?"

Patty's smile widened. "That would be nice. I enjoyed our brief meeting the other day. Do you mind waiting?"

"Not at all." Stephen pointed to the nearby stacks. "I'll ramble through the Texas History section."

As Stephen and Patty stood waiting for the elevator, she asked, "What's in your bag? It looks heavy."

Stephen blushed. "Cat food. I feed a small clutter of homeless cats that live along the river on the northern edge of King William."

"I knew when I met you that you were a kind man." Patty nodded. "After years of dealing with the public, I'm a pretty good judge of character. Have you fed them this evening?"

"No. I was planning to, but found myself here instead." He blushed again but smiled.

"I'd love to go with you, if you don't mind. Is your car in the garage?"

"Actually, no, I walked from my apartment. I live in the Casino Club building."

"I love that building. I especially love the multi-colored dome on the roof."

Stephen laughed. "There was quite a controversy among the residents when they did that. Some thought it made the building look like a night club. Personally, I kind of like it. I think it gives the classic old building a touch of whimsy."

"It's quite a walk to King William from here. We can take my car if you like."

"That would be very nice. Thank you."

The two walked the short distance to the library employee's small parking lot. It pleased Stephen to see that Patty's dark blue Jetta was immaculate inside and out. His own OCD tendencies would have made it difficult for him to ride with her—or even continue spending time—if she was messy or unkempt. He shook his head, knowing his reaction and thoughts were petty, but helpless to control them.

"Is something the matter?" Patty asked.

"No, not at all." Stephen smiled. "Quite the contrary. I was actually admiring your car. It just made me think of something else." He widened his smile. "But everything is just fine."

"I'm pleased to hear that."

They exchanged brief background stories on the drive to King William. Stephen learned that Patty grew up in Tulsa and ended up in San Antonio as a young girl when her father was stationed at Fort Sam Houston. She'd been there ever since and had worked at the library for twenty years, long before the new building was built.

He, in turn, told her about growing up in Terrell Hills and becoming a successful CPA in Austin. He deliberately avoided mentioning anything about his dad's murder and sister's abduction. He desperately wanted a friend, or perhaps more than a friend, who didn't feel sorry for him. He did admit to Patty that he'd returned to San Antonio after his mother died.

As they approached the King William area, Stephen directed Patty onto the appropriate street. They found a nearby parking space and walked down the dirt trail to the river.

"I've always come here alone," Stephen admitted. "I hope they'll be brave enough to eat with someone else present."

"I'll stay back." Patty paused beside a tree. "To avoid scaring them."

Stephen walked into the small clearing the cats had made as a result of months of eating in the same place. He opened five cans of the inexpensive, aromatic food and plopped each one on the ground. He'd barely stepped away from the clearing when cats started trotting from the surrounding weeds and bushes. Soon, the little clearing was full of hungry cats of every size and color.

Stephen stood for a moment, admiring his feline friends, then rejoined Patty beside the tree.

"They're so pretty," Patty whispered. "I wish they didn't have to be homeless. But it's almost impossible to tame wild cats."

"I know." Stephen frowned. "I've tried hard, but this is as relaxed as they've become. Even after several months, I can't get closer than five feet, depending on the cat." He turned and looked at Patty. "I'm glad you're here, although I must admit I'm a bit surprised you'd come to such a secluded place with a stranger."

Patty shrugged. "As I said, I'm a pretty good judge of character. Besides," she admitted with a small laugh, "I prepared myself just in case." She raised her hand, in which she held a small black can. Stephen didn't need to ask. He knew it was mace or pepper spray.

"I hope you aren't offended," Patty said. "But you're right. It's always better to be safe than sorry."

"No need to apologize." Stephen waved in dismissal. "I completely understand, and I'm not offended. In fact, I'm glad to see you're cautious." He gave her a warm smile. "I'd hate for something bad to happen to you."

They watched the cats in silence for a few minutes. Patty pointed to a family of ducks paddling in circles near the opposite shore, chasing and gobbling up bugs or minnows.

"It's so peaceful here." She sighed in relaxation. "It's hard to believe we're on the banks of one of the biggest tourist attractions in the country."

"That's why I started walking this direction in the first place." Stephen glanced around. "Living on the River Walk has many plusses, but it also has the minus of never really being quiet or empty. Coming here gives me a break from so much civilization."

Patty laughed, which scared the cats back into their hiding places. "Oh no, I'm sorry."

"It's all right." Stephen smiled. "They spook easily, but they'll be back. Could I still buy you that cup of coffee, or perhaps dinner?"

"Dinner sounds nice."

"How about that little Italian place on South Presa?"

"La Parmigiana? That sounds good."

They spent over two hours at the restaurant, eating a delicious dinner and sharing delightful conversation. Stephen was sorry when their coffee and dessert dishes were cleared away, signaling that the evening was drawing to a close.

"I had a wonderful time, Patty. May I see you again?"

"I'd like that." Patty took a small notebook from her purse and jotted down her phone number. "I work Wednesday evenings at the library, but the rest of the week, I get off at four. And I graduated long ago from having to work weekends."

Stephen walked with Patty to her car and held the door while she slid in. He didn't circle to the passenger side.

"Can I give you a lift home?" she asked.

"Thank you, but I think I'd like to walk. It's only half a dozen blocks from here, and the evening is lovely." Stephen patted his stomach. "Besides, I need to walk off that half loaf of garlic bread I just ate."

"Remember I ate the other half." Patty laughed. "I should leave my car and walk with you. But it's late, and I really need to get home."

"Where do you live? I hope you don't have a long drive."

"Out North New Braunfels Road, not far from the military base. It was our family home when my father was stationed here. After my parents died, I stayed on. It's a lovely home, and it makes me feel closer to my parents even though they're gone."

Stephen nodded. "I understand. That's why it was so hard to leave my home in Austin. But I needed to get away from the memories of watching my mother slowly waste away."

"I'm so sorry." Patty put her hand to her chest. "I didn't mean to remind you of—"

"No, no, it's really okay. I'm doing fine these days." He leaned down and kissed Patty lightly on the cheek. "I'll call you soon."

By the time he got home, it was after eleven. He realized he'd forgotten all about Ms. Morgan's message concerning Tom Darnell, and was sorry he'd remembered it now, when it was too late to do anything. He'd call Ms. Morgan back tomorrow.

MY NEW FRIEND PAM

Strangers are just friends waiting to happen. ~unknown

I didn't hear back from Davidson until nine Thursday morning. He sounded tired and stressed.

"I'm sorry I missed your call yesterday. You caught me in between locations, and I forgot to turn my cell phone back on after a meeting," Davidson said.

"No problem." Not being able to communicate with a client could be a problem, but I didn't say that. "I'd like to talk to you now, if you have a minute."

"Now is fine. You asked about Tom Darnell. Yes, I remember him. What makes you believe he may be connected with my case?"

"Do you remember my telling you that I'd been run off the road Saturday afternoon?"

"Yes. I hope you're feeling better."

"Healing more every day, thanks. In any case, the man who ran me off the road was Darnell." I paused to gauge his reaction.

"My goodness, how did you find that out? Did they catch him?"

"In a way. They found his body in his truck outside Whiskey Smith's bar Sunday morning. He'd been shot twice in the head."

"Oh, dear God. What made you think I'd know him?"

"Because he was last seen with a woman that I believe may be your sister."

"What! Stephanie would never have anything to do with a lowlife like Tommy Darnell."

"C'mon, Stephen, you can't know what she's like these days, or who she may be friends with. You said yourself that if she lived through her ordeal, she may have changed in terrible ways."

Stephen uttered a long, despairing sigh. "You're right. I just can't imagine Stephanie as anything but my happy, loving sister, even if it was only for a few short years. Please tell me what you learned."

I filled Davidson in on my visit to the impound yard and to Whiskey Smith's. "How well did you know Darnell, and when did you last see him?"

"I didn't really know him at all. We certainly weren't friends. He moved into our neighborhood after Stephanie was ki…after the burglary in our home. He quickly took over as the school bully. No one liked him. I still remember the day a puppy got run over in front of the school. Darnell laughed. Anyway, he reined supreme for months before finally being sent away to a ranch for troubled kids. I never saw him again, not then, and not recently."

"Okay. Somehow, Stephanie's hooked up with Tom. I don't know how yet, but I'll find out. For your sake *and* mine. I still have no idea why Tom ran me off the road. I hate to believe that Stephanie had anything to do with it, but signs sure point that way right now."

"I know, and it makes me sad to think of her that way. What do you plan to do?"

"I have some errands I must run this morning, but I'm going back to San Antonio this afternoon. Unless you have a better idea, I'm parking outside that gray door until she shows up."

I'd planned to run errands all morning and meet Judy for lunch, but I was tired of not knowing what was going on, and the only place I knew to look was inside a locked room behind the Bargain Mart. I gassed up Judy's car and headed straight for San Antonio. I passed the time by calling with apologies to Judy and the people at the other places I'd been scheduled to stop.

It was only eleven when I hit San Antonio, but I was already hungry, so I swung through a Dairy Queen and got a D.Q. Dude, fries, and Coke to go. I circled the block around the Bargain Mart's strip center and cut through the parking lot. I saw no sign of Stephanie's blue Taurus, so I parked beneath the Chinaberry tree. It was just past eleven-fifteen. I reclined my seat back a bit, unwrapped my Dude—a chicken-fried hamburger patty on a bun—and got comfortable, figuring I was in for another long wait.

I'd just mangled open a small pouch of ketchup/catsup/whatever when I saw the gray door open. I tossed the Dude and ketchup on the passenger seat, dribbling bright red tomato sauce across my leg and shorts as I did.

"Shit!" I hissed as I scrambled to simultaneously wipe it off with a napkin and grab my crutch. I was clambering awkwardly out of the car when the woman I'd decided was Stephanie backed out through the door, her arms laden with a large, overflowing paper bag. From across the street, I couldn't tell what was in the bag.

"Wait!" I yelled as I stepped off the curb and tried to hurry across the street. Then I took a chance. "Stephanie, wait!"

The woman jerked her head around and looked directly at me. She quickly kicked the gray door shut and started to run in the opposite direction. She wasn't very fast, thanks to the bag in her arms, but I was even slower, thanks to the damn crutch under my arm.

She reached the corner at the next block, turned and disappeared. I stopped in the middle of the street. It wouldn't do any good to continue the chase. I jumped a foot when a car rounded the corner and honked as it swerved close around me.

"Dammit! Dammit all to hell!!" I needed a break in this case and my best chance at one had just gotten away. Again.

I stood in the middle of the street until a second car nearly ran me down, then I slowly trudged my way back to my car, shaking my head and muttering at the ground. I ate my half-squashed, mostly cold Dude and fries, with no ketchup, since most of *that* had ended up marinating my thigh. I saved one small chunk of Dude for Deke. I always saved him snacks from Dairy Queen, since he'd been scrounging food from their dumpsters before I rescued him.

She must have parked the blue Taurus some distance away—I hadn't spotted it when I'd first arrived. I wondered what had changed for her, or if she normally parked different places and distances to prevent someone from taking too much interest in her comings and goings.

"Time for action," I said to the angry-looking woman in the rearview mirror. "I think I know just who can help me." I wiped the last of the grease off my hands, clambered out of the car again, and headed to the Bargain Mart.

The air inside was as cold as I remembered, but the place was less crowded today. I spotted an orange-smocked employee and approached. "Excuse me, can you tell me if Pam is working today?"

The pimply-faced, skinny young man blankly stared at me, mouth slightly agape.

I spoke slowly. "You know…Pam? Sings country and western songs? Handles the stock in back?"

"Oh. Yeah. Pam. She's in back."

"Thanks." I drew the word out, to be sure that his synapses had time to receive and translate. I probably sounded condescending, but I didn't care. I was having a crappy day—might as well take a few folks down with me.

I poked my head through the Employees Only door and saw Pam sitting at the battered, puke-yellow table. This time she was filling out official-looking forms. "Pam? Can I come in?"

"You!" She said with a toss of her head. "I remember you. You got me in so much trouble. You said you'd cover for me, but Woody came in and caught me doing my nails. I almost got fired. I had to beg to keep my job. And I had to work overtime, *without pay*, rearranging displays to make up for it. I even had to cancel a date."

I couldn't imagine begging for a job at Bargain Mart. Still, I felt bad for what'd happened. "I'm sorry, Pam. I never meant to get you in trouble. I was in trouble myself at the time, but I couldn't say anything. Please, can I talk to you now?"

"Yeah, okay. I guess so." Her voice softened and she shrugged her shoulders. She pointed to my crutch. "What happened to you?"

I sat on one of the other metal chairs. I figured the direct, blunt approach would reach deeper into Pam's emotions, giving me a better chance to get beyond the fact that she was pissed at the trick I pulled on her last time we met. "I was run off the road by a real asshole who was murdered by someone else that same night." I was right—her eyes grew big and round and her mouth fell open.

"What are you? Some kind of cop or something?" I could hear the awe in her voice.

"Something." I gave her my warmest smile. "I'm a Private Investigator. And I need your help."

"*My* help? How in the world can *I* help? And why should I believe you, after you lied to me. I don't even know your real name."

"First, my real name is Marianna. I didn't completely lie, at least I said my name was Mary. Well, okay, Rosemary. But it's pretty close. Second, I'm really sorry for last time. I was on a case, following a woman. I was only trying to see if there was a way to get from the back of this store to wherever that exterior gray metal door leads. I didn't expect there to be anyone back here. I was just trying to cover my ass. I sure didn't mean to get you in trouble."

Pam stared at me silently, chewing on her lip, her brow furrowed. I guess she was sizing me up, or thinking really, really hard. Finally, she smiled. "Okay, I accept your apology. Now, what did you mean by needing my help?"

"I still need to get into the room behind that gray door, even more so now that there's a dead body involved in the case. Do you know what's in there, or can you get me inside it?"

"I don't know, but I'll bet I can find out. Follow me." Pam stood and circled the table, patting me on the arm as she passed.

I shrugged and followed. I had no idea what she was up to, but her plan was better than mine, since I didn't have one. We re-entered the main store and Pam made a beeline for Woody.

"Excuse me, Mr. Greenwood This customer has alerted me to a prowler hanging around."

"Prowler? Where?" Mr. Greenwood had a whiney, nasal voice that made my eye twitch. "Is this the customer?" His contempt was clearly stamped on his face as he looked me up and down.

"Yes." I nodded. "I saw a woman carrying a full paper bag exit out the gray door down the side of this building. When she saw me, she kicked the door closed and ran. She disappeared around the corner. It may be nothing, but she sure looked suspicious to me."

"What's that door lead to?" Pam asked.

"It's the electrical and phone access room for this complex," he responded. There's nothing in there to steal." He looked directly at me again. "Are you sure of what you saw?"

I stood as straight and dignified as possible, considering that I was on a crutch, remnants of bruises and scabs dotted my legs, my hair was stringy from sweat, and there was a large ketchup stain on my shorts. "As I said, I was getting ready to cross the street when I saw a tall, long-haired woman exit through that door. She was carrying an obviously full shopping bag, although I couldn't see what was in it. I was only trying to be helpful. I'm sorry I wasted both your and this thoughtful and helpful employee's time."

Pam, who was standing just out of Mr. Greenwood's view, grinned from ear to ear. I started to turn away.

"Wait. I'm sorry." His entire demeanor changed. "I appreciate a customer taking time to alert us about potential problems. My apologies for my initial reaction. You caught me by surprise."

"Of course." I flashed him a toothy smile.

"Do you have a key, Mr. Greenwood?" Pam asked. "I know you're very busy, and I'd be happy to take Ms., um—"

"Morgan," I said.

"Yes, Ms. Morgan. I'd be happy to walk outside with Ms. Morgan to check on the equipment room for you."

Mr. Greenwood raised his eyebrows and smirked, but he pulled a keyring packed with what looked like fifty keys out of his pocket, flipped through them, and handed the whole mess by the selected key to Pam. "This one."

"Yes, sir. I'll only be a few minutes. I doubt we'll find any problems, but it doesn't hurt to check."

We left Mr. Greenwood to continue straightening and organizing customer-mangled displays and made our way outside.

"That was smooth." I grinned at Pam. "You could be a Private Investigator if you wanted." I figured she deserved some extra kudos, since I was still feeling guilty about getting her in trouble.

"Really? You think so? Cool."

When Pam inserted the key in the gray door's lock, I couldn't help but feel a tingle of excitement at finally seeing what was behind it. She pulled the door open and we bonked heads trying to look in at the same time.

"Sorry!" we said simultaneously.

"You go ahead, it's your case." Pam extended her arm toward the room. "Besides, it's dark in there."

"Thanks." I stepped inside and felt around the wall for a light switch. Once lit, I saw that the entire room was perhaps eight feet wide and fifteen feet deep. Along the length of one wall were banks of alternating boxes—telephone connection racks with their miles of multi-colored wire in a tangled chaos, and large, closed boxes that I assumed contained electrical circuit breakers. But it was the back end of the small room that caught my attention.

Stretched between the side walls, a couple of feet from the back wall, was a heavy rope. Hanging on the rope were half a dozen empty wire clothing hangers. Taped to the back wall with duct tape was a dirty mirror. On the floor was a red and purple print scarf, trampled into a wrinkled, ruined mess. In the corner behind the scarf was a crumpled piece of paper.

"Wow." Pam said from behind me. "What was going on in here?"

"Hard to say." I bent to pick up the paper.

"What's that?" Pam asked.

I extended my hand toward her. In it was a brochure for the Snake Farm. "My next destination."

"What's at the Snake Farm?"

"You mean besides *over 500 animals on display?*" I said as I read the brochure. "I'm not sure yet, but if the woman who's been using this room went there, then I've gotta go there, too."

"Wish I could go with you. Private investigation seems like fun."

I cringed. The last thing I needed was a loopy sidekick. I decided to nip her ambitions in the bud. "I wouldn't call it fun." I pointed to my ankle. "You should have seen me a few days ago." I told Pam all the gory details of my accident and injuries. I emphasized all the worst parts, hoping to discourage her from following in my footsteps. She was too innocent and trusting, at least for now. Maybe when she was older.

When I finished my story there were beads of sweat running from her forehead, and she was breathing in little short gulps.

"Hey, are you okay? I didn't mean to scare you."

"No, no, it's okay. I guess I didn't think about the bad parts of the job. I, um, guess I'd better get back to the store. I'm sure Woody's watching for how long I'm gone."

"Sure." I gave an enthusiastic nod. "I don't want to get you in trouble again. I really appreciate all your help, though. You've helped me with one of the biggest breaks I've had so far."

"Really?" Pam squealed. She clasped her hands and bounced two or three times on her toes.

"Really." I nodded again. Poor kid. Her life must be pretty mundane.

As I pulled onto northbound Interstate 35, I glanced at the time. It was already after four, so I'd have to hurry if I was going to make it to the Snake Farm. I had no idea what time they closed. Then the light bulb went on in my head, and I smoothed open the brochure.

> Come to the Snake Farm! We feature more than 500 reptiles, as well as a variety of monkeys, exotic birds, Llamas, and Texas Longhorns.
>
> Open weekdays during summer 10am-7pm (winter hours Mon.-Fri. 10am-6pm). Closed Tuesday. Year-round on weekends (Sat. and Sun.) 10am-6pm. Exit 182 on I-35 south of town.

Okay, so I wasn't almost out of time, but I was still anxious to be on my way, and not because they had monkeys, birds, Llamas, and Longhorns, in addition to snakes.

ESCAPE

Little thieves are hanged but great ones escape.
~14th Century French Proverb

After he got off the phone Thursday morning with Ms. Morgan, Stephen felt restless and anxious. The lonely, angry memories from his childhood flooded his brain like a roaring river overtaking a weakened dam. It wasn't even noon yet, but he already felt ragged and tired.

He should drive to his office, but there was still one day to go before the weekend. *I'll work on Friday.* He paced through his small apartment, rubbing the top of his head. When his scalp began to burn, he self-consciously jerked his hand away.

He needed to get away, but he couldn't bring himself to venture onto the River Walk during the middle of the day. Instead, he walked to his kitchen, opened the refrigerator, and removed a chilled bottle of chardonnay. He pulled a wine glass from the cabinet over his sink and poured it full.

As he raised the glass to his lips, he remembered Ms. Morgan's suggestion that he stop drinking for a while to see if the alcohol was triggering his Lost Times.

"I'm sorry Ms. Morgan, I guess I'm not as strong as I thought." He took a deep swallow of wine. He drained the glass with his second swallow and poured it full again. He didn't remember much after that.

Stephanie threw the bag on the floor and kicked it. "Dammit! Damn, damn, damn." She had better things to do with her Thursday, but she had no choice. She was losing control of the situation. She quickly gathered the few personal things in the room and shoved them into the shopping bag. She wasn't sure where she'd move them to, but she knew she had to get them out of here.

She yanked off the clips that connected the answering machine's power cord to a bare spot on the electrical line in the breaker box, and pulled the jumper wire off the telephone-switch patch-panel where she'd tapped into the emergency phone line for Tan-UR-Hide's alarm system. She unplugged the phone and answering machine and shoved them into the paper bag.

She needed to think. She dug inside her large purse, pulled out her comb, and ran it through her hair. She was not about to consolidate everything into one location—she wanted several safe places to go. She'd just have to find a new place for this particular stash.

She leaned back against the wall, closed her eyes, and sighed. Life wasn't supposed to be this complicated. Whatever happened to that little girl she once was. Too much had happened, too much time had passed. That happy, carefree little girl was dead. Now, leaning against the wall, she felt as hollow as a mannequin.

She sighed again and pushed off the wall. "Enough!" She dropped her comb back into her purse. "Enough feeling sorry for myself. I've got to keep my head on straight and move on. Everything's going to be just fine." She reached for the bag. "Yep, just fine."

SNAKES OF A FEATHER?

Birds of a feather, flock together.
~Robert Burton (1577-1640)

Thirty five minutes after leaving the Bargain Mart, I reached exit 182. I was moving right to take the exit when a memory flooded into my brain with such intensity that I almost went off the road. I knew Tom Darnell's truck had seemed familiar. I just couldn't place it, thanks to post-accident stress and drugs.

Taking the Snake Farm exit finally triggered my addled memory. The Killer Pickup Truck that zipped around me at this very exit a couple days ago, and the truck Darnell was driving when he ran me off the road, were one and the same. It was another clear indication that Stephanie and Darnell had something to do with each other. Whether or not the Snake Farm had anything to do with whatever was going on remained to be seen, but I was definitely on the right track.

I circled under the highway and looped back to the Snake Farm. I was about to find out if the whore-house legend was true. I pulled into the dusty, caliche parking lot and parked between a beat up Chevy Impala and a Ford Explorer that still had paper tags.

As soon as my crutch and I exited the car, I was greeted by the strong smell of eau-de-animal, which I guess I should have expected. You can't confine large numbers of animals—or people for that matter—without their combined scents permeating the air.

I walked to the main entrance and stopped at the ticket counter. It was staffed by a bored-looking teenage boy with a spike-topped haircut that made him look like he'd been caught in a blender. The outside edges of both ears were lined with small silver hoop earrings. *I wonder how he'd manage at airport security?*

"How many?" He stared droopy-eyed at my crutch.

I started to say there were to many earrings to count, then realized he was talking about tickets. "One."

"Four-ninety five." He stifled a yawn as he spoke.

Good help sure is hard to find these days. I handed over a ten. I counted my change before pocketing and shifted my crutch to a more comfortable underarm position. "And awaaaaay we go!"

"Huh?" said yawn-boy.

I just laughed and moved toward the exhibit area. Even though I was supposed to be strictly on business, I found myself fascinated by the place. The largest indoor exhibit was the snake room, which consisted of row upon row of small cages. Their ads weren't lying when they said *more than 500* snakes. There were snakes everywhere, in every possible combination of colors and patterns.

The reticulated python looked big enough to swallow me whole. She—according to the placard on her glass-walled cage—weighed two hundred and seventy-five pounds (three hundred and twenty-five after a rabbit and chicken lunch) and was twenty feet long.

There were also other critters in the snake room—baby alligators that stared with hungry interest as I walked by, giant tarantulas, scorpions as big as salad plates, and turtles, four of whom were stacked one atop the other. On my way outside, I passed a cage full of Egyptian fruit bats, who were in the middle of a squeaky argument over elbow space.

The outside grounds included dozens of large cages and pens containing everything from different species of monkeys and apes to exotic birds to farm animals like Llamas and Texas Longhorns. Dwarf Bantam chickens with fat, fluffy feet, and regal peacocks in full fan-tailed display wandered free around the grounds.

The peacocks reminded me of my favorite skirt when I was six. It was a full circle and patterned like a peacock's tail feathers. When I twirled, it flew high up in the air. I felt exotic when I wore it.

That memory made me think of Stephanie as a little girl. What had she been like? How close had she and Stephen been? He'd talked about the *twin bond* they'd had and how that was influencing his belief that she was back. It sounded pretty iffy to me, but my brother and I were six years apart. Dwelling on this wasn't doing me any good, so I returned my attention to my surroundings. I scanned for employees, but the place looked deserted.

The next cage I passed was filled with ringtailed lemurs, all leaning back on their haunches with their arms lazily draped across their stomachs and their two-foot-long tails waving slowly behind them. The lemurs were conversing with an adjacent cage full of red and blue macaws. The macaws exactly mimicked the lemurs' coyote-like calls. I approached the macaws and said, "Hello." I got a chorus of simultaneous *hellos* in response.

Beyond the cages was a large, fenced cement pond full of crocodiles and alligators basking in the hot sun. One six-foot croc had a turtle happily sleeping on its back. Nearby, a giant tortoise, probably eighty or ninety years old, munched on a head of lettuce.

I glanced at my watch and was shocked to realize I'd been wandering around for over half an hour. Time to get back to work. One thing was sure, the whore house legend was just that—likely started by teenage boys in the throes of raging hormones.

I retraced my steps and spotted a young man raking the path next to a cage of foot-tall, jet black and cobalt blue jays. They stared at me with beady yellow eyes.

"Excuse me, could I ask you a question?" I asked the young man. Unlike blender-hair at the front counter, this young man was well-groomed with neatly trimmed brown hair, jeans, and a vintage Houston Oilers T-shirt.

He looked up and grinned. "Sure, anything to get a break from raking duck and chicken shit for a few minutes." He leaned his rake on the cage.

"Do you know someone named Stephanie Davidson or Tom Darnell?"

"Same person? What is he/she, a cross dresser?"

I laughed. It wasn't especially funny, but I was hot and tired and my ankle was throbbing. "No, two different people, a woman and a man."

"Oh. Well, I haven't worked here but a couple days. Hang on." He shifted his gaze to over my shoulder and hollered, "Hey Yolanda, got a second?"

"Sure, why not." Yolanda set the bucket she was carrying down with a plop and trotted over. "What's up?"

She was Hispanic and looked around twenty. She had thick, mahogany-colored, shoulder-length hair that framed her heart-shaped, olive-toned skin. Her eyes were bright and alert, and she wore just a hint of liner and blush. She, too, wore jeans and a T-shirt, but her shirt was from the musical *CATS*. I repeated my question.

"Yeah, Tom used to work here." She shrugged. "I guess he quit, cuz I haven't seen him at all this week."

"That might be because he's dead." What the hell, going for the shock value worked with Pam, maybe it'd work with these two.

"Oh God." Yolanda reached out and grabbed a cage for support. The guy just stood there and gaped at me.

"When? What happened?" Yolanda asked.

"Late Saturday night. He was shot outside a bar." I'd hold off on any more details until I knew more about what Yolanda knew.

"That's awful." Yolanda shook her head.

"Look, I gotta get back to work." The guy picked up his rake and hurried away.

Yolanda gave me a wry smile and tipped her head in the direction of her departing co-worker. "He's pretty simple-minded. He can't handle much stress, but he's a hard worker."

I shrugged. He hadn't known Tom anyway, so I didn't need him to stay around. It was probably better that Yolanda and I could talk alone. "How well did you know Tom?"

"We have…had, worked together for about eight or nine months. He was one of the caretakers around here. He wasn't really my supervisor, but he sort of had seniority over me. Why?"

Ah, that's the question, isn't it? I wish I knew the right answer. I decided to go for broke. I gestured at my crutch. "He ran me off the road last Saturday afternoon, a few hours before he was murdered. And no," I added quickly when I saw a look of concern cloud Yolanda's face. "It wasn't me. I'm a private investigator, working on a case that might involve him somehow. I'm trying to find out how he fits in, why he went after me, and why he was killed. I'd appreciate your help."

"I'm not sure what I can do. You should probably talk to John or Sue, the owners."

"Thanks, I will. But co-workers almost always know more about each other than bosses know about their employees."

Yolanda laughed. "You've got that right. Bosses are clueless."

"Please tell me whatever you can about him. What he was like, where he hung out, who his friends were, anything at all."

"I didn't know him that well." She shrugged. "He could be okay when he wanted to, but mostly he was an asshole. He was good with the snakes and animals, though. Always made sure they had food and water and that their cages were clean. He sure came down on us if he found a dry water bowl or empty food pan."

"Snakes of a feather," I mumbled.

"What?"

"Nothing. Sorry. What about friends?"

"Not many. Couple of lowlife guys he hung around with, a skinny chick who wore too much make-up, and a strange woman."

That perked up my ears. "Strange woman? What do you mean?"

"Hard to say. There was just something not quite right about her. When she looked at you, her eyes had a hard, mean look, you know? And she hardly ever spoke, at least not that I heard. She didn't come around here very often, and when she did, it was almost always at night. Maybe she came up after she got off work, but I never knew for sure."

"Can you tell me what she looked like? I don't suppose you know her name."

"No, sorry, I only heard the name of the skinny one—Melissa. The strange woman was tall, and she had waist-length, dark-brown hair. I'd kill for hair like that." Yolanda flounced her own hair for emphasis. I thought Yolanda's hair was pretty, but I didn't say anything. I didn't want to get her off subject. "And her purse!"

"What about her purse?"

"It was *huge*—she could have put *you* in it. I always wondered what she carried in there."

"Probably stuff that would scare most men to death." I laughed.

Yolanda laughed, too. "I'll bet. Anyway, I never knew if she or the skinny chick were employees or girlfriends."

"Employees?" I was confused. Or at least slow on the uptake.

"Yeah, if that's the right term for, well…" Yolanda pursed her lips. "You know…"

I stared for a beat, maybe two. "Oh. Do you think they were?"

"Tom was into extra ways to make money. Working at a place like this, you know, doesn't pay much, and Tom liked his gambling.

He was always griping about needing more money to place a bet or pay off a loss with his bookie. He dealt a little dope, sold hot items, that sort of thing. For all I know, the women *were* hookers and he was their pimp, although I doubt it. Creepy as he was, he just didn't seem the type to deal in human goods and services."

"What kind of stuff did he usually sell?"

"I only know a little. Sometimes I'd overhear, sometimes I'd snoop, once in a while he'd show me something and try to get me to buy it. He sold everything hot he could get his hands on—stereos, jewelry, guns, even art and antiques, or what he called *collectible garbage*. I'm sure he had no idea what most of the stuff was worth. He just took the best offer he could get. I'm not surprised he was murdered." Yolanda's eyes briefly clouded over, and she stared into the distance. "He wasn't a very good person."

"Well, he sure wasn't to me. I'm on this crutch thanks to him, and the accident totaled my motorcycle."

"I'm sorry that happened to you. I sure hope you find out how he was involved. I wish I could be of more help." Yolanda's smile was friendly and warm, but I got the feeling she was wrapping up the conversation, not because she wanted to get rid of me, but because she'd said all she knew.

"You seem, I don't want to sound insulting, quite literate to be hauling a bucket full of food pellets around. What keeps you here?"

Yolanda laughed and gave me a wide smile. "I'm studying herpetology at Texas State University in San Marcos. Working here part time provides me with valuable hands-on experience."

"Makes sense." I nodded and returned her smile. "I appreciate all the time you've given me. I should let you get back to work."

I left Yolanda to her feeding and returned to the main building, cutting through the gift/souvenir shop on the way. I approached the ticket counter and found the same bored teenager still there. *Highway to Hell* was playing on the CD player he had on a shelf behind the counter.

"Can you tell me where to find John or Sue?" I almost had to yell over the volume.

"Yeah, John's through there." He waggled his head toward a door that said Office.

"Thanks." I crossed to the door, knocked, and heard a muffled, "Come in."

"John? I'm sorry, I don't know your last name. Yolanda said I should look for you."

He motioned me in. "How can I help you?"

John was maybe mid-forties, trim and tanned, with sandy brown hair, and a neatly trimmed goatee. He wore a light blue, short sleeve, western cut shirt and khaki shorts.

"My name's Marianna Morgan." I extended my hand. We exchanged a quick handshake and I perched on a guest chair. "I'm a private investigator working on a case in San Antonio. I believe that an employee of yours, Tom Darnell, may be involved."

"Tom." He spit the name out as if it tasted bitter. "He was pretty unreliable about most things, and mostly standoffish with co-workers and customers alike." He sighed and his voice softened. "In spite of his personality flaws, he seemed to care about our menagerie. That's why I kept him on. But he hasn't shown up this week. Or called. That's it. I'll fire him, if he shows up again."

"That's not likely, since he was murdered last Saturday night."

"Well! I can't say I'm surprised, but I am sorry. What happened?"

"That's still a little unclear, but he was shot outside a bar. I believe a woman who was with him in the bar may also have come to the Snake Farm. At least Yolanda's description seems to match."

"I wish I could help you, but I never saw him with anyone. If he had friends meet him here, he kept it out from under my nose. I'm sorry I'm not able to help you."

"Maybe you still can. Could you give me directions to his home? I only have a route and box number."

"Well, I'm not sure that's… I don't know if…"

"I can understand your reluctance." I nodded and frowned, doing my best to look sympathetic and understanding. "But Detective Fincher and I are trying to find out who might have been angry or upset enough with Tom to kill him. We're hoping something in his home might provide a valuable clue." Hey, I'm not above stretching the truth, especially if it nets the right results. It did —I watched John's demeanor change right before my eyes.

"Of course, I want to help the investigation in any way I can. His trailer is just a couple of miles from here. One of the local ranchers lets him live on a corner of his property in exchange for some basic handyman services." John stood and shuffled through a file drawer, extracted a manila folder with Tom Darnell written on the tab, and sat back down. He tore a page off a calendar and wrote direction's to Tom's house on the back of it.

"This is a tremendous help." I took the paper. "You've saved us a lot of time, and I'm sure you can appreciate that time is of the essence in a murder case." I stood and extended my hand.

John stood and we shook hands again. "Glad I could help. Let me know if there's anything else I can do."

As I pulled back onto the interstate I thought about what I'd learned, which wasn't much. What I did get was valuable. Tom seemed somehow or other to be hooked up with Stephanie. It was unlikely that any of his other friends were involved in my case, but I'd keep them in mind.

I looked at the paper John gave me. It was from a word-a-day calendar. Today's word—deceptive. *Yep, that's about right.* I flipped the page over, studied John's simple map, and then glanced at the clock. It was still a couple hours before dark. I figured, what the hell, I might as well go trailer trawling.

TRAILER TRASH

Be it ever so humble there's no place like home. ~unknown

I drove along the graded caliche road leading to Tom's trailer, kicking up a white dust plume behind me, which meant I'd have to wash Judy's car before I gave it back. Half a mile up the road on the right, I saw a battered metal mailbox with a large Box 14 painted on the side. I turned into the rutted driveway and stopped in front of a beat-up, single-wide mobile home. I sat for a few minutes and looked around.

There was no sign of life, and no indication that anyone had been by lately. There were no fresh tire tracks, and the trailer itself was closed up tight. The half dozen scraggly tomato plants that grew in the front yard were shriveled and bent over from lack of water.

Just to be on the safe side, though, I pulled my trusty Sig Sauer 380 semi-automatic from my briefcase, checked the clip to be sure it was fully loaded, and slipped the handgun into the back of my waistband. I tucked a pair of latex gloves into my pocket.

I made my way completely around the place. It took a while to traverse the weeds and rocks with my crutch. I guessed the trailer was probably manufactured in the mid-eighties, when house trailers were long, skinny, sheet-metal covered boxes of paper-thin walled rooms. Trailers from that period probably inspired the term *trailer trash*. They were butt-ugly, at best.

This particular trailer was once white, but now faded from age and weather to an ugly yellow. It had small, filthy windows spaced unevenly down the two long sides. Each window was surrounded by dark green sheet-metal shutters for that homey, welcoming look.

On a barbed wire and cedar post fence a couple dozen yards behind the trailer were three faded paper targets, liberally peppered with holes. The center of all three was shot clean away. I whistled. *Someone's a damn good shot.*

When I was satisfied the place really was deserted, I climbed the homemade, rough wood steps and used my shirttail to turn the doorknob. It was unlocked. God bless country folk who still trust others, even if they are scum like Tom.

Now I had to make a decision. The police hadn't found out yet where Tom lived, or at least they hadn't taken the time to visit. They would soon, though. If I entered now, and they found out, I'd be charged with breaking and entering. Of course, if they never found out…

I glanced over my shoulder and then slipped inside. It was a wreck. There were empty beer cans on every horizontal surface. The floor was littered with fast food bags and dirty napkins. The furniture was strewn with dirty clothes. The place reeked of spoiled food, stale beer, and body odor. I felt my gag reflex surging to life and stifled it through a conscious effort.

There was a small A/C in the window to the right of a tattered sofa, but it was off. Plus, the place had been closed up tight for nearly a week. It felt like a sauna. *Oh well, I've got a job to do, and the sooner I get to it, the sooner I can return to my air conditioned car.*

I made a cursory pass through the entire trailer, which took about thirty seconds, given the cramped size of the place. I didn't see anything obvious, so I slipped on the gloves and began exploring more closely.

I started in the sparsely furnished living area—sagging, stained sofa in avocado green brocade, mismatched end table and coffee table that both looked like they were made from varnished plywood, and a monstrous, brown vinyl recliner.

I looked under all the cushions and inside the end table drawer, carefully rearranging everything when I was through. I found flyers for so-called escort services and video stores that probably didn't carry Disney movies.

I moved into the bedroom, which sported an unmade double bed, another end table, and an unfinished pine dresser. I didn't want to touch the filthy, stiff sheets, even while wearing gloves, so I convinced myself that there was nothing in the bed.

Under the bed was a stack of porn magazines and half a dozen dirty socks. In the nightstand were fifteen condoms. I had to wonder what kind of woman would enjoy having sex in a pigsty like this, but maybe *enjoy* didn't have anything to do with it.

The bathroom was small and looked and smelled like a port-a-potty. I found nothing of interest there, either, unless you count the wilted marijuana plant growing in a pink plastic pot in the window.

I moved into the kitchen area and checked all the drawers and cabinets. Tom didn't have much in the way of dishes or cookware, but judging by the quantity of junk food bags in the place, that hadn't mattered much.

I was just about to decide there was nothing worthwhile in the whole dump when I saw a torn piece of yellow tablet paper sticking out from under the refrigerator. There were four names and phone numbers scrawled on it. *Well, well, well. Pay dirt. And just when I was about to give up.*

I tore another sheet off the tablet on the counter and quickly wrote the numbers down.

Melissa - 555-5081
Stephanie - 555-3483
Carlos - 555-1984
Virgil - 555-9757

I carefully repositioned the original paper under the fridge. The police would want the numbers, too, and I wanted to leave the place just as I'd found it.

As soon as I was back in my car, I stripped off the gloves and tossed them on the floor. Then I started the engine and cranked the A/C to full. I just sat for a few minutes and inhaled deep breaths of the clean, icy air. When I was cooled off, I pulled away from the trailer and headed for home.

Once on the road, I debated whether I should wait until the police found Tom's place and the list of phone numbers before I made any calls. It wouldn't be in my best interest to have the cops find out I'd already called the people on the list—that would lead to questions about how I got the numbers in the first place. *What the hell. I'll deal with that problem if and when it occurs.*

I flipped open my cell phone and called each number. No one was home at any of them, and only Melissa had an answering machine. I listened to the most annoying announcement I'd ever heard.

"Howdy-do, this is Melissa. I am *so* glad you called. Bubbles and I must be out having lots and lots of fun right now, so please-please-please be sure to leave a message so I can call you back and tell you all about the fun I was having. Say hi, Bubbles."

This final bit was followed by a series of rapid, shrill, ear-piercing barks before the beep finally ended my suffering. God, I'd take cats over dogs any day, especially over one of those hyper, yapping, pee-on-the-floor beasts.

"Hi, Melissa, my name's Marianna," I began in my best sing-song voice. "I'm a friend of Stephanie and Tom's. I lost the paper where I'd written their numbers down. I kind of need to talk to Stephanie. I stopped by the Snake Farm, but Tom wasn't working today. Yolanda suggested I call you. Could you either call me with Stephanie's number or have her call me? My number is 512-555-5968. Thanks bunches!"

It was all I could do to keep from gagging. I realized as I was finishing that I'd been waggling my head back and forth as I talked, which made me laugh out loud.

I next called Davidson, who wasn't home. At least his announcement was short and professional. I left a message for him to call. I didn't leave any details or reasons. I figured I'd best fill him in live rather than having a digital representation of me share everything I'd learned today about Stephanie.

My cats were all major pissed at me by the time I wheeled into the driveway. I'd forgotten to fill their dry food bowls.

"Aw, poor babies." I smirked. "Without food for an entire day. I'll bet y'all nearly starved to death." I opened three cans of Friskies, though instead of the usual two, to appease my guilt.

After I'd fed the cats, I pulled out the yellow paper with the phone numbers I'd found in Darnell's trailer. It wouldn't hurt to try Stephanie again. I dialed the number. It rang twenty-three times before I sighed and hung up. *Oh well, that'd've been way too easy.*

I opened a can of tomato soup for supper and curled up on the sofa. I slurped soup and thought about the day. I'd learned a lot, but nothing of earth-shattering—or case-solving—proportions. Apparently Stephanie was alive and kicking and hanging out with decidedly unsavory folks. But I wasn't any closer to actually finding her. This cat and mouse game was driving me crazy. Sooner or later I *would* catch up with her, but I'd just as soon it'd be sooner.

DIGGING UP FACTS

A little learning is a dangerous thing.
~Alexander Pope (1688-1744)

Friday morning, Stephen worked at home. He'd promised himself that Friday would be a work day, so he didn't even take the time to return Ms. Morgan's call. Her message was short and vague, which normally would have piqued his curiosity, but today he was burning with anticipation for other reasons—he was anxious to finish work and start his search for the rifle.

After three hours of toiling over numbers, he tossed his client folders back into his briefcase. He should have worked longer, but he'd done all he could tolerate. He opened his desk drawer and removed the police report.

While stroking his head, he looked at the pages, flipping quickly past the Xerox copies of crime scene photos, unwilling to subject his fragile emotions to their raw images. He read every word, however, of the notes and reports about the investigation into the missing rifle. It seemed to him that a visit to Trinity University's Archeology Department was as good a place as any to start.

Stephen loved the Trinity campus, built in 1952 and modeled on an Italian village. Even Murchison Tower, rising prominently in the center of the campus, has an old Europe feel. The spacious campus, shaded by towering live oak trees, and peppered with gorgeous fountains, undulates across some of the highest hilltops in San Antonio. Most of the campus's red brick buildings overlook the nearby Alamo Stadium and offers a commanding view of the San Antonio downtown skyline three miles to the south.

Stephen had spent many hours sitting on the Alamo Stadium's painted wood bleachers, cheering on the Terrell Hill's Tigers. He'd often imagined what his sister would have been like as a cheerleader. He knew she'd have loved it. The stadium still hunched below the heights of Trinity, but these days it looked tired and worn out, its limestone sides gray with decades of accumulated dirt and car exhaust. Seeing it now reminded Stephen just how much time had passed.

He drove the winding road through the university's main entrance and past the Eugenia Miller fountain, which bubbled with light blue water. He remembered many fun splashing wars with his sister at that fountain, when his mother would bring them by to visit with his dad. Stephen parked in front of the sprawling Coates University Center, the hub of campus life and the location of the university's main information center.

The woman at the information desk smiled as Stephen approached. "May I help you?"

"Where would I find the archeology department offices?"

"They're located in the Cowles Life Science Center, which houses the departments of biology, sociology, anthropology, and psychology." She spoke with efficiency but also with a slight rote sound to her voice, as if she'd memorized the campus directory and no longer really listened to her own words. "Archeology is included in anthropology here at Trinity. The four-story Cowles building is just southeast of the Chapman-Cowles fountain. Here, I'll show you on a map."

"Thank you, you've been quite helpful." Stephen left the building, map in hand.

Stephen entered the Cowles Life Science Center and looked around for the building's directory. The anthropology/archeology department was on the third floor. He took the elevator to the quiet, seemingly deserted floor and poked his head in the first office he encountered. "Excuse me, I'm looking for someone with the archeology department."

"Found someone," replied the man behind the small, wooden desk. He was poring intently over a pile of papers on top of his cluttered desk.

Stephen waited for the man to say more, but was greeted only with silence. After several seconds, Stephen said, "I'm looking for Professor Jonathan Wagner."

"Down the hall, third door on the left." The man didn't look up.

"Thank you."

"Mmm-hmmm."

Stephen found Professor Wagner's office and knocked.

"Come in." The voice was a rich basso, with just a touch of a southern accent.

When Stephen opened the door, he found himself looking at a smiling, portly, middle-aged man, whose black, horn-rimmed glasses accentuated a smooth, shiny bald head.

"Professor Wagner?" Stephen asked. "I understand you can tell me about the archeology digs during the construction period before the 1968 HemisFair World's Fair opened."

"Happy to. I was a graduate student back then. Working on the HemisFair sites was research for my thesis. If I can't answer your questions, I'm sure I know someone who can. Please sit down." He extended his hand. "And please call me Gordon."

"Thank you, and please excuse my manners." Stephen shook Gordon's hand and sat on the hard, wood guest chair. "I'm Stephen."

"Okay, Stephen." Gordon leaned back and put his hands behind his head. The armpits of his white cotton shirt were yellow with accumulated sweat stains. "What's on your mind?"

Stephen cleared his throat and stroked his head a couple of times. "My father was an Assistant Professor here in the mid-sixties, and—"

Gordon's smile faded. He rocked his chair forward, dropping his hands on the desktop with a loud thump. "You're Stephen Davidson? Your father was Chester? I'm so sorry about what happened back then. Such a terrible tragedy. A great loss. A sad—"

"Yes, it was." Stephen tersely cut Gordon off. He couldn't stand to hear another stranger spouting sympathetic platitudes. "I've read the old police reports and I know that an antique rifle was stolen from our home the night of the burglary. The report described the rifle as a Brown Bess. I remember the bayonet had a bent-tip and there was an engraving on the lock plate of the Mexican eagle with a snake in its claws. Can you tell me about the Brown Bess?"

A tentative smile twitched at the corner of Gordon's face. "Ah, yes, the Brown Bess. It's actually a musket, not a rifle. And to be technically correct, it's an East Indian pattern musket. Brown Bess was a nickname. It was originally used by British soldiers during the colonial wars. They also sold many of the muskets to the Mexican army, so it's sometimes called the Mexican musket."

Gordon turned his chair around and fumbled among the books in his bookcase. "Here we go." He turned to face Stephen again, and set a large, leather-bound volume on his desk. He began to flip through the pages. "Read this." He rotated the book to face Stephen.

The smoothbore flintlock musket was the firearm of choice for all 18th-century armies. The Long Land Pattern Musket, the firearm style most commonly used during the Revolutionary War, was affectionately known as the Brown Bess. The name Brown Bess comes from the German word *busche*, which means *gun* and the browning, or coloring on the gun's barrel. (Prior to the Brown Bess, stocks were painted black.)

The Brown Bess was mass-produced and designed for combat. It was not accurate; in fact, the expression "Can't hit the side of a barn" originated with the Bess. Soldiers carrying the 10-pound Bess muskets never took a bead on anyone; they simply pointed their guns in the general direction of the enemy and fired, counting on mass volley. But an experienced soldier could fire the Bess 2 to 3 times in a minute, making up in volume for the loss of accuracy.

A 17-inch, triangular-blade bayonet was fitted onto the end of the 46-inch barrel, making the .78 caliber Bess also useful in hand to hand combat.

Stephen's brow furrowed. "So a rifle, er, musket like the Brown Bess would have been worth a lot of money to a private collector."

"Yes." Gordon nodded. "A private collector would pay good money for an authentic Brown Bess, even if it was not in good shape. Few of the muskets were found intact, and one found in ruins that linked it to the Alamo could easily fetch thousands."

Stephen hung his head and rubbed his eyes. "It pains me deeply to admit it, because my father was an honest, honorable man, but he must have taken the musket after it was excavated at the HemisFair construction site. He was desperate for money back then, and perhaps it clouded his judgement. Now I'm determined to track it down and see that it's returned to the Alamo Historical Society. I was hoping you could help me."

Gordon removed his glasses, wiped them with a wrinkled, yellowed handkerchief, and pushed his glasses back onto his nose. "Yes, well, no one was ever sure where the musket came from. We certainly found it hard to believe your father took it. And we definitely did not see it at any of the sites. The police asked everyone working on the digs at that time. None of us saw anything. I'm terribly sorry."

"I understand. I didn't expect this to be easy. I guess my next step will be to seek out antique dealers who deal with private collectors. Can you suggest anyone by name?"

"No, no, I'm sorry. I wish I could be of more help. But I'm just an academic, I don't follow the world of private antique dealers or collectors."

"May I call if I have additional questions?"

"Of course." Gordon smiled, but Stephen noted it didn't spread to the man's eyes.

Stephen retraced his steps through the building and back to his car. He rested his forehead on the steering wheel and sighed. His only movement for several minutes was to lightly stroke his head. He had no idea what his next step should be. His sleuthing skills were definitely deficient. He decided to call Ms. Morgan as soon as he got home.

REMINISCING

Home is where the heart is.
~Gaius Plinius Secundas–Pliny the Elder (AD 23-79)

Stephen pulled onto Divine Road, planning to take the McAllister freeway back to downtown. Instead, he impulsively bypassed the freeway entrance and instead cut through Brackenridge Park.

Stephen smiled as he drove through the beautiful grounds. Brackenridge Park had existed in San Antonio for over one hundred years. The city's first water supply came from pump houses, raceway canals, and gates located in the park. It's even where the San Antonio river begins, a mere three miles north of where it snakes through downtown San Antonio.

Stephen's class had taken a field trip there to see the remains of the old water system. He'd been surprised when his teacher showed them the *blue hole* where the meandering river begins its life, bubbling forth from a series of artesian springs. He'd thought the teacher was lying, but his dad had reassured him it was true.

The three-hundred-forty-three acre park also includes a carousel —featuring antique Bradley-Kay horses, a skyride filled with Swiss manufactured cable cars, and even a miniature railway, which carries replicas of antique steam locomotives on a scenic four mile ride through the park.

Stephen remembered the many lazy Saturdays his family had spent in the park, riding the train and skyride—the carousel wasn't built yet—and then picnicking at a stone table under a live oak. He wished now that those fun times had lasted longer. His mother tried once to bring him back after that awful night, but neither of their hearts were in it. They'd returned home after less than half an hour.

He drove past the entrance to the San Antonio Zoo and pulled into the parking lot of the adjacent Japanese Tea Gardens. Walking through the massive, ornate gate, he frowned as he tried to pull a forgotten memory. *Now I remember. When I was a boy, the entry sign welcomed everyone to the Chinese Sunken Garden.* The name had been changed after America entered war with Japan, and wasn't restored to its original until 1984.

Stephen wandered among the winding walkways, past waterfalls and over bridges spanning tranquil pools. The garden looked exactly the same as it had when he and Stephanie ran along these same walkways. He paused on a stone bridge. Birds sang from the nearby trees and koi half as big as he was swam lazily among the tire-sized lily pads. The air was pleasant, protected from the blazing July heat by the sheer cliffs of the old quarry and cooled by the mists from the waterfall that cascaded from the cliff's precipice.

He'd hoped to find out more at Trinity, but his life had been nothing but disappointments lately. He *would* prevail. He had to—he believed with all his heart that his very sanity depended on it.

Stephen impulsively reached into his pocket and tossed a shiny penny into the water. He watched it do a slow motion, end-over-end fall and settle to the bottom. A large white koi with a tennis ball-sized red spot on its head came over the see if the coin was edible. "Sorry, fellow, just a coin for luck," Stephen said. The koi turned and glided silently away.

After half an hour, Stephen returned to his car. He exited the park and headed north to Terrell Hills. He drove the once-familiar streets of his old neighborhood, his head flooded with a torrent of happy and sad memories. His left hand slipped to the top of his head and made slow circles around it.

The neighborhood hadn't changed much. The low-slung, ranch style houses were well-maintained. The wood trim around the shallow-pitched rooflines painted in earth tones and subdued blues.

He drove slowly through the hilly neighborhood, turning on first one bumpy street and then another. Even today, the neighborhood streets were the only choice for evening walkers, kids on skateboards, and little ones on tricycles—no community sidewalks paralleled the curbs.

The trees were certainly larger than when Stephen was young. The mesquite provided paltry shade, thanks to their elongated, rice grain-shaped leaves. Most of the Arizona ash, now pushing well beyond their average age limit of twenty-five or thirty years, were sparsely leafed. Many included dead, bare limbs and amputated stumps. *Dying slow deaths, in bits and pieces. Like me.*

It was hard to believe that a mere one block away, Terrell Hills blossomed into monstrous, two-story, upscale brick homes and colonial mansions that sold for anywhere from hundreds of thousands to millions of dollars. That part of the neighborhood was where the area's *landed gentry* had once lived, employing domestic and landscape help from the lower middle class neighborhood Stephen now cruised.

He turned down Cragmont and slowed to a crawl. As he approached the house at 566, his heart pounded a jungle-drum rhythm in his chest. He could hear the hollow beat inside his head. He took a couple of deep breaths and pulled to a stop at the curb.

Whoever lived in the house had painted it light blue with dark navy trim. When he was a boy, the bulk of the house was tan, the trim a dark brown. The blues gave it a cheery, friendly look.

A riotous, colorful collection of zinnias, daisies, and snapdragons grew in amoeba-shaped beds around three trees—one mesquite and two ash—and in two curved beds below the old-fashioned, crank case windows on either side of the concrete porch.

Bird houses and feeders hung from various tree limbs. As he watched, a bright red cardinal flew to one feeder and proceeded to dine. Stephen smiled. Whoever lived here now must be happy. They certainly went to a great deal of effort to make it attractive.

His memory of the house was of a gloomy, depressing place. No flowers ever brightened the front—his mother had stopped planting them—and there certainly weren't any bird houses or feeders placed around, either.

He momentarily debated whether to ring the doorbell, but what would he say? "Hello, I used to live here when I was a boy. My father was murdered in your hallway. May I come in for old time's sake? And by the way, you haven't seen my missing sister have you?"

He uttered a derisive laugh at the absurd thought of his sister returning to the family home after many years, like a dog or cat who is relocated far away and slowly finds its way back to the only home it'd ever known.

The black humor made him realize how close he was to losing touch. He sniffed and wiped his eyes with the palm of his hand. He absentmindedly stroked his head until it was shiny. His logical mind knew it was time to move on—time to put the past behind him. Of course, he also knew that he could not do so until he discovered the truth about his sister.

And now he truly wanted to find the lost rifle…musket. This latter task now seemed as important as the former. Maybe he needed to see for himself the object that had instigated so much pain and suffering.

He had no intention of discontinuing either search, but he had to keep them in perspective. The woman was probably not his sister, all grown up and running around town doing who-knew-what. It was more likely his imagination and wishful thinking run amok after seeing a woman who struck a subconscious chord of recognition.

Yes, that has to be it. She's just a look-alike. Although he knew that, deep down, he didn't believe that. Didn't *want* to believe it.

Stephen took a ragged breath and exhaled slowly as he pulled away from the curb, leaving the cozy home behind him. He turned onto Thacker Street and realized he was only a block from Whiskey Smith's. He debated as he sat at the light. When the light turned green, he turned and shortly pulled into the bar's parking lot, without realizing he'd decided to do so.

He approached the fifties-vintage, black and white checkered tile entrance slowly, still unsure of what he'd do once inside. When he pulled open the front door, the blast of icy cold air washed over him as it rushed past him to be swallowed by the intense summer heat.

The cold revived and refreshed him, and he entered the establishment with a clearer head and less trepidation. He found an empty bar stool and sat. An attractive bartender finished pouring drinks for a small group on the other side of the U-shaped bar and approached Stephen with a smile. "What can I get you?"

"What's your house chardonnay?"

"Screw top." She laughed. "Sorry, just joking. Our house is Cap Rock, which is actually a pretty good wine. Would you like a glass?"

"Sure." He laughed, too. "It's hard to beat a vintage wine imported from the Texas panhandle."

When the bartender returned she set the glass in front of him and said, "I'm Tammy. What's your name?"

"Stephen."

"Well, Stephen, welcome to Whiskey Smith's."

"Thank you." He sipped the wine and looked around. It was hard to think of Stephanie having been here, especially with a low-life like Tom Darnell. But Ms. Morgan sounded pretty convinced.

"I guess most of your customers are regulars," Stephen said.

"Yeah, pretty much. Once in a while we get someone who's passing through. How about you? I haven't seen you in here before."

"I grew up in Terrell Hills. I was over this way for business and decided to check the old neighborhood out."

"What's your conclusion? Has it changed much?" Tammy asked.

Stephen shrugged. "These kinds of neighborhoods cycle up and down as families move in and out. It'll be a good neighborhood for a while then it'll go to pot, then a new round of folks move in and it's good again. But for the most part, yeah, it looks pretty much the same."

Tammy laughed. "These days it's becoming Yuppie Central. It's full of young married couples looking for something they can actually afford and still have some money left to raise their kids."

"That's quite an astute observation."

"I've been told I'm the neighborhood authority." Tammy grinned and made a small curtsy. "Well, actually, I think the term most often used is Head Gossip."

Stephen smiled. "That's okay. There's nothing wrong with being interested in other people. Speaking of which, did you know Tom Darnell, the man who was murdered last Saturday night?"

Tammy laughed. "Sorry, but that seems to be this week's most popular question. Anyway, I wasn't here Saturday night, and I don't recall him ever coming in on my shift."

"What about a woman named Stephanie, Stephanie Davidson?"

Tammy frowned with concentration. "I'm not sure. What's she look like, or better yet, what does she drink? I always remember a drink, even if I don't remember the name."

"Sorry, I don't know what she drinks, but she has long, dark hair. Here I'll show you." Stephen opened his wallet and removed a folded piece of paper on which was a copy of a newspaper photo. "Her face is pretty small in this photo, but I hope it helps."

Tammy studied the face Stephen pointed to. "Oh, sure, she's been in several times. Drinks Tanquerey and tonic with a twist. Leaves big tips. Ya know, you look a lot like her. You two related?"

Stephen opened his mouth to speak but found himself mute with shock. He stared at Tammy, the first person he'd found who'd been face to face with his sister. The revelation was more than he could bear. He went cold. The room swayed. The last thing Stephen remembered was hearing a voice that sounded distant and shrill.

"Sir? Stephen? Are you okay? Hey Maggie, call nine-one-one…"

"He's okay, Joe. He's coming around now."

Stephen looked up and found himself eye to eye with someone in a white coat. He blinked his eyes into focus and realized it was an EMT. A second EMT was next to Stephen's left side.

"Welcome back," EMT 1 said. "You're lucky. You only lightly bumped your head on the bar when you passed out and fell off your stool. Could've been a lot worse. You feeling better now?"

"Yes," Stephen said, although it came out as a whisper. He cleared his throat, rubbed his head vigorously a couple of times, and tried again. "Yes, thank you. I guess I shouldn't have had alcohol on such an empty stomach. He saw the look on the face of EMT 2 and added, "I only had the one glass of wine. Maybe I'm fighting a bug or something."

Both EMTs nodded as if in understanding, but Stephen could read the *yeah, sure* expressions on their faces. He decided not to pursue it any further. As his eyes focused more clearly, he could see Tammy looking on from the background, and he smiled at her. "I'm very sorry, Tammy. I sure didn't mean to cause such a stir."

"That's okay. I'm just glad you're all right."

Probably out of your fear of lawsuits. The cynical thought made Stephen feel ashamed. "How long was I out?"

"About twenty minutes," EMT 1 replied. "You might have a headache from where your forehead hit the bar, even though it doesn't look bad. Best to take it easy tonight, and maybe even tomorrow."

Stephen stood to go, but the EMTs both grabbed his arms. "You need to sit here for another few minutes," EMT 2 said, guiding Stephen to a nearby chair, "so we can make sure you're all right before we okay you to drive."

When the EMTs were satisfied, they packed up their bags. EMT 1 said, "You take care."

"I will." Stephen slowly got to his feet. "I appreciate your help. I intend to go straight home and straight to bed. This is definitely enough excitement for me for one day."

"If you feel disoriented or your headache lasts for more than a day, be sure to see a doctor," EMT 2 said. "Pretty sure you don't have a concussion, but you never know."

"Yes, I will, and thank you again." Stephen tried to pay his bill, but Tammy waved him off.

"Don't worry about it. I'm just glad you're okay," she said.

As Stephen moved toward the exit, he wondered how he'd distinguish concussion-related disorientation from the disorientation he'd been feeling every day for several months.

As soon as he got home, Stephen tried to call Ms. Morgan. She didn't answer her office or cell phone. He left the same message at both locations. "Ms. Morgan this is Stephen Davidson. I've just finished speaking with a former colleague of my father's at Trinity University. I have some information to share with you. Please return my call as soon as you get a chance. I'll be home all evening."

PATTERNS OF TWO

When choosing between two evils, I always like to try the one I've never tried before. ~Mae West (1892-1980)

I decided to spend Friday in Austin, I was tired of driving back and forth to San Antonio. I normally try to get to my office every day, but pursuing a case in San Antonio had totally screwed up my schedule—well that, and being in a temporarily debilitating accident. I headed to my office after a breakfast of a strawberry Pop Tart and an entire pot of coffee.

I watered my palm, which was wilted again, before I even checked for messages. If my schedule stayed this crazy, I was going to have to take the poor plant home, or ask Jason Storga to water it for me.

I'd missed four calls. The first was, coincidentally, from Jason, asking if I was available to help on another case. I rarely turn down his requests, and as long as the job didn't prevent me from continuing my work for Davidson, I'd definitely say yes.

The second was from Aunt Louise. *Damn! I forgot to call her back.* The third was from Patrick, asking if I was feeling up to our date tomorrow night. I grinned—I'd have to be on my deathbed before I'd turn down my first date with him.

The last was a hang-up. I pressed the Caller ID button and jotted down the number. It came from San Antonio and looked vaguely familiar. I opened Davidson's case file and did a Find command. Sure enough, the hang-up came from the same place as the one I'd received a couple days ago—the pay phone outside Martin's Drug Store in Terrell Hills.

"Who the hell keeps calling me from Terrell Hills?" I asked the palm, which ignored me, probably payback for my neglecting it.

"Hrmph." I was frustrated and restless. I got up and headed down the hall to Jason's office. He was successful enough that he had an administrative assistant, and a door separating his waiting area and his office. "Hi, Rebecca, is Jason in?"

"Hi, Marianna." She smiled, then raised her eyebrows. "Wow, what happened to you?"

For what felt like the thousandth time in a week, I explained why I was on a crutch. I'd be glad when I saw Dr. Von Rueden this afternoon, so I could stop using the damn thing. I ended my tale of woe. "So, anyway, is he in?"

"Sure is. I think he's surfing eBay. Just go on in."

I poked my head through his door and smiled. "Jason? Busy?" He jumped like a teenage boy caught snooping through daddy's girlie magazines. I widened my smile. "How's the bidding going?"

He blushed, then grinned. "Okay, fine, I have a weakness for Star Wars collectibles. Shoot me."

"Not today. I don't feel like having to clean my gun."

He laughed. "Fair enough. Come on in. What's up?"

"Sorry I've been slow with your latest request. This injury-recovery business is cramping my style."

"No problem, I completely understand. Sit down for a bit, and I'll tell you why I called."

Jason's jobs were rarely complex or long-term, but they were lucrative. Since his clients paid my fee, he made sure I got every penny he possibly could. This time, he wanted me to do some hoofing through the record archives at the Travis County courthouse, gathering information for a client who was suing someone else for breach of contract, after the someone else suddenly filed bankruptcy.

Jason needed previous bankruptcy records, tax liens, and judgments on his client's former associate, to see if there was a pattern of fraudulent business practices. I was always amazed at the things people neglected to look into before throwing large sums of money at someone they barely knew.

"Do you need it right away or can it wait a few days?" I asked

"Any time in the next two weeks is fine." Jason waved his hand. "Don't stress over it."

"Okey dokey." I returned to my office. Davidson's file was still open, so I scrolled to the bottom and added all the information I'd learned, including a recap of my experience with Pam and the gray door, my conversations at the Snake Farm, and a detailed description of Tom's trailer, including the phone numbers I'd found there.

Since it'd been over a week since I began working for Davidson, I prepared a summary report, along with an invoice for my time and expenses so far. I printed both of these and stuffed them in a manila envelope. I debated with myself and decided to address the envelope to Davidson's office.

I ripped a page from my joke-a-day calendar and wrote a note on the back reminding myself to verify he'd received the information by Tuesday of next week. As an afterthought, I flipped the calendar page over—it was dated three weeks ago. I guess I was behind on jokes. I tore off a small piece of Scotch tape and stuck the note to the front of my file cabinet.

Accounting chores done, I next returned Patrick's call. He wasn't in so I left a confirmation message on his voicemail. After I hung up I leaned back and closed my eyes. The time of reckoning had come. I picked up the phone and dialed Aunt Louise's number.

"Halloooo," Aunt Louise sang into my ear.

"Hi, Aunt Louise, it's Marianna."

"Hello, Luv, how are you? I've had you on my mind all week. You haven't called."

"I know, I'm sorry. I, um, I guess I didn't want to admit that you were right about killer pickups."

"Oh, dearie, I'm so sorry. Please tell me what happened."

I gave Aunt Louise a basic rundown of my experience. I figured she didn't need to hear the specific gory details. I concluded with, "So I guess now I'm in the market for a new motorcycle."

"Must you? You know how dangerous those things are. You could have been killed."

"I love riding motorcycles, and I'm not going to let some goddamed asshole ruin one of my greatest pleasures. Besides, he's dead." *Damn. I didn't mean to let that out.*

"Dead? What did you… What happened?"

"As much as I might have liked, I certainly didn't do anything. He was killed outside a bar in San Antonio."

"Well, if he was as bad as you say, I guess I'm not surprised." Aunt Louise *tsk-tsked* a few times. "You know, I've had another vision about you."

"Can't the visions pick on someone else for a change?"

"That's not the way it works, Luv, the spirits pass on the information they receive. They don't pick and choose."

"Of course. What is it this time?"

"Patterns of two," Aunt Louise almost whispered.

"Huh?"

"I keep getting the number two with respect to you. The two of swords and two of wands in tarot spreads, two fuzzy images in my crystal ball, patterns of two over and over in the I Ching. I don't know what it means. Are there two people involved in your current case, or is it possible you're being double-crossed?"

"Well, to answer the first part of your question, no, I'm only working for one man right now. As for the second part, not that I know of. But Davidson certainly hasn't been the model client. I suppose anything is possible. I appreciate your concern. I'll tell you if I learn anything. Can I buy you dinner next week?"

"I'd like that very much."

We set a date for the next Thursday at seven at Chuy's Tex-Mex, Aunt Louise's favorite restaurant. I glanced at the clock as I swiveled away from the phone. *Yikes!* I realized I only had twenty minutes to make it to Dr. Von Rueden's office. I grabbed my purse and hurried out.

Dr. Von Rueden was on time today, meaning I only had to wait forty-five minutes sitting on an examining table in a thin paper gown, reading through a six-month-old *Sports Illustrated*. He hurtled through the door like a small, red-headed tornado. He flipped quickly through my chart, then looked up and smiled. "How are you feeling? You look better."

"Thanks. Everyone else I've seen this week has said I look like hell."

Dr. Von Rueden laughed. "They should spend a day making rounds with me."

"Please tell me I can get rid of this damn crutch. I can't take it anymore. And can I please shower without mummying my thigh?"

"Well, it's a little early to drop the crutch, but let me see how you're doing." He proceeded to perform atrocities on me that could qualify as torture in some countries—namely, he examined my ankle. He looked up when I winced for the third time.

"I can tell it isn't bothering you at all," he said in an official, dry tone.

I flashed a crooked smile.

He stood up and crossed his arms. "Would you consider a cane?"

The look on my face must have said all he needed to know, because he sighed. "Okay, if you promise to take it easy, I'll let you drop the crutch *and* forego the cane. You'll probably do what you want anyway, no matter what I tell you. Let's at least get those stitches out of your thigh."

I only winced a few times as he cut and tugged the stitches out of my skin. When he was done, I sighed with relief.

"Now you can shower without covering the wound. It's healing good, although it's going to leave a significant scar." He turned toward the door then turned back. "But the ankle brace stays on at least one more week."

I sighed. "Okay. I guess I can live with that."

"That what? The scar or the brace?"

"Both. No choice on the first. Probably stupid to choose otherwise on the second."

He rolled his eyes and left the exam room.

I checked my cell phone as I waited for the elevator. Davidson had left me a message, returning my call from Thursday. I should have called him back from the car, but Aunt Louise had spooked me just enough that I decided to wait and let him call me again. But then that would mean two calls, patterns of two. *Sheesh…*

I drove home to the tunes of the local oldies station surrounding me at full volume, happy to be alive and thrilled to be crutchless.

It wasn't until I was pulling into my driveway that it hit me. Davidson was a twin, and it was apparently her I was trying to find. I might only be working for one client, but the case most definitely involved a very big *pattern of two.*

TUCKING IN

The power of hiding ourselves from one another
is mercifully given, for men are wild beasts,
and would devour one another but for this protection.
~Henry Ward Beecher (1813-1887),
Proverbs from Plymouth Pulpit

Stephen woke up Saturday morning with the expected trauma-induced headache. He decided he simply could not manage to get any work done feeling as he did, so he arose just long enough to drink some juice and take four aspirin before crawling back under the covers. He fell asleep almost instantly and slept until late in the evening.

When he got up the second time, he found his head still pounded like a pile-driver. The knot on his forehead wasn't bad. Maybe the headache was more from stress and shock than his forehead's impact with the bar. Not that it mattered. The pain still made his vision blurry and ruined his day.

He took a cool shower and fixed himself a cup of canned split pea soup, something he generally loathed. He only kept a few cans on hand for times when he was too ill to prepare fresh food. Today definitely qualified. He sat by the living room window and looked out over the River Walk as he ate.

Twilight was descending rapidly on the river level, blocked as it was by the surrounding tall buildings and almost equally tall cypress trees. The tops of the buildings were still glowing brightly from the early evening sun, while the river was already shrouded in shadow.

When he was done with his soup, he cleaned up the kitchen and took a slow walk around his apartment, both to check that everything else was in order and to stretch his legs. Stephen took two aspirin and returned to his bedroom and the safe cocoon of his bed.

Stephanie drove around the city for two hours Saturday afternoon, pondering what to do with the things she'd removed from behind the Bargain Mart. She wanted to choose the best—and longest term—of the several options she considered.

She was still angry that she'd been forced to move in the first place, but determined not to let it slow her down. She swung through a Whataburger and ordered a large soda so she could take two more sinus pills. Her allergies were killing her today. A mega-sinus headache pulsed behind her eyes, which didn't help her mood.

Sipping on her drink, she headed toward the older suburbs, where the houses were small, but today's residents owned ever more crap. When she turned onto West Avenue, she smiled and nodded. Half a block down was the Pack-and-Store self-storage facility, draped with a giant banner reading *First Month Free!!!*

She pulled in and parked. *This will be perfect.*

Thirty minutes later, Stephanie hummed as she left, her bag of supplies safely tucked into a five-by-five storage room. She'd have to figure out how to reconnect her answering machine and phone, but she felt better already. She absentmindedly ran her fingers through her long hair as she scanned for a pay phone, harder than ever to find these days. She finally spied one near the front door of a 7-Eleven. She stopped and called Melissa, who answered with her usual bubble-headed, "Howdy do."

Stephanie sighed. "Hello Melissa."

"Stephie! How are you?"

Stephanie sighed again. *God I hate this girly crap.* "I'm fine. Have you heard about Tom?"

"Heard what? That jerk was, like, supposed to take me out Wednesday night but he, like, stood me up."

"He's, like…dead."

"Wha… Whe… Oh my God." Melissa's voice hitched and ground to a stop with a squeak.

Stephanie smiled, happy to have shut the young girl up. "He was shot outside a bar in San Antonio. I just learned about it today."

"Ooooooohhhhhhhhhh."

Stephanie winced as Melissa's wail pierced her ear. "Please Melissa, get hold of yourself."

Melissa sniffled and snuffled for a another minute, hiccuped once, and sighed. "I guess I'm, like, not surprised."

"I may need your help. My phone line is temporarily down, so I may need to have a couple of people call you, if that's okay."

"Why don't you get a cell phone? Like, everyone has one." Melissa's tone was patronizing.

Stephanie's upper lip curled in anger. "I. Don't. Like. Them." Her voice was measured and clipped. "Are you going to let me have people call you or not?"

"Sure thing, Stephie. I didn't mean to piss you off. I'll call if you, like, have any messages."

"You cannot call me, Melissa, because I do not have a phone right now. I'll be sure to call you every day or so."

Melissa giggled. "Oh, yeah, right. I forgot."

"That's all right. Please don't forget to get both the name and phone number of anyone who calls."

"You bet. Oh, wait! I almost forgot. You already got a message. From, like, some chick named Marianna. She asked you to call. You want her number? It's an Austin area code."

Melissa's words penetrated into Stephanie's brain with the power of a high-caliber bullet. She shook her head hard and took three slow, deep breaths.

"Stephie, are you there? Do you, like, want the number or not?"

"Yes, yes I do." Stephanie dug through her bag and found a pen and pad. "Go ahead." She jotted the number down. "Got it. Thanks for remembering to tell me."

"Sure thing."

Stephanie checked her watch. She'd been out most of the day. "I've got to go. I'll call soon." She returned to her car, already planning what she'd do next.

A DATE TO REMEMBER

It is better to look ahead and prepare than to look back and regret. ~Jackie Joyner-Kersee (1962-)

I started Saturday morning by heading to Eagle Nest, an outdoor gun range off 1431, about ten minutes west of Cedar Park.

"Hey Marianna." Dee, the owner, nodded when I entered.

"Hey Dee." I love the fact that a woman with the honest-to-god real name of Dee Day runs the place.

"I haven't seen you here in a while. What happened to you?"

"Motorcycle accident."

"I told you those damn things are dangerous."

I couldn't help but laugh at the absurdity of that statement coming from a woman standing amidst a plethora of handguns, rifles, and ammunition of every conceivable caliber.

I paid my range fee and headed toward the firing line. I decided to start at the seven-and-a-half yard distance and selected an empty booth. I stepped away from the booth to a dirt waiting area, signaling my desire for the firing line to go down.

Within a couple of minutes the other five shooters also stepped away from the booths. We moved together toward the targets. I tacked up a couple of target sheets and returned to the waiting area. When all were done posting targets, we returned to our booths.

I spent the next two hours firing rounds at twelve-inch, red and white ringed circles. I was a little out of practice, but I managed to get eight or nine out of every ten shots into the center circle of the target. Even the shots that strayed a bit were still somewhere within the target's concentric rings.

I figured they'd be more than sufficient if my target was human. Since becoming a private investigator, I'd never had to shoot anyone, and I didn't look forward to the day when it might finally be necessary, but that didn't mean I wasn't going to be ready.

Although target shooting requires full concentration, it's also oddly relaxing. Unless the range is crowded, shooters space themselves out, so there's usually no one else within a couple of booths of me. And wearing earplugs reduces outside noises. The loudest sound in my head was my own breathing, followed by the dull crack of my weapon when I fired it. The scuba-mask-sized plastic eye protectors provided their own unique sense of isolation.

As I reloaded, I looked up and down the line. Two solitary guys were also on the same yard line as me. One couple was taking turns at the fifteen yard line. Even between the two of them, less than a dozen shots had actually hit the target.

One guy was hunched in a booth at the twenty-five yard line, shooting at a target printed with a photo of a *menacing hoodlum* in a hooded sweatshirt. I never understood the guys who used targets with photos of real people on them. I always wondered if they were living out some creepy, secret desire—but I wasn't about to ask.

After two hundred rounds, my trigger finger was sore and I was sweating buckets. I retrieved my targets one last time and returned to the office. "All done."

"How'd you do today?" Dee asked.

"Not bad, considering how out of practice I am."

"Come on back more often, hon, and you'll be up there with those ex-Marine sharpshooters in no time."

"I'll do that."

The first thing I did when I got home was jump into a nice, long shower. I let my hair air-dry while I cleaned and polished my gun. When my Sig was all clean and shiny, I stowed it in the nightstand next to my bed and headed to the kitchen.

I fixed my favorite home-made lunch—a tuna sandwich made with sweet pickle relish, Miracle Whip, crispy canned onion rings, and chopped boiled egg—and curled up on the sofa. I found I was the center of attention, or at least my dead-fish sandwich was. Deke, Georgie, Cooper, and Boggle took turns trying to weasel their way onto my lap. Polly and Mayfly—dainty girls that they are—sat and stared at me, obviously hoping I'd either drop or spit out a morsel they could then claim.

"Beat it." I yelled through a mouthful of food. It came out sounding like *eegit*. But the cats got the point, they at least momentarily scattered to beyond arms length.

I spent the afternoon catching up on reading and watching one of my favorite old Bogie movies, *The Maltese Falcon*. I took a little time and did some leg exercises, mostly stretches and bends, to loosen up my ankle, which had grown stiff, and I did some rudimentary house-cleaning in preparation for Patrick's arrival in a few hours.

My last chore was to spend two hours getting ready for my date. I normally don't primp and fuss, but it'd been a long time since I'd been on a date, so I was a little out of practice. I changed clothes three times and finally settled on black slacks and a short-sleeved, aqua and cream sweater. It was flattering and casual at the same time—at least that's what I hoped.

I fidgeted and fussed around the house, too restless and nervous to sit. The cats made a little parade behind me as I paced from room to room, clearly as restless as I was.

"Sorry, guys, I won't be at your beck and call tonight. I have a date." Georgie responded with a loud *mreowr* just as the doorbell rang, which scatted all of them into the far reaches of the house.

"Hi," I said as soon as I opened the door. God I felt like a teenager on a blind date. Shouldn't dating be like bicycle riding, shouldn't you never forget? "Come on in."

"You look wonderful." Patrick grinned. "And you're off your crutch!"

"Just yesterday, so I'm still a bit gimpy, but feeling great." I wanted to tell Patrick he looked great, too, in his navy slacks and peach Polo shirt, but I didn't want to get into one of those awkward compliment-swapping moments. Instead, I changed the subject. "Can I get you a glass of wine? I have red and white."

"White would be nice."

I got us both a glass of wine and we sat on opposite ends of the sofa. We sat silently for a minute, then both started to talk at the same time, which made us laugh. The laughter seemed to finally break the ice. We made small talk about safe, innocuous topics like the weather and the current water level in Lake Travis.

While we chatted, all six cats slowly came out to say hello, which relaxed us even more. As cats jumped onto the sofa, we found ourselves scooching closer together until we were finally sitting side by side, although still a bit self-consciously, at least on my part.

After an hour of chatting, Patrick said, "Ready?"

"Sure." I set our wine glasses in the sink and grabbed my purse. "Bye guys. Be good."

The evening was pleasantly warm and the stars were out in force. We climbed in Patrick's Ford Classic Thunderbird and headed south.

I stroked the dashboard. "I've never been in one of the new *old* T-Birds before. This is really killer. I love the port hole window."

"Thanks." Patrick laughed. "I always wanted a vintage fifty-five or fifty-six Bird, but couldn't afford one. I figured when they came out with the retro Classic model, it was just the thing. It isn't quite the same as having an authentic classic, but it'll do. Besides, this one has a CD player instead of just an AM radio!"

We chatted about cars we'd owned and cars we dreamed of owning. We talked about motorcycles, and I told Patrick about my plans to buy another motorcycle soon.

"Are you sure? I'd hate to see you have another bad accident." He reached over and lightly patted my knee.

"You sound like my Aunt Louise." I grinned and shook my head. "Seriously, I'm a good rider, and I love motorcycles. I'd feel trapped if I couldn't get out and ride with the wind flowing around me and the sounds of nature filtering into my ears."

"You could roll down your car windows."

We both laughed. Again. *So far so good.*

We made it to Macaroni Grill and searched for a close parking space, which rarely exists outside the popular restaurant. Patrick insisted on dropping me at the front door and hoofing alone from the space he found half a lot away.

We had another glass of wine with our dinner and talked about our careers and aspirations. I told Patrick how I'd gotten started as a private investigator in California, my desire to return to Texas, and my happiness at getting my career ramped back up after my move. He told me how he'd become a cop.

"I was pretty rudderless when I graduated from college." He shrugged. "I'd gotten a degree in chemistry and then realized too late that I had few choices—teach or work for a big oil company or bio-research firm. I had no desire to do any of those, so much to my father's consternation, I interviewed for every job offer I saw that didn't require much experience or training, and I accepted the first offer I got. That's how I became a night watchman. It was a stroke of luck, really, because I discovered I loved it. After six months, I applied to the Austin Police Department and was accepted into their police academy."

"Larry Morrow said he was a rookie with you."

"Yeah, we worked out of the same precinct for about a year, but then I bought a little house near Georgetown and transferred to Williamson County. Of course, counties don't recognize each other's police training, so I had to go through academy all over again."

"That's terrible."

"Yeah, it kind of sucked, but they at least accelerated the program for me. I've worked the county ever since. Working a mostly rural beat is a whole 'nother world from working a contemporary, high-tech city like Austin. I've handled everything from drug busts, to breaking and entering, to removing a raccoon from an elderly woman's bedroom, to rescuing fair maidens who've been run off the road by evil white trucks."

As he finished, Patrick reached out and squeezed my hand. His smile was wide and his eyes sparkled, but his hand trembled the tiniest bit. I could feel my heart doing little pitter patters, and from the warmth on my cheeks I knew they were bright red.

I opened my mouth to speak and couldn't think of a single intelligent thing to say. Instead I dropped my eyes and smiled back. I was behaving like a smitten schoolgirl. I was most certainly glad that Larry and Judy would never know how demurely I'd behaved. They'd never let me hear the end of it.

We ended the evening with two cappuccinos and one monstrous slab of tiramisu. The drive home was the first time I relaxed all evening. I hadn't realized how awkward I felt about simple, friendly boy-girl conversation. Patrick also seemed a bit uncomfortable throughout the evening, but whether he was out of practice too, or my lack of skills was affecting him, wasn't a question I was about to ask.

When we got back to my house, we held hands as Patrick walked me to my door. We paused on the porch. I thought about asking Patrick inside, but I wasn't ready to take the next step, whatever that might be. "I, um, would, ah…"

Patrick, bless his heart, understood my nervousness and reluctance. "I'd love to visit more, but I've got a special assignment in the morning and haven't finished preparing for it."

I exhaled with relief and smiled. "Oh! That's too bad. I had a wonderful time tonight."

"I did, too. And I'd really like to see you again." He put his arms gently around my waist and eased me toward him. He leaned down and kissed me firmly, but gently.

I shivered with excitement. It'd been too long time since I'd had even a hint of a sexual relationship. Good thing he didn't use any tongue—I might have fainted from the overwhelming sensuality.

"I'll call tomorrow." His voice was husky and soft.

"Okay." My own voice was a bit husky, too.

I unlocked my door and turned to watch as he returned to his car. I automatically noted his license plate—H57 SDT—which instantly came to mind as *Heinz 57 Super Duper Trooper*. I blushed at the meaning, glad Patrick couldn't see it, and waved as he backed down the driveway. "I have *got* to get out more." I mumbled.

I closed the door, flipped the lock, and turned. No cats were waiting for me. *Lazy butts. Probably all asleep on my bed.* I tossed my purse and briefcase on the sofa and headed to the bedroom. No cats on the bed, either. I bent down and lifted the edge of the bedspread. Five sets of eyes peeked out at me. "Hey, guys, what's up?"

At the sound of my voice Boggle came flying out from under the bed and hurled himself at me, yowling and pawing at my leg. Mayfly remained under the bed, but added her own cries to those of her brother. Cooper and Polly stayed silent and stared at me as if I were a ghost. Deke began to growl.

"What's wrong?" They were clearly upset and frightened. "Where's Georgie?" I gathered Boggle into my arms and hugged him. He was trembling, and his paw pads were hot and damp. "Boggle, what's the matter?" Something was terribly wrong. I set Boggle on the bed, reached into the nightstand, and removed my Sig. I racked the slide to chamber a round.

Having the Sig in hand gave me some confidence, but I didn't know what, if anything was amiss. Was somebody in the house? I consciously switched into Stealth Mode, a calculated and unemotional behavior I'd spent years training my brain and body to reach. I turned off the bedroom light so I wouldn't be silhouetted as I moved down the darkened hallway. I stood silently and listened for strange sounds, but the crying of the cats made that useless.

I moved quietly and methodically through the house, reaching around the door of each room to flip on the light before entering. I inspected the other bedrooms and the guest bathroom—everything looked normal. Nothing out of place, no unusual sounds.

I headed down the hall to the living room, which had seemed fine when I walked through it earlier, but now I was moving slowly and deliberately, scoping out every room for any misplaced or disturbed item. The living room still looked okay. I turned into the kitchen and stopped short.

A small furry body lay on the island in the center of the room. Stealth Mode slammed against Maternal Instinct. Maternal Instinct won as a scream rose in my throat. I stopped it with a choked sob. "Georgie, oh God, oh God."

Adrenalin poured through my system. My mouth went cotton-ball dry. My vision blurred. My heart began pounded in my ears.

I leaned against the wall until my vision cleared. I forced control back into my body and my heart back into my chest. I moved slowly forward, the hand holding the gun twitching, ready to fire.

Georgie was splayed on the middle of the island countertop. He'd been gruesomely slaughtered. His body was disemboweled and dismembered, his limbs and internal organs laid out with an obscene neatness across the counter.

One of my expensive Henkel knives lay beside Georgie's head. The knife was spotless, wiped clean of blood. A disconnected part of me noticed that the entire scene appeared to have been carefully cleaned, with one exception—writing was scrawled in blood on the island next to Georgie's mutilated body.

I warned you to leave me alone

next time it'll be you!

A shiny brass bullet punctuated the exclamation point. I recognized it as a forty-five caliber.

I felt another sob rise in my throat and this time let it out. "Georgie, I'm so sorry. I'm so sorry. I'm so sorry. Please forgive me." I wiped my eyes and nose with the back of my hand and glanced out the solid glass kitchen door. The gate was open.

I moved in slow-motion to the living room sofa, retrieved my cell phone from my purse, and dialed.

"Nine-one-one. What is the nature of your emergency?" The voice was matter-of-fact and monotone—professional and neutral.

"My home has been broken into." My voice hitched. How do you describe having your cat mutilated as a lesson to you? "My cat has been killed and someone has left a threat on my own life."

"Yes, ma'am. What is your name and address."

I answered, trying to sound as calm and collected as the operator.

"We'll dispatch an officer immediately. Are you alone?"

"Yes."

"Have you been through the house?"

"Yes, I'm a licensed private investigator, that was the first thing I did." I hoped that bit of information gave me some credibility. Based on the dispatcher's response, it didn't.

"Of course. Please do not touch or move anything. An officer will be right there."

I wanted to say *I'm not stupid,* but decided it would get me nowhere. I was spun up enough without adding my own fuel to the fire. Instead, I said, "Thank you." I sat on the sofa, and dialed the phone again. It wasn't until it began to ring on the other end that I realized it was after midnight.

"Hello." Larry's voice was slurred and dull with sleep.

I was doing pretty good until I heard his voice. Then the tears started to flow. "Larry, it's Marianna."

"Hey, Cutie, what's wrong?"

I opened my mouth, but couldn't get my voice to work.

"Marianna?"

I tried again. "Georgie's dead. He was murdered."

"What do you mean murdered? When? How?" His voice was now alert and crisp.

"It happened while Patrick and I were out to dinner. Georgie was on my kitchen counter when I got home. I think the woman I've been following did it. She left a warning on the counter. It was written in…" my voice hitched, "in Georgie's blood." The tears flowed steadily now, and I found my voice had stopped working again.

"Have you called the police?"

I managed a confirming gurgle.

"I'll be there as soon as I can." The line disconnected.

Even if he left immediately, it would be another twenty minutes before he arrived. I set the phone on the coffee table and placed my gun beside it. I put my hands around my knees and rocked while tears fell in steady streams onto my lap. I could do nothing but wait.

GOODBYE SWEETIE

Life is pleasant. Death is peaceful. It's the transition that's troublesome. ~Isaac Asimov (1920-1992)

I was only a mile from the Cedar Park Police Department. In less than five minutes my numbed brain vaguely registered a car pulling up out front. I heard two sets of footsteps on the front sidewalk, a hard knock on the door, and then, "Police."

I yanked a tissue from the box on the end table and dabbed my nose and eyes. I forced myself off the sofa and opened the door. "I'm Marianna Morgan. I'm the one who called."

"Yes ma'am. This is Officer Bradley and I'm Officer Hawkins."

"I'm glad you got here so quickly. Before we proceed, I want to be sure to let you know that I'm a licensed private investigator and my loaded gun is right over there on the coffee table."

Both officers snapped their heads in the direction I was pointing. "Okay." Officer Hawkins nodded. "Thank you for letting us know. I assume you'll leave it sit while we are here."

"No problem. If you'll follow me I'll take you to the kitchen." I led the way around the corner, stopped in the doorway, and gestured. "If you don't mind I'd rather not go back in there just yet."

Officer Bradley moved toward the island. He whistled softly under his breath.

Officer Hawkins turned to me. "I'd like to ask you a few questions, if you're up to it."

"Of course. We can go to the living room. I think I'd better sit down again."

"I understand." He nodded and offered a comforting smile.

I sat on the sofa near my gun. Officer Hawkins slid the gun to the opposite side of the coffee table, then sat on the loveseat and flipped open a notepad. "Can you tell me what happened?"

I gave Officer Hawkins a rundown of the evening, including the time we left for dinner, the time I returned home, and what happened after Patrick left me in my doorway.

"Do you know who did this?"

"Sort of." I gave a brief description of my case. "As far as I know, the woman is my client's long lost sister. Based on her recent behavior and activities, though, she isn't the sweet sister he remembers. Seems to me she's pretty damned emotionally disturbed or unstable."

"How would she know about you, if her brother hasn't been able to locate her."

"That's the sixty-four-thousand-dollar question. I don't know yet, and it's driving me crazy. There's something odd going on here, and I haven't been able to figure it out. My lack of success just cost my cat his life."

I bit my lip hard in an attempt to staunch the tears that welled again. I looked away and blinked rapidly to keep the tears from rolling down my cheeks. I didn't want these cops to see me cry. I wasn't exactly a fellow officer, but being a private investigator still gave me an odd kind of kinship. And I didn't want to come off as just another weak female.

A camera flash filtered into the room from the kitchen. "I'm going to check on how things are going. Excuse me." Officer Hawkins stood and in one quick move scooped up my gun and took it with him to the kitchen.

I quickly dried my eyes again and used a fresh tissue to blow my nose. I heard the two men talking in hushed tones and went to join them. I knew I should be in there, whether I wanted to or not.

As I crossed the living room, I heard a car pull into the driveway. It had to be Larry, so I opened the door and stepped onto the porch. I breathed a silent prayer that he'd arrived just in time to save me from the carnage in my kitchen.

He trotted up the sidewalk and surrounded me in a warm bear hug as soon as he reached the porch. I melted into his arms, buried my face in his broad chest, and sobbed. "Oh Larry, Georgie didn't do anything to deserve this. If I was a better PI he'd still be alive."

"Hush." He hugged me harder. "You can't blame yourself. You're dealing with a very bad and deranged person. She did this, not you. You can't predict people like that, and you can't control their behavior. Come on, let's go inside. The cops'll wonder where you went."

The officers must have heard the door close behind us because they both hurried into the living room. "Officer Bradley, Officer Hawkins, this is Detective Larry Morrow with APD. He's here strictly as a friend." I added that last sentence when I saw the confused looks on their faces.

The men shook hands, then Larry eased me back onto the sofa. He sat close beside me and put his arm protectively around my shoulders. Officer Hawkins returned to his spot on the loveseat. Officer Bradley sat on the rocker. "We have a few more questions."

They asked me about the knife, which I confirmed had come from my kitchen. "Of course we'll have to take it as evidence." Officer Bradley sounded apologetic.

"Keep it. I don't ever want to see it again," I said through gritted teeth.

"Why do you believe," Officer Hawkins glanced at his notes, "that Stephanie Davidson is the person who broke in and killed your cat?"

"This is the third threat." I dug through my briefcase, which was still on the end of the sofa, and extracted the threatening letter I'd received less than two weeks before.

"Mind if I keep this?" Officer Bradley tucked it into his notebook without waiting for my answer.

"That's fine," I answered anyway. "But I'd like to make a copy first."

"I'll do it." Larry took the letter and moved down the hall to my home printer/copier combo.

"You said third threat." Officer Hawkins cocked his head.

"Yes." I told them about my accident and Tom Darnell's subsequent murder. "Deputy Patrick O'Meara with the Williamson County Sheriff's Office was one of the responding officers. He and I drove to the San Antonio impound yard, where I confirmed that Darnell's truck was the same one that ran me off the road."

I didn't mention my visit to Darnell's trailer, which would have gotten me in a lot of trouble. The SAPD would find the trailer, and the list of phone numbers, soon enough. They probably already had.

Officer Bradley was busily writing down everything I said. When Larry returned, he gave Officer Hawkins the original letter, handed me the copy, and returned to sit by my side.

Officer Bradley looked up and asked the question I most dreaded, "Whoever did this entered through the side gate and came in through the kitchen door. I didn't see any evidence that the door had been forced. Is it possible that Ms. Davidson had a key?"

I sighed and shuddered. "No. The door wasn't locked. I rarely lock my back door. The house shifts so much, depending on the weather, half the time that door doesn't lock anyway. I kept the gate latched, but not locked. I always figured that by the time someone got into the backyard, a glass door wasn't going to stop them anyway. I never expected something like this." I saw the officers exchange a look, but neither said anything.

"Marianna, we've talked about this." Larry shook his head and pursed his lips.

"I know." I stubbornly pursed my mouth back at him. "But Austin is a big city. Cedar Park is still mostly a small country town. There just isn't that much crime out here. And besides, I'm surrounded by retirees and stay-at-home moms. Someone would have to work hard not to be seen entering my backyard."

Officer Hawkins said softly, "Someone succeeded."

I felt my face grow hot as I blushed.

Officer Bradley cleared his throat. "We'll dust for prints on the door, the knife, and the bullet, and we'll take samples of the blood, in case your cat fought and drew blood from the assailant. We consider this a terroristic threat rather than a breaking and entering or cruelty to an animal. We'll follow up with both the San Antonio Police Department and with Deputy O'Meara."

"Thanks. I'm going to continue looking for her myself, too."

"Be careful," Officer Bradley said. "She clearly seems to be unstable, and you could easily get hurt."

"I agree." Larry nodded. "This chick is a kook."

"I'd originally planned on confronting her when I finally found her. I was hired to track her down for her brother. It's much more personal now, and much more dangerous. When I find her, and I will, dammit, I'll call for help."

All three men nodded in agreement. Officer Hawkins spoke in a soft, gentle voice, "Would you like us to call Animal Control for you?"

"No." My tears started again. "I'll bury him in my backyard." I turned to Larry, who squeezed my knee.

"Of course I'll help," he said with a twitching smile.

"We'll finish bagging and tagging and then be on our way." Officer Bradley stood. The two men returned to the kitchen. I sat silently, staring at nothing.

Larry let me be for a couple of minutes before speaking. "You'll find her. She won't get away with this."

I nodded, unable to form words.

After ten minutes the officers re-entered the living room. "We're done," Officer Bradley said, "We've got photos, bagged evidence, and fingerprints, although the perp did a very through job of wiping everything down. We found almost a full roll of paper towels soaked in both blood and cleaning solution in your trash can. We're taking them to check for a blood match. I assume your prints are on file."

"Yes, since I have a concealed carry permit."

"We'll pull them for elimination purposes," Officer Hawkins said.

"Of course." I nodded.

"The perpetrator took her time," Officer Bradley said. "She had to have known she wouldn't be disturbed. Do you know how she might have known that?"

"I don't know, unless she's been following and watching me. She drives a light blue Taurus, license H59-VBW."

"We'll implement a high intensity patrol of your house and this part of the neighborhood." Officer Hawkins jotted in his notebook. "And we'll put out an APB on her car. Tomorrow, we'll check with your neighbors to see if anyone saw or heard anything. In the meantime, I suggest you keep your eyes open and your windows and doors securely locked."

"Thank you." I smiled sheepishly.

"Oh, and you'll want this." Officer Hawkins placed my gun back on the coffee table.

I nodded but said nothing.

After the officers left, Larry pointed at me. "Stay here. I'll be right back." He walked toward the kitchen. I heard his gasp and shuddered at my own memories of the view he was seeing. I heard him shuffling around and then I heard the refrigerator open. He returned a couple of minutes later with an iced-tea-sized glass filled to the brim with a dark liquid. "Here, you need this."

I took the glass, it smelled of bourbon and Coke. I drank half the glass in two swallows and felt the hot rush of alcohol hit my system.

"I have to bury him. Tonight. Now." I said through speech that was already slightly slurred from shock, stress, and the sudden onslaught of alcohol.

"Okay, but you stay here. I'll get him ready."

I nodded, knowing that by *get him ready* he meant *gather up all his parts*. I took another big swallow of the drink. Larry pivoted to leave, turned back, and took his own long gulp of alcohol from my glass. Then he shuffled back to the kitchen.

I followed his actions in my mind by the sounds he made. He got a garbage bag from under my sink and fluffed it open. My stomach roiled at the sounds that came next. I heard wet plops as pieces of my feline friend were dropped into the plastic bag. And I heard the squishy wet sounds of a sponge being dunked into water and rinsed out. Finally I heard running water and knew he was washing his hands. When he returned, his face was grim, his mouth turned down in a deep frown. "Whoever did this is a big-time sicko."

"I know."

"Ready?"

"No, but let's go on anyway." I followed Larry into the kitchen, where he picked up the garbage bag he'd carefully rolled and sealed with tape. We moved through the kitchen door—now covered with dark, fingerprint-powder stains—into the backyard. Larry pulled a shovel out of the storage shed, and we walked to the far back corner.

"Let me do that." I took the shovel. "I need to be the one." It was hard work, and I hit a rock every few inches, but Larry stood by patiently while I dug. After thirty minutes, I was sweaty and tired, and my hands were burning and blistered, but the hole was big enough for Georgie's body.

I stepped back while Larry gently placed the bag into the hole. He silently took the shovel and filled the hole back in. I stared at the small mound of fresh earth and whispered, "Good-bye, Sweetie. I'll miss you." My eyes welled up with tears. I tried—unsuccessfully—to hold them back.

"Come on, let's go in." Larry took my hand and led me back to the kitchen, stopping only long enough to put the shovel away. I followed numbly. When I sat on the sofa, I realized how drained and tired I was. The adrenalin rush was gone. I felt as if someone had pulled a plug out of the bottom of my foot and all my energy had drained out. I let out a deep sigh, slumped my shoulders, and let my head drop.

"Not the sofa, you're going to bed." Larry cupped his hand under my elbow and gently helped me to stand.

I obediently followed Larry down the hall to my bedroom. "Where're your T-shirts?" he asked.

I pointed to the right dresser drawer. He reached in and extracted a white shirt that said *Mermaid from Hell*. "This should be good for tonight." He waggled his fingers in a gimme signal. "Okay, pants and sweater. Off."

I removed my outer clothes and bra. Larry pulled the T-shirt over my head and helped me push my arms through the sleeves. "I feel like I'm six," I mumbled through the shirt, which still covered my face.

Larry pulled the shirt down the rest of the way and my head popped out like a turtle. "Sometimes it's good to feel six. Six year olds rarely have the kind of problems you're having these days." He removed my shoes, pulled back the bed covers, and pushed me onto the bed. "In you go." He tucked the covers around me and kissed me on the forehead. "I'll turn out the lights and lock the doors. Even the back door. You get some rest. I'll call you tomorrow."

I opened my eyes to pitch darkness. My remaining cats were tucked tightly around me. I wiggled myself to a sitting position and looked toward the clock. Larry had covered its glowing numbers with my sweater. I swatted the sweater to the floor. It displayed an ungodly 3:14. I slipped out of bed and padded into the living room. My gun still lay on the coffee table. I picked it up and checked it—a bullet was still in the chamber.

Even though I was sure Larry had checked everything, I was too restless to go back to bed. I moved systematically through the house, checking every window and exterior door. None of the cats followed me—they seemed to sense my tension.

I'd grown complacent living in safe, *countrified* Cedar Park. It had never occurred to me that it didn't matter how safe Cedar Park was, my job made *me* unsafe no matter where I lived. To top it off, Cedar Park was changing—fast. The population was exploding, which meant crime rates were rising.

As I checked the deadbolt on the French doors, I wished for an alarm system, which up to this moment had seemed like ludicrous overkill. But tonight even the illusion of tight security mattered—a lot.

I reluctantly entered the kitchen and found that Larry had scrubbed everything down after he'd put me to bed. Even the garbage can was lined with a fresh bag and heavily sprayed with Lysol. I turned on the back light and looked out the kitchen door. Larry had also closed the gate. I didn't go outside, but I was willing to bet the gate was secured with the lock that normally sat unused on the fence rail. I hoped I knew where the key was these days. I turned off the light and left the kitchen. After prowling the entire house, I returned and sat on the bed.

"Mreowr." Boggle rolled over and patted my leg.

"Hey, buggy." I reached out and tickled his stomach. He purred and stretched full length. I sighed, knowing I'd never feel Georgie's headbutts in my tummy or see his cute head bobble again. At least I still had my other five babies. I crawled back under the covers and slipped the 380 semi-automatic under the pillow next to mine.

The rest of my night consisted of nightmares interrupted by frequent tossing, turning, sitting up suddenly at every noise, and reaching out every few minutes to feel the reassuring nearness of a cold steel butt. Well, okay, the handgun's custom grip was really room-temperature rubber, but its nearness was reassuring anyway.

BREAKFAST OUT

Just for once, don't you want to try something new?
~Lisa Simpson, The Simpsons (1989)

Stephen woke up Sunday morning with only a bare trace of a headache, much less severe than the day before. He was pleased. He wasn't normally a lay-about and had no intention of succumbing to that behavior two days in a row.

He was anxious to continue his search for the musket, although he doubted he could accomplish much today, and he still wanted to talk to Ms. Morgan about his revelation at Whiskey Smith's. It was the first honest evidence he had that his sister really was alive.

It was only seven, too early to call Ms. Morgan, so he decided to allow himself a treat—he'd go out for breakfast. Most tourists would still be tucked in their respective hotel rooms, so he didn't have to worry about crowds.

He cleaned up and dressed and headed down Presa Street to Shilo's Delicatessen. He'd always intended to eat at the classic German restaurant, but had avoided it because it was always crowded with locals who lived or worked in the area. Today, he decided to brave the place thanks to the lighter crowds. German food sounded good.

When Stephen walked through the entrance, he felt as if he'd stepped back in time. Fritz Shilo had opened the restaurant in 1917 and it had been in its present location since 1942. The floor was the original mosaic tile, a busy pattern formed from one-inch, earth tone octagonal tiles that almost made Stephen dizzy.

The walls were covered with framed postcard collages, each a photo of a vintage San Antonio skyline. Dominating the longest wall were three large flags—the red and white striped Austrian flag, the U.S. stars and stripes, and the black, red, and yellow German flag.

The waitresses looked as if they'd been working there since the place opened. A short-haired, blonde, woman with a name tag that said *Marie* smiled brightly at Stephen as she bustled by, effortlessly toting a a tray loaded with heaping plates of food. "Good morning, sir. Breakfast? Table or booth?" Her German accent was heavy and authentic.

Stephen returned her smile. "Booth, please."

The waitress gestured her head toward an empty booth. "Have a seat. I'll be right there."

He settled into the hardwood booth and scanned the menu already on the table. He was amazed at the prices. It looked as if he'd accidentally picked up a menu from the sixties. When the waitress walked over, she was already carrying a pot of steaming coffee and a cup and saucer. "Coffee?"

"Yes, please." She set the cup on the table and filled it all the way to the top. He'd have to pour a bit onto the saucer before he could add creamer. But he smiled at her anyway. "Thank you."

He ordered the Papa Fritz breakfast and fiddled with the cream and sugar for his coffee while he waited. It wasn't long before Marie returned with a plate spilling over with eggs, bratwurst, hash browns, and biscuits, as well as a glass of fresh orange juice. He ate slowly, relishing each bite of the heavy but delicious food.

When the waitress brought the check, he couldn't believe the total was only $5.45—coffee and juice included. Many River Walk restaurants catered to the convention crowd and charged an arm and a leg for one scrambled egg and dry toast. But Shilo's was a local's place and their menu, quality, and prices reflected that fact. He was so pleased he left a twenty percent tip on the table.

He laughed out loud as he approached the register. A sign on the wall by the door explained in no-nonsense terms that the restaurant name was pronounced ShEElows, NOT ShYlows. In response to the curious look he received from the waitress, he pointed to the sign. She smiled and nodded.

Stephen paid his bill and left, whistling a lively tune as he walked down the sidewalk. He felt rejuvenated by the filling breakfast and fresh morning air. The streets were still mostly empty, the waitress had been friendly, and no one had bothered him. Maybe he *would* start getting out of his apartment more during the day. He might even find an excuse to return to the library so he could see Patty again.

By the time he dropped his keys on his dining table, he saw that it was almost nine. Good, he could try Ms. Morgan now. He crossed the living room to the telephone, noting he had one message. He pressed Play. "Hello Mr. Davidson, this is Marianna Morgan. I'm leaving now to drive to San Antonio. It is absolutely imperative that I meet with you. Please call my cell phone as soon as you get this message."

Stephen sat down slowly. He could tell by the tone of Ms. Morgan's voice that something was terribly wrong. Visions flashed quickly through his mind like a slide show—Stephanie dead or injured, Ms. Morgan's life threatened again, Tom Darnell back to life and coming after one of the three of them.

His pulse quickened and he felt beads of sweat break out on his forehead. He grunted and stood up. He was being paranoid. She probably had reached an impasse in the case and needed to talk to him.

Yes, that's it. Nothing more. He rubbed his head with gusto, then took several slow, deep breaths to force himself to relax. He picked up the phone and dialed Ms. Morgan's cell phone.

"Hello. This is Marianna."

"Good morning, Ms. Morgan, this is Stephen Davidson, returning your call."

"Oh good. I'm already heading toward San Antonio. I need to meet with you. Will you be there around eleven?"

"Yes, I have errands to run, but I can take care of them later. I'll be here when you arrive."

"See you soon."

TRUTH OR DARE

Well I double-DOG-dare ya! ~Schwartz,
A Christmas Story (1983)

I was staring at the clock when it clicked from 5:59 to 6:00. An indecent hour, especially for a Sunday. I crawled out of bed, exhausted and drained, and staggered to the bathroom. My head throbbed dully, a combination adrenalin and alcohol headache.

Cold water on my face helped, but not much. I needed caffeine and I needed it *now*. I headed to the kitchen and brewed thick, strong coffee. I sat at the table and stared out the window at the brightening sky. Birds were stirring and starting to gather at my three feeders. I could hear their happy chirping through the closed window.

I couldn't see Georgie's grave from here, which was just as well. I needed to think about what my next move should be. Well, it *should* be telling the police about the phone numbers I found in Tom's trailer. I decided to think about what my next move *would* be.

After three cups of coffee, my hands were shaky but my mind was firm—I needed to return to San Antonio and have another long talk with Davidson. I was going to demand some answers, or else.

Like how he knew about the car and the gray door behind the Bargain Mart, and how Stephanie knew where I lived, and how she knew I wouldn't be home.

If he refused to talk, I was going to give him back his retainer—like hell I would—and tell him to find another investigator. This was no longer just a weird case that was making me lots of money. Things had turned very personal.

I showered and scrubbed from head to toe with a harsh, abrasive loofah, trying to wash away the last of my grief and fear. By the time I reached for a towel, my strongest emotions were anger and determination. I was going to find this bitch, for Davidson, for me, and for Georgie.

I dressed quickly in jeans and a *Scuba Maui* T-shirt. I'd have worn the *Mermaid from Hell* shirt but I had, unfortunately, slept in it. I pulled my gun from under the pillow and grabbed the extra magazine out of the nightstand.

I wasn't going to screw around anymore. I'd turned a corner last night. My career choice had never before been responsible for a death, human or animal. I wasn't going to let that happen again, at least not out of my own carelessness. I intended to take advantage of my concealed carry permit, and I was going to update my household budget plans to include an alarm system.

By the time I was done getting ready to leave, the cats had gotten active and were milling about the bedroom. I set my gun and ammo on the bed and dropped to my knees, hugging each cat in turn and tickling and petting them in their favorite spots.

When I'd showered love on all five of them, I stood and gathered my things. "I'll be gone for a good part of the day, guys, but I'll be sure all the doors are locked."

I wished I could have ridden my motorcycle. The fresh air and speed would do me good. Unfortunately, Max was now a memory, and I hadn't had time to go shopping for a new ride. *Soon. I need to do it soon. I miss riding.*

I called Davidson without looking at the clock. I didn't give a damn what time it was. His cell phone went straight to voicemail, so I assumed it was off. I called his home number, but he didn't answer. Maybe he was an early bird. I left a terse message that I was on my way, then made good on my word.

I was merging onto Interstate 35 when my cell phone chimed. I answered to find Davidson was returning my call. He was polite, but his voice was strained, nervous. He probably wondered why I was coming on such short notice. I wasn't about to get into it on the phone. I wanted to look him square in the eye when I asked my questions. I let him know what time I'd arrive and rang off.

Davidson was waiting in the hallway outside his door when I stepped off the elevator.

"Good morning, Ms. Morgan, please come in."

I'd forgotten how small his apartment was, and how the carefully arranged furniture gave it the illusion of being much larger. I sat on the same rocker as last time. I seemed to be establishing a pattern of confrontation whenever I was in Davidson's apartment.

He sat on the sofa. "What can I do for you today?"

"I have reason to believe that your sister entered my home last night and ritually slaughtered one of my cats. His name was Georgie, and he was dismembered and disemboweled. She left a threat written in Georgie's blood on my counter top. She said I'd be next." I stopped so I could size up Davidson's reaction.

He stared at me with a gaping mouth and wide eyes. "I... I can't believe she'd do such a thing. My sister—"

"Is a fucking lunatic." I cut him off. Maybe I should have held my tongue, but I didn't feel much like making the effort.

"Please, Ms. Morgan, I hardly think you can make that determination. You don't know that the person who entered your home was my sister." He started to nervously stroke the top of his head.

I shot to my feet, sending the rocker into a frenzy of motion. I wanted to slap his hand away and yell, *Stop with the head job already.* Instead, I forced myself to speak in a measured, non-screaming tone. "Look. I. Have. Had. It. Your sister—and I am convinced to the core that it was her—*was in my home*. She murdered my cat and told me I'd be next. Do you understand? That's way too personal for comfort. So I'll give you two choices, and those are your only two. One, you can tell me every damn thing you know. Two, you find another investigator."

Davidson stared at me for at least thirty seconds, then dropped his eyes. I saw tears land on the tops of his shoes, but it didn't move me—much.

"I'm so sorry. I truly am." His shoulders sagged. "I thought everything would be okay. I was at Whiskey Smith's on Friday and learned that the bartender knows Stephanie. Tammy said my sister had been there several times. It startled me, to finally learn such a concrete fact, but I took it as a good sign. I was excited that I finally had proof she's alive. Now you tell me she's become some kind of a monster. It's just hard to accept."

He tilted his face up to mine. The tears now fell down his cheeks and dripped off his chin. "Please sit down. I promise to tell you everything."

I was still angry enough that I stared for a few seconds before returning to my chair. I sat, but I kept my back stiff and my posture erect, just to show I meant business. "Fine. You can start by telling me how you knew about the car and the gray door. You've never fessed up to that."

Davidson bit his lip and looked away. "I was afraid you'd think I was crazy. But I guess that doesn't matter now. The truth is the truth, no matter how it sounds." He sighed and looked directly into my eyes. "I dreamed about them."

"Oh, puh-lease." I rolled my eyes. "Saying *I dreamed it* is your way of coming forth with the truth?"

"I'm quite serious." Davidson's forehead was drawn down, his eyes intense. "When we were little, we really did have some type of psychic connection to each other, although I hate to use that word. It always makes me think of late night infomercials. But we could finish each other's sentences, we knew what the other was thinking. One time I even knew the instant she fell off her bike and broke her wrist, even though I was at the store with my mother at the time. All of those *insights* stopped when she disappeared. But they started up again shortly before I saw her for the first time in the background of that news story. I told you about that already, about seeing her in the background during a local television news story."

"Yes, I remember."

"If it *is* true, if I *am* having psychic connections to my sister again, that means she's close, and that perhaps she's in trouble, and that the dreams are her subconscious reaching out to me. Please believe me. Please don't think I'm just being foolish."

I sat back, thinking. There were many documented reports of twins sharing thoughts and visions across the miles. Could he and Stephanie be sharing them after so many years of separation? Maybe he had a point. After all, the gray door and Taurus turned out to be true. But if I found out he was still jerking me around…

"Okay, let's pursue this for a minute." I tapped my chin. "If you're somehow getting this information from your sister, then why aren't you also getting a sense that something's not right with her anymore, that's she's somehow disturbed? Can you explain that?"

"I… No, I can't. I have no answer for you. I wish I did."

I stood and paced Davidson's small living area. "I don't have another answer for how you knew Stephanie's location, unless you've somehow been in contact with her and—"

"NO! I HAVE NOT!" he hollered.

"OKAY!" I hollered back, then lowered my voice. "All right."

"Please don't give up now." Davidson reached out like a street beggar.

I stopped and turned toward him. "I'll keep at it, but I'm doing it for Georgie."

"Yes, I understand. I'll help however I can."

I nodded, sat again, and leaned forward. "We need to discuss where to go from here. Let's put every fact we have on the table. You started already, so finish."

Davidson filled me in on his visit to Trinity and Terrell Hills. He told me about stopping by his old house and Whiskey Smith's. He unconsciously touched his forehead as he described his fainting spell.

"You're lucky you didn't give yourself a concussion. No real damage?"

"Only a headache." Davidson made a wan smile. "Anyway, that's it for me. I'd planned on spending more time today looking for the rif…musket. I thought I'd start by talking to antique dealers." He shrugged. "I guess my priorities have changed."

"Not necessarily. But let me tell you what I've learned." It took a while to fill Davidson in on everything, including my seeing Stephanie, my subsequent examination of the electrical and phone room she'd been using, and my visit to the Snake Farm and Tom's trailer. I only elaborated a little, figuring it couldn't hurt to ensure he was satisfied enough with my efforts to pay the bill I'd dropped in the mail. By the time I was done, his eyes were as big as salad plates.

"You've definitely been busy. I can't believe how much you learned. What's your next plan for contacting Stephanie?"

"I'll keep calling the other names on Tom's list until I reach one of them. But that may take time."

"Yes, you're right. In the meantime, where do we go from here?"

I smiled. "We go antiquing."

ANTIQUE HUNTING

Research is what I'm doing when I don't know what I'm doing. ~Wernher Von Braun (1912-1977)

It was after two when Davidson and I left his apartment, armed with the list of antique shops the police had investigated thirty-five years earlier. Most were probably long gone, but it was a place to start. Besides, I was restless and glad to be out of our one-on-one isolation for a while. I imagine he was, too.

"Are you hungry?" Davidson asked. "Let me buy you lunch."

"All right." I figured he was trying to make amends for what Stephanie had done, and I also figured I'd let him, even though it wasn't his fault. As if in agreement, or protest from only being fed one lousy Pop Tart hours earlier, my stomach growled. "Where to?"

"Do you like German?"

I smiled and nodded. "Sehr."

"Excuse me?" Davidson raised his eyebrows.

"A lot." I laughed. "It's one of the few German words I know."

"I know just the place."

When we stepped into Shilo's, it was like stepping into a timewarp. I hadn't been there in years, since long before I moved to California. The first thing that rattled my memory was the tile floor. "Wow, I'd forgotten about that. The pattern reminds me of the braided rug in my Aunt Louise's living room. They both look like a series of alien eyeballs."

"Yes, well, I never thought of it quite like that, but now that you mention it..."

An attractive, past-middle-age blonde noticed us staring at the floor. She waved. "Back again so soon! Sit wherever you like. I'll be right there."

I glanced at Davidson as we wove through the crowded tables to the back, where one of the few remaining empty ones was located. "You a regular here?"

"No, but I was just here at breakfast. My first time, in fact. I left that meal feeling happy and lighthearted." He huffed with sarcasm. "Didn't last long."

I shrugged. "Sorry."

I ordered a Polish Neighbor, a Polish sausage on a toasted bun with a deviled egg and cup of soup. I was debating which soup to try when Marie, the waitress, said in a no-nonsense voice, "You must have Mama Shilo's split pea soup."

"Okay." I wasn't willing to argue with her, considering the stern look in her eye.

Davidson ordered the Papa Fritz lunch, a ham, turkey, and both Swiss and American cheese sandwich on rye, with potato salad and soup—Mama Shilo's split pea, of course.

"Papa Fritz would be proud!" Marie exclaimed. She and Davidson both laughed.

When she'd walked off, Davidson explained, "I'm having a Papa Fritz day, I ordered the Papa Fritz breakfast just a few hours ago."

We both decided to treat ourselves to a Spaten, a German beer they had on tap. The waitress brought our beers almost immediately and we sipped in silence. I glanced around as we waited for our food, not ready to continue our conversation. There were hat hooks everywhere, harkening, I supposed, back to the pre-Kennedy days when every man wore a hat.

When Marie brought our plates, we spent another couple of minutes busying ourselves with salt, pepper, and thick, spicy mustard. Finally out of excuses, we chatted, but kept our conversation casual, not wanting to discuss private topics in such a public place.

After lunch, we moved onto the tourist-crowded sidewalk. Stephen seemed nervous and edgy.

"You okay?" I asked.

He nodded. "I'm not good with crowds."

"Want to cancel?"

"No. I want to make some progress. I'll manage my stress."

"Good. I want progress, too. Walk behind me if it helps. I'll part the waters, so to speak."

At least today I didn't see anyone wearing alien-inspired hair or clothes. They might have sent Stephen fleeing in terror. Nearly everyone was wearing a plastic badge around their neck proudly proclaiming National Concrete Masonry Association. *Well, probably hard to get more mundane than that.*

One by one, we checked each name on the list and walked to the specified address. As I feared, we struck out time after time. After two hours and six non-existent stores, we stopped for an iced tea in a small cafe tucked between a souvenir shop and a quilt store.

"You know…" I wiggled my tired, aching feet. "We could have done this faster with the phone book."

"Yes, but we both needed to get out of that apartment."

"You're right." I sighed. "What's the next place?"

"Kathy's Kollectibles," Davidson said. "And we're in luck, it's only two blocks from here."

Kathy's was no longer there. In its place was Kay's Keepsakes. Kay's was on the first floor of the Stackner building, a beautiful granite and marble structure built in a strange art-deco/Middle-Eastern hybrid style.

Stephen pulled open the glass door and we simultaneously sighed as the chilled air rushed out and over us. We entered the store and approached the checkout. The woman at the register completed the transaction for a twenty-something, male customer, who was purchasing a handful of old record albums.

She thanked the young man, then turned to us. "May I help you?"

"Yes," I said, before Davidson could take charge. "We're interested in old handguns and rifles. Do you have any here we could look at?"

"Yes we do." The middle-aged woman smiled warmly. "They're all located in Mr. Pitt's display areas. He keeps them locked in a case, but you're welcome to look at them. If you want to examine one closely, I'll have to call Mr. Pitt. He doesn't allow anyone but himself to show his guns."

"Thank you," Davidson said. "We'll let you know if we'd like you to call him."

We moved in the direction the woman pointed. We passed a series of three-sided stalls. Each was labeled with the dealer's name and stall number. One stall displayed old decorated tins, jars, and glass high-voltage insulators. Others were filled with old books. A few were overflowing with dried flower wall hangings, door toppers, and wreaths. Those stalls looked like tacky-bombs had gone off in them.

We finally found ourselves in front of a massive oak and glass gun cabinet. Inside was an impressive collection of muskets, shotguns, and rifles. All of them looked very old, very ornate, or both.

We spent a few minutes reading the descriptions of each gun. Most were World War I and World War II era items, but there was also one Civil War musket.

Davidson whistled softly as he leaned over for a closer look at the price tags tied to each gun. Most of the weapons were priced in the middle to upper four-digit range. "My. Do people really pay these prices?"

"That and more," the employee said from behind us.

Davidson and I both jumped a foot.

"Didn't mean to startle you." She laughed. "I thought I'd see if you'd like me to call Mr. Pitt."

"Yes, please." I pointed. "We're especially interested in this Civil War musket."

She excused herself to go place the call. We hung near the back of the store, casually perusing the displays of bottles, books, figurines, plates, and other collectibles my father would have called *trashables*. She returned after a few minutes. "Mr. Pitt will be here in about twenty minutes. I hope you don't mind the wait."

"Not at all." I figured it would give us an opportunity to find out what we could from the woman running the store. "Are you, by chance, Kay?"

"That's me." She smiled.

"Didn't this place used to be Kathy's Kollectibles?" Davidson asked. I was impressed. He managed to sound innocent and only casually interested.

"You have a good memory." Kay nodded. "I bought out Kathy when she retired fifteen years ago. Many of the spaces in the store are still rented by the same people, though."

"Was Mr. Pitt one of those who had a space when this was Kathy's?" I asked.

"My, yes," Kay answered. "Mr. Pitt was one of Kathy's first renters. I believe this display case has been here since shortly after the store opened."

"And when was that?" Davidson asked.

"Nineteen-sixty-five, I think," Kay said after a moment's pause. She didn't see Davidson and I exchange a quick, surprised look.

"Yes, I remember now," she continued. "Kathy opened about the time that the excavations were going on all over downtown. She originally carried the largest inventory in the city of Alamo-era items. I've seen photos and reviewed her original journals. She had cookware, jewelry, buttons, and even boots from that era. Mr. Pitt managed all of the weapons that were brought in."

"Brought in?" I asked. "By who? Whom?"

"Well…items that were excavated were supposed to belong to the city, or the university, I forget exactly, but many amateur scavengers brought in items with dubious stories of how and where they'd been found. Kathy did her best to verify stories, but mostly she took them at face value." Kay smiled crookedly and shrugged, as if to dismiss any questionable ethics Kathy might've had.

Before we could ask any more questions, the front door jingled. We followed Kay and found a tiny old man standing by the counter. He looked like a life-sized version of a wrinkled-apple doll. He was wearing a plaid western-cut shirt and unfaded jeans that were pressed to military precision. Below the hem of the pants I could see highly polished, alligator-skin cowboy boots.

"Mr. Pitt." Kay reached out and patted the man's shoulder. "These are the customers I called about."

Mr. Pitt approached us with a walk that was much steadier than I expected. I reached out and we shook hands. Mr. Pitt's skin was baby-soft, but his handshake was firm and strong. "I'm Mary, and this is my husband Steve," I said quickly.

Davidson, to his credit, didn't flinch or bat an eye. "Hi." He shook Mr. Pitt's hand. "It's nice to meet you. You have quite an impressive collection back there."

"That's just a small bit of it, too." Mr. Pitt hooted with laughter. "The wife, may she rest in peace, used to say our house looked like we could protect Fort Knox."

"Kay tells us you've been handling collector's pieces and antiques since the sixties," I said.

"Oh, long before that, honey." He smiled and winked. "I started collecting guns right after the war."

I wasn't about to ask which war, although I assumed World War II. "That's a long time. I can see why you've amassed such a large collection."

"Yep." He straightened his shoulders with pride. "I have hundreds of World War II weapons, but my favorites have always been the Alamo-era muskets and rifles. They're much more rare, and some of them were downright beautiful."

"We're especially interested in the Mexican muskets," I said.

"Ah, yes, the Brown Bess," Mr. Pitt interjected before I could continue. "Should be plentiful because the Mexicans had thousands of them, but they're still rare because their wooden stocks didn't often survive the test of time. I believe I have two of them, though not here at the store."

"We're hoping to find one Brown Bess that was particularly unique," Davidson said.

I held my breath, hoping he'd be able to maintain his innocent buyer personae.

"We like to collect antiques that have a quirky or unusual aspect to them," Davidson continued. "They make wonderful conversation pieces in our home."

I have to admit, I was impressed, not that I'd ever actually admit that to him.

"We heard about a Brown Bess that had a bent-tipped bayonet," Davidson said. "We were hoping you could help us locate it."

Mr. Pitt stroked his chin and looked at us a long time before speaking. His eyes were intense and piercing. "Can't say as I've seen one exactly like that. But you know, that's the oddest coincidence. I had a feller come in just the other day talking about that same Bessie."

"You mean someone else is also trying to buy it?" I asked.

"Nope," Mr. Pitt said. "Claimed he had one like it to sell. Said except for the bent tip on the bayonet it's in great shape, although I ain't seen it yet."

"Someone has one to sell?" Davidson asked with a gasp. He stepped back and grasped the edge of the counter to steady himself.

Mr. Pitt furrowed his brow and frowned.

Before he could start worrying too much, I said, "That's great!" I reached out and grasped Davidson's arm. "I can see how excited you are honey. You know, Mr. Pitt, we heard about this musket years ago, but Steve had pretty much decided it didn't really exist. I guess you shocked him. And I guess I win the bet." I squeezed Davidson's arm tightly as I said, "Isn't that right honey."

"Huh?" Davidson stammered. I squeezed harder. "Oh." He uttered a nervous laugh. "That's right. You win the bet."

Mr. Pitt stared at us for a bit, then laughed. "Hope the bet isn't too big!"

"Just housecleaning for a month." I grinned. "I'm going to enjoy the break. Can you tell us about the seller? We sure would like to talk to him. And we'd be happy to pay you a finder's fee or commission for your help."

"He didn't want to give me his address, or even his phone number." Mr. Pitt shook his head. "Don't know why. Said he'd be back by in a week with the musket. Sure hope he's legit."

"Did you get his name?" I asked.

"Can't rightly remember," Mr. Pitt continued. "I remember he said he's a perfessor at Trinity, though."

"Was his name, by any chance, Wagner?" Davidson asked softly as he began to stroke the top of his head.

"Why, now that you mention it, I believe it was."

I wasn't sure what the hell was going on, but I could tell from the ashen look on Davidson's face that it wasn't good, and that I better get him out of there. I quickly promised Mr. Pitt that we'd be back in touch a week later, after he'd had a chance to meet again with Mr. Wagner.

I hustled Davidson out of the antique shop, steering him by the elbow down the crowded sidewalk, since he didn't seem to be paying the slightest attention to where he was. I didn't slow our pace until we were half a block away, when I finally pulled on Davidson's arm.

"Okay, stop for a minute." I looked into his eyes. He had the look of a deer caught in headlights. "What's going on? Who is Wagner and why does that name sound familiar to me?"

"He... He..." Davidson took a deep breath, stroked the top of his head a couple of times, and tried again. "He's the professor at Trinity University I told you about. I went to see him last Friday because he and my father had both been Assistant Professors during the HemisFair construction years. I was hoping he could help me find the missing musket. He told me he'd never seen the musket, although I must say he certainly was an expert on the Brown Bess."

"Now that is interesting." I raised my eyebrows. "Did he act nervous or upset that you were asking him about the musket?"

Davidson rubbed his head again. I badly wanted to slap his hand away. Finally, he said, "Yes. No. Maybe. I'm not sure. I mean, he kept wiping his face and cleaning his glasses, but maybe those were just nervous habits." As he finished his sentence, he blushed and quickly pulled his hand away from his now-shiny dome.

"Okay, I need to go see this Professor Wagner. He obviously knows more than he was willing to tell you, and he may be much more involved than either of us care to guess. Not much reason to do more antiquing this afternoon." I looked intently at Davidson's strained face. His skin was pulled so tight it looked like it had shrunk a couple of sizes. "Are you okay?"

He turned to me, but his eyes looked as if he were staring into another dimension. I don't think he really saw me at all. But he said, "Yes, I'm just in a bit of shock, I guess, that Wagner may somehow be involved. I remember him coming to the house when I was a kid. He and his girlfriend had dinner with our family on many occasions. Of course, I never saw him again after Dad's mur…after the incident. I guess he didn't have a reason to socialize with a widow and her childre…child." Davidson visibly shuddered. "I think I'll go home. I'm getting a serious headache."

"Sure, sure." I patted his arm. "I need to head north anyway. I'll call you tomorrow as soon as I've talked to Wagner."

Davidson nodded and walked off, rubbing his head and mumbling as he left. I scooted my ass back to my car and made a beeline to Trinity.

BACK TO COLLEGE

College isn't the place to go for ideas.
~Helen Keller (1880-1968)

Even though it was Sunday, I was hoping to at least get the lay of the land. I circled through the campus, following the Information arrows to the Coates University Center. I was in luck. The regular receptionist obviously didn't work weekends—a security guard sat at the information desk. He looked up with a bored, sleepy expression.

Good, maybe I can catch him off guard.

"May I help you?" he asked as I approached.

"Could you direct me to Professor Gordon Wagner's office?"

"Can I see your campus ID? We're closed on Sunday to all but students and faculty."

Well crap. So much for the direct approach. Okay, time for the big guns. Nothing like a nice, rambling female to relax a male's guard. Luckily I have one of those in my Trusty Personae Kit that I'm very good at playing when necessary. I pulled out my Distressed Sweet Female personality and put it on.

I took a nice, long inhale and spewed forth. "Oh, well, gee, I don't have one yet because, you see, I decided after my husband left me for his secretary that I'd go back to college and finish the degree I never got to complete after we married because I got pregnant almost immediately and my jerk ex decided I had to give up all my dreams and stay home but now he's gone so I made an appointment with Professor Wagner in archeology for tomorrow morning at nine and I don't want to be late but I have no idea where his office is and this is such a big campus I'm lucky I even found this building so I was hoping to stop by today and get a kind of lay of the land and maybe even find out where his office is located."

I was about to turn purple, but I took a quick breath and added, "Could you help me?" I ended with my warmest, most sincere artificial smile. I even bit my lip, but only briefly, just for good measure.

The middle-aged, toupee-topped guard stared at me as if I was speaking Martian—a good sign. Sure enough, he winked and leaned forward. "Of course, honey, I'd be happy to help you out."

Talk about a quick one-eighty. But then, most men can be manipulated, if you know how to do it. I winced inwardly, though, at the sexist endearment, but managed to hold my smile steady.

He pulled out a campus map and hot pink highlighter and began marking the exact route I should take to the archeology building.

"Now don't let the signs fool you, sweetie, 'cuz the archeology department is part of anthropology here, so watch for the sign that says *Anthropology*. The building you want is this one." He stabbed a chewed-to-the-quick fingernail on the map. "The Cowles Life Science Center. Wagner's office is on the third floor, room 311."

I frowned in mock concentration at the simple directions he'd indicated. "Do you maybe also have his office number, so I can call and leave a message today confirming tomorrow morning's meeting? Maybe I saw the Absent Minded Professor one too many times, but I'd rather remind him, just in case. I'm afraid I left the note I wrote it on at home." I widened my smile until I felt one of my cheek muscles start to twitch.

"Well, now, let's see, honey…" The guard thumbed through a large black vinyl binder labeled *Campus Directory*. "Yep, here it is." He wrote the number on the edge of the map and then pushed it toward me.

"Thanks!" I said brightly. "This is a big help. I'm sure I won't be late now. I think I'll drive by there on my way out. Bye!" Before he could throw more endearments at me, I blew him a kiss, spun on my heel, and hurried out the door.

I glanced briefly at the guard's map and quickly found Wagner's building. I grabbed a notepad off my backseat to give myself a more official look. I pulled my handgun out of my purse and tucked it under the seat, since even with a license it's illegal to carry on a college campus. I cringed, realizing I'd had it on me when I entered the Coates University Center.

I trotted up the stairs to the main entrance. Luckily, the door was unlocked. Jogging up the stairs to the third floor, I dodged around a scattering of men and women carrying everything from armloads of books to boxes of rocks. The third floor was as busy as an anthill. Dozens of people bustled up and down the hall, popping in and out of doors. *No rest for the weary, or those working on doctoral theses, I guess.*

No one looked my way, so I squared my shoulders, lifted my chin, and strode smoothly down the hall. I glanced as subtly as possible at door numbers, lest someone see that I was unsure where I was going and ask what I was doing there.

I was fortunate that room 311 was only the fifth door down the hall. I could see as I approached the frosted glass and wood door that Wagner's office was dark.

I tapped lightly on the glass panel and leaned in as if listening for a response, then I tried the knob. The door was unlocked, bless his heart. I glanced around once more, then slipped through, and locked the door to ensure privacy. The light filtering through the glass from the hallway was just enough for me to move around without banging into anything.

Wagner's office was a tidy mess. Although there were piles of papers, magazines, books, and computer printouts everywhere, each was stacked with military precision. I shuffled through some of the stacks but found nothing unusual. The file cabinet was locked. I scanned the few tabbed folders laying loose on top of the cabinet but didn't see anything anywhere that raised an eyebrow.

I moved quietly around the large wooden desk and sat in his black, faux-leather chair. The right side of the seat cushion was compressed much flatter than the left. I gathered from the way it made me list to starboard that Wagner was a lefty and spent most of his time leaning on his right arm while writing with his left.

Wagner's desk was neat, except for the cluttered bin—labelled *Student's Inbox*—on the corner nearest the door. The mesh bin held no surprises, just the usual requests for help, papers with *sorry this is late* notes affixed, and proposals for new studies. I tried to search the desk, but it was locked.

When I turned my attention to the row of bookcases behind the desk, however, the ol' eyebrow shot right up. One entire case was dedicated to books about Alamo-era relics. Two books were pulled forward, as if recently removed and hastily returned to the shelf. One was *The Brown Bess Bayonet - 1720-1860*. The other was *Texas Antique Dealers Directory*.

I quickly scanned through the other titles. Wagner had research books about archeological digs where muskets had been found, collectibles books that showed various states of decay and applicable monetary value, reference books that included photos and detailed information about muskets that had been donated to museums or sold at public auctions, and a host of brochures, pamphlets, white papers, and theses.

He was certainly a musket connoisseur, if nothing else. And the Texas directory was a pretty strong indication that Wagner was more than just an interested professor.

I debated leaving a business card, but decided I didn't want Wagner to know that I was a private investigator. Instead, I tore a sheet off the notepad I'd brought and wrote a short note, using my cell rather than office phone number:

Professor Wagner, I stopped by hoping to catch you in the office while I was in town. I'd like to talk to you about Brown Bess muskets. My professor said you can help answer some questions for my masters thesis. Please call me at 512-555-5968. I'm in Austin but I'll drive back down at your convenience. Thanks, Marianna Morgan

I stood and glanced around the office one last time to be sure Wagner wouldn't be able to detect my rifling, no pun intended, and that I hadn't missed anything. Satisfied, I stepped back into the hall. There was a lull in the people traffic, so I took the opportunity to quickly fold and tuck my note into Wagner's door.

He should find the note first thing Monday morning. Although I didn't know what his lecture schedule might be, I hoped he returned my call soon. Things felt like they were speeding up, or maybe it was just my own impatience at the case's lack of progress.

❧❧❧

Two hours later, I walked in the door at home to a chorus of hungry meows. I took a few minutes to appease the hoard before pulling my cell phone and notebook from my purse.

I had two messages. I hadn't heard it ring. One from a telemarketer. *Why do they even leave messages? Does anyone return their calls?* Not me—I pressed Delete. The second message was from Wagner. My heart did a little pitty-pat as I listened.

"Ms. Morgan, this is Professor Wagner at Trinity. I had to stop by my office this evening and found your note. I see my students on Mondays from nine to one. I have an opening tomorrow at nine, if you really want to drive back down so soon. I'll be in my office."

I paced for a minute, debating what to do. Of *course* I was driving back down. But I couldn't decide whether or not to tell Davidson. I glanced out the back window and my heart did another pitty-pat—this time for Georgie. Everything about this case seemed to be spiraling toward Wagner. Davidson was my client, so I guess he deserved to be included.

I dialed Davidson's number but got no answer. "Mr. Davidson, this is Marianna. I have an appointment at nine tomorrow morning with Professor Wagner. You're welcome to meet me there if you want."

CONFRONTATION TIME

Since I got here, I have done nothing but underhanded, despicable, not even terribly imaginative things.
~Julianne, My Best Friend's Wedding (1997)

It was barely after dawn Monday morning. Stephanie had already paced a circle inside the small storage room for hours. She vigorously brushed her hair the entire time, as if she could brush the frustration and anger from her body. She walked to the open door and stopped. The tops of the nearby trees were just starting to glow from the sun, and the leaves were rustling as the birds began to stir.

She stood perfectly still except for the arm that held the brush, which continued its up and down rhythm. She made a conscious effort to change from the frenzied hair brushing to long, gentle strokes. After a few minutes, she took a deep breath and emitted a long, anguished sigh. She dropped her arm to her side and barely noticed as the brush fell with a plunk to the concrete floor.

She'd hoped that bitch Marianna would drop the case after finding her precious cat laid out, buffet-style, across the kitchen counter. She'd also hoped that Stephen would insist on discontinuing the case after realizing how much danger he'd put the private investigator in. But, dammit, both of them were determined to press on. She'd kept an eye and ear on them all day Sunday, although it was very hard to do so without being detected.

At least she'd learned something that made the difficult day worth the effort. She couldn't help but smile, but the smile didn't reach her eyes and left her with a menacing, dangerous look.

Well, well. Gordon Wagner. Who would have suspected gentle, quiet Professor Wagner. She spat indelicately on the ground and then continued, speaking aloud to the wall of closed storage sheds before her, "Dad trusted you—you were his best friend. I guess I'd managed to forget all about you. Were you the one who broke in that night, or did you just buy the musket from the person who did?"

No matter how hard she'd tried, she had no memory of that night, or of its aftermath. She guessed she'd passed out. But perhaps her mind had blocked that part of her memory as a survival instinct.

Stephanie bent and retrieved the brush from the floor. She resumed her brushing, and her pacing. After another ten minutes, she dropped the brush on the only chair in the small room. She quickly and efficiently went through several of the boxes that were neatly stacked along one wall.

She was intimately familiar with the contents of each box, so it didn't take long to assemble the items she needed for later that morning—her gun, an extra clip of ammunition, nondescript clothes that would blend in on a crowded campus, a floppy-brimmed hat that would help to conceal her looks.

As she changed and applied her makeup, her heart rate quickened with anticipation and excitement. She'd waited a long time to know the truth. She wanted to believe it hadn't been Wagner who'd entered their home that terrible night. But somehow she felt it really was him, although the feeling could be due to a buried memory or even to morbid thinking.

Either way, Wagner was the first person that even stood a chance of being able to tell her the truth about what had happened to her, and why her years after that night were hidden behind a vague gray cloud, out of reach of her conscious mind.

Stephanie packed her oversize purse with her gun, brush, and makeup, and pushed the floppy hat onto her head. She hated hats—they messed up her hair—but she worried her older face could stand out at Trinity, and she wanted to minimize any attention directed her way.

She glanced at her watch. It was just after seven. Good. She needed to be at the university first thing so she could catch Wagner the moment he arrived. The last thing Stephanie'd learned the day before was that Marianna planned to drive down sometime this morning to have her own talk with Wagner.

Stephanie locked the storage room door and hurried to her car. She had no intention of arriving after Marianna. She wanted to be there and gone before Mizzz Morgan even arrived. She didn't know what Marianna's agenda might be, but she sure as hell knew what her own was—she couldn't wait to see the look on Wagner's eyes when a *dead girl* walked into his office.

SHOWDOWN

I don't know why we are here, but I'm pretty sure that
it is not in order to enjoy ourselves.
~Ludwig Wittgenstein (1889-1951)

I was in the shower by six, in spite of the stiff drink I'd downed before bed. I still wasn't fully awake until seven, and only then because traffic was getting heavy as I crossed downtown Austin.

I zipped down Interstate 35, doing my best to maintain a psychic cop-invisibility-shield around my car. I could have made even better time on Max, or any bike for that matter, but I was still cycle-less so I was stuck on four wheels. I managed to hit Trinity at eight-thirty.

Thanks to my previous day's foray, I knew exactly where to go. I wound through the campus at what felt like a snail's pace, dodging hordes of students. I got stuck at one point behind a couple of bleached-blonde bimbos who were sashaying in spray-paint-tight jeans down the middle of the road. They were probably only attending college to find a man.

I got close, sat on my horn, and swerved around them with only inches to spare. Both girls yelled and shot the finger at me. The one with the biggest tits slapped my fender as I went by.

I'd have hollered back that they should plan on going to finishing school to learn some manners, but I didn't have time. Instead I shot the finger back at them. Hey, I *didn't* attend finishing school and *didn't* give a damn about manners at the moment. I rounded the last bend and made an indelicate stop in front of Wagner's building.

I scanned the parking lot for Davidson's car. His car wasn't there, but then I hadn't heard back, so didn't know if he even intended to show up. I was turning toward the building when the back of a light blue Taurus caught my eye.

What the hell is she doing here? Is she following me? Is she after the same information I am?

Law or no law, I leaned down in my car and dug my gun from under the seat. I tucked it into my purse and bounded up the sidewalk, happy my ankle wasn't complaining too much.

I had no clue what to expect, but I figured it wasn't good. I elbowed my way up the narrow stairs to the third floor, earning several *heys* from offended students. I tossed a couple of *sorrys* over my shoulder for good measure, but kept running.

When I reached Wagner's office, I could hear voices through the door. They were too muffled to follow the conversation. I leaned in a bit, careful that my presence didn't show through the frosted glass. The conversation grew more distinct.

"I searched for so long," a woman's voice said. "And here you were, all along."

"I don't understand," Wagner said.

"What are you doing with the musket that was stolen from our house? Did you steal it yourself or buy it from the person who did?"

So it was Stephanie.

"Musket?" Wagner said, "I'm not sure I—"

He should've known better. I heard a quick shuffle and crack. She'd apparently slapped the rest of the sentence from his mouth.

"Please," he whimpered. "I can't help you. I don't—" His pleading was interrupted by the sound of another slap. He whimpered again.

I debated whether to knock or just barge in. I opted for the surprise-but-prepared approach—I pulled my gun from my purse, turned the doorknob, and stormed in.

Even though the woman wore a large hat that heavily shadowed her features, I could tell I was face to face with Stephanie Davidson, alive and in the flesh. Her first words convinced me.

"Hello, Mizzz Morgan." She exaggerated *Ms.* as if it was a dirty word. "Come in. We've been expecting you. Have a seat over there."

Since she emphasized the invitation by waving a large handgun in my direction, I figured I'd best do as she asked. I wasn't going to argue with what looked like a forty-five caliber, which would do a nasty number on Wagner's bookcase-lined walls, not to mention my personal person. I eased into the chair and casually tucked my purse onto the chair beside my leg.

"How about tossing that purse over here." Stephanie gave a tight nod. "I don't think you'll be needing to powder your nose, or use anything else that might happen to be in there."

Damn. So much for taking advantage of my concealed carry license. But I didn't see much of a choice, so I kicked the bag—it stopped a couple of feet in front of her.

Stephanie used her foot to slide the purse under the edge of Wagner's desk. She then moved toward the open door, which she closed and locked. She also lowered the shade over the door's frosted window, ensuring total privacy for our little party. The windows that overlooked the campus had already been covered with lowered shades.

I took the opportunity to catch Wagner's eye. I raised my eyebrows in a *what gives* signal. He only returned my look with the barest shake of his head. His eyes looked like a pig in a slaughterhouse who's just realized it's next up for the electrocution butt-probe.

Stephanie caught our brief exchange and uttered a cackling laugh. The sound was bone-chilling. "You two have no fucking clue, do you. Poor Gordon has been sitting there all pasty-faced, because I wouldn't tell him anything until you arrived. Although, we've spent the last two hours having a lovely conversation about the Snake Farm and its wonderful collection, haven't we? We were just discussing muskets when you finally made your appearance."

Wagner's lips were set in a thin line, and his face was ashen, but he gave a short nod.

Stephanie continued, "Let's get this show back on the road."

"Why me?" I asked. "Why do you care if I'm here?"

Stephanie chuckled, although coming from her it sounded menacing rather than cute. "My dear Ms. Morgan, you've been spending all your time trying to find me. I knew you wouldn't want to miss this opportunity. I'd planned to be long gone before you arrived, but decided to wait for you strictly out of kindness and courtesy."

"You mean like the courtesy you showed when you slaughtered my cat?"

She grabbed the most convenient item on Wagner's desk, a magnetic paper clip holder, and threw it at my head. I ducked and the heavy plastic box slammed into the bookcase behind me, sending a shower of silver curlicues onto the carpet.

"Enough!" she spat. "You got what you deserved, you nosy bitch. And you'll get the rest of it, too. I'm not done with you yet. But now I'm just getting started with old Wagner, here. So sit still and shut the fuck up."

I stared intently at Stephanie. She was wearing a baggy khaki shirt, faded jeans skirt, and the over-sized hat. Even through the shadow I could see she had a pencil thin smirk and cold, hard eyes. Her long hair and bangs framed her heavily-made-up face, giving her a boxy, angular look. Her skin was pale, making her dark eyes look like the holes in a bleached-out skull. But I could also see a strong resemblance to Stephen. Yep, there was no longer a shred of doubt in my mind that I was looking at his twin.

I debated what to do and decided to see if I could wrest a bit of control from her before she went any further. I pointed casually toward her gun. "If it were me, I'd have dumped that gun after killing Tom Darnell. It's never a good idea to re-use a gun that's being sought by police." I *tsk-tsked* for emphasis. "And leaving Tom in the cab of his truck right in front of the bar. Well that was just sloppy work. I'd have at least made his body a little harder to find." I smiled broadly. I even showed my teeth.

Stephanie laughed again. "You would, sweetie, because you haven't got the balls it takes to be the bad guy. You'd spend half your time trying to cover all your tracks instead of moving forward and finishing the job. I've got plans, and they don't include buying a new gun every few days, or worrying about bodies after the occupant is done with it."

She slowly rotated the gun in her hand, seemingly admiring it from multiple angles. "Besides, there are still perfectly good bullets in here. Maybe I'll show you in a bit. If you like, I'll even move your car when I'm done. Just to make it harder for the police to find."

So much for trying to dazzle her with brilliance. Maybe I can baffle her with some bullshit. I started with a casual shrug, just to show I didn't care. "I'm tired of that car anyway. But you might want to be careful when you go for it, since I called campus security on my way here to let them know where I was going and to ask that they send a couple of men around to check on Professor Wagner's office."

Stephanie's eyes narrowed as she studied my face. I summoned every bit of willpower I had to maintain an honest, sincere expression. I sure didn't want an eye tic or deep swallow to give away my lie. I sat stock-still and maintained eye contact. I'd played Don't Blink with my cats many times so I was pretty good at maintaining a stare. The measured tick-tock from Wagner's wall clock filled the room.

After at least a minute, Stephanie blinked and looked away. "Fat chance," she mumbled. But a bead of sweat rolled from beneath her bangs and traced a trail through the makeup on her cheek. I'd won that round, although I wasn't sure that it had actually bought me anything.

My victory didn't last long. Stephanie pushed herself off the wall and stepped toward Wagner. "Let's get back to you." She waved her gun in his face.

"Want to try that again?" She leveled the forty-five so that she was sighted directly at Wagner's head. She grinned so broadly that her eyes crinkled at the corners. She was obviously enjoying the hell out of whatever game she was playing. I felt the hairs on the back of my neck stand straight up.

Wagner's chin quivered and a soft whimper escaped his lips. He looked like he was about to piss himself. Or maybe he just had. He removed his glasses and used a tissue from the box on his desk to wipe them clean. He also took the opportunity to quickly wipe the corners of his eyes and dab at his lip, which was already sprouting a dark purple bump.

"I'm waiting." Stephanie tapped her toe loudly on the tile floor. "And I do *not* have infinite patience."

Wagner quickly replaced his glasses and dropped the wadded tissue onto the floor. "It…it was me." His voice was so soft I found myself trying to read his lips. "I was young and stupid. And in deep debt. I couldn't see any way out of the hole that tuition and gambling losses had left me in."

Stephanie snorted but said nothing.

"I watched your father slip the musket into the trunk of his car." Wagner kept his eyes down as he spoke. His hands fidgeted in his lap. "I checked the site records and saw he hadn't logged it. I figured it wouldn't hurt anyone if I took it and sold it. All of you were supposed to be at the symphony or ballet or something that night. I just remember he'd talked about it that afternoon, because you so rarely got to go out as a family. Money was too tight. But he'd splurged and purchased the tickets, because it meant so much to Nora. Maybe that's what drove him to steal the musket. His desire to provide more than the basics for his family. I don't know. I sure never meant for anyone to get hurt. I swear." He looked pleadingly at Stephanie and tears welled in his eyes.

"I'm touched." Stephanie's voice was as flat and cold as steel. "But people *did* get hurt. Me included." She waggled the gun. "Go on. I'm dying to hear the rest of your poor-poor-pitiful-me story. And make it good or I'll find some way to persuade you."

Wagner swallowed hard and licked his lips. "I parked around the corner and walked to your house. I knew your parents kept a key under the pot of red geraniums on the porch. I'd seen Chester use it more than once when he'd misplaced his keys. I guess he didn't hear me when I came in. Even though I didn't think anyone was home, I still moved softly through the house. I found the musket inside your parent's closet. I was on my way out when I ran into Chester in the hallway outside your bedroom."

"He always read to us and kissed us good night." Stephanie's voice sounded faraway as she shared that small memory. I could see she was having trouble maintaining control. It was like watching a television whose image wavers in and out because of an unstable signal.

I thought her distraction might give me an opportunity to do something. But the second I shifted, which caused the cheap Naugahyde-covered chair to utter a rude-sounding squeak, both Stephanie's head and gun snapped my direction.

"Don't even twitch your big toe." She leveled the gun at what looked like a convenient spot between my eyes.

I nodded and slipped back into the chair, wiggling my butt a couple of times just to annoy her with some additional fart-sounding squeaks. I shrugged and smiled innocently.

Stephanie glared at me. I could see her trigger finger actually twitching. I decided I'd sit very still for a while, and for good measure I wiped the grin off my face. After a few more seconds, she turned her attention—and the forty-five—back to Wagner. "Keep talking."

Wagner stared at the gun and nodded. "At first, Chester was just startled at seeing me—then he noticed the musket. I'd tried to hide it behind my back, but it was just too big. I tried to think up a quick excuse, but nothing even remotely reasonable came to mind. He ordered me to hand over the musket and leave. I was scared, and that made me angry, so I pushed him. That set him off. He cursed and yelled as he grabbed for the musket. He was between me and the front door. I lunged, hoping to knock him down and run past him. Instead, I slipped. He came at me at the same time. The musket's bayonet went straight into his chest. He went down hard and lay there groaning. Blood pooled around him fast. I knew there was nothing I could do to help him."

"So much blood." Stephanie's voice was haunted, hollow. "It soaked into the hardwood, making it look like rusted iron. It spread all the way into my room. I remember the smell. It was just like the smell that came from our neighbor's cat when it got hit by a car right in front of our house one time." Her body was rigid and her eyes were vacant, as if she'd left present time and returned to that night of terror.

Wagner stopped speaking at the sound of Stephanie's first word. He stared at her, his mouth gaped at the gruesome picture her words painted.

Stephanie shook her head hard and cleared her throat. "Go on."

Wagner hesitated and started to remove his glasses again.

"NOW!" Stephanie hissed. She tightened her grip on the gun for emphasis. I could see her jaw muscles pulsing, and her bangs were stringy with sweat.

"Yes. Okay," Wagner stammered. "The musket had fallen on the floor beside your father. I was bending to pick it up when you started screaming. I was scared that it would attract the neighbors, so I told you to shut up. But you kept screaming *daddy* over and over. Finally, you stopped screaming and just stared at me with wide, frightened eyes. You said *Oh, Uncle Gordon* once, then you fainted dead on the floor."

Wagner stopped speaking and used a fresh tissue to wipe his sweating brow. He also dabbed at his lip, which now sported a bump the size of a Corn Nut. It probably hurt to talk, but the furrowed brow on Stephanie's face told him he didn't have a choice.

"I felt Chester's neck and found no pulse. I was really scared by then, so I grabbed the musket and wrapped it in an old yellow rain slicker. I knew I couldn't leave you there, because you could identify me, so I had no choice but to take you, too. I wrapped you in your bedspread so I could control you better if you woke up, and I slipped out of the house and hurried to my car."

I stole a glance at Stephanie. She was quivering all over, as if Wagner had touched her with a live wire. She was staring at Wagner through eyes that were narrowed to small slits. The gun she still pointed at Wagner's head shook in her hand. And her hat had sagged just enough that it was partially blocking her view of me.

As much as I wanted to hear the rest of the story, I wanted more to live to talk about it. And I knew that whatever Wagner had to tell next was likely going to be the undoing of Stephanie's fragile mental state. I decided to take a chance. I briefly considered going for my purse, but I quickly realized I'd be dead before my hand ever so much as touched it.

Instead, I launched from the chair and lunged for Stephanie's thighs. I hit her with my left shoulder football-tackle style and forced her hard into the wall. She grunted, dropped the gun, and slid down the wall. She wasn't knocked out, but she was stunned, and that was enough. I grabbed her gun and pointed it at her chest.

"Well, Miss Stephanie, looks like your party's over. Professor, please call nine-one-one." When he didn't respond, I glanced quickly in his direction. He was staring catatonically at Stephanie.

His lips were moving in a rhythmic pattern, but I couldn't make out the words. I eased a bit his direction and finally heard. He was whispering *not you, not you, not you* as if it were a mantra.

I turned to Stephanie and saw that she was still disoriented. I could almost see the little cartoon birdies circling her head. Her hat had slipped off and was lying in a heap on her lap. "Well I'll be damned," was the best I could do as I stared closely at her.

The full light from the overhead fixture glaring down on Stephanie's face left no doubt in my mind what I was seeing. I reached out and yanked at the now-tangled hair. Sure enough, the long, dark tresses came off in my hand, exposing Stephen's shiny bald spot.

UNCOVERED

In archaeology you uncover the unknown. In diplomacy you cover the known. ~Thomas Pickering (1931-)

Stephen...Stephanie...Whoever-the-Hell sat at my feet and stared blankly up at me. The haughty look was gone. So was the arrogance.

"Where am I?" The voice was now unmistakably Stephen Davidson's.

At least I know what name to use. For now.

"Where am I?" Davidson repeated. "What's going on? Professor Wagner? Ms. Morgan?" He looked around. His expression was one of confusion and bewilderment. He glanced down at his denim skirt, gingerly touching it as if it might burn his fingers.

When he looked up at me again, his eyes were clouded with confusion. And probably denial. It seemed clear to me he truly had no idea what was going on. It wasn't an act.

As if magnetically attracted, his hand slipped up and began to stroke his bald spot, which was shiny with sweat from being held captive under the wig.

The absurd image was enough to make me bust a gut laughing, but I bit my tongue and swallowed hard. I knew absolutely zip about the psychology that was involved here and didn't want to do anything stupid. I figured that brevity and low volume were my best defenses against ignorance.

"Easy now." I turned again to Wagner, who still looked like a badly-posed mannequin. "Professor Wagner." I spoke softly, so as not to upset Stephen. Wagner didn't respond. I increased my volume and lightly tapped Stephanie's gun on his desk. "Professor Wagner." This time he looked at me, but his stare was still blank and his lips still silently moved. I gave up and leaned for the phone, trying not to lose sight of Stephen.

"Campus Security Emergency Services. Please state the nature of your emergency."

I'd forgotten that we were on campus and nine-one-one wouldn't reach past its boundaries. But I really didn't care. The professional, steady male voice that answered my call sent a flood of reassuring warmth through my body.

"There's been an attempted murder." It was close enough to the truth to ensure a quick response. I identified myself and provided our location.

"Whose attempted murder? Who else is with you?"

Good question. "A former associate was…accosting Wagner with a gun. I arrived just in time to stop it. It's just the three of us." *Should I have said four of us?* This was all so confusing.

I promised to stay at the scene until the police arrived. There was no way I was going to miss whatever would happen next.

I unlocked the door, but didn't raise the shade, for fear that students would take it as an invitation Wagner was available for drop-ins. The last thing any of us needed was a distraught student arriving to beg for a better grade.

The campus cops arrived within minutes. Ten of them. They probably hadn't had much excitement all year, and none of them wanted to be left out of an attempted murder investigation.

A beefy-armed, barrel-chested, black male was the first through the door. He was followed by the other nine cops, who crowded into the room like a scene out of a Marx brother's movie. Except all ten cops had their hands on their respective holsters. I sure wasn't about to laugh at my mental analogy.

"What's going on here?" the black cop asked. Folks might make jokes about rent-a-cop types who work campus and mall security, but this guy left no doubt that he meant business.

I quickly placed Stephanie's gun on Wagner's desk and stepped forward. I kept my hands front and center, so they could see I was unarmed. "I'm the one who called. My name is Marianna Morgan and I'm a licensed private investigator. This man." I waved toward Stephen, who sat like a rag doll on the floor, except that he was still rubbing his head, "is my client. It's a rather complicated story, but he's the one who was holding Professor Wagner at gunpoint."

I waved again, this time toward Wagner, who sat in his chair, looking just as stunned as Stephen. "My client had Wagner summon me here to hear Wagner's confession of murdering my client's father years ago. I believe that Stephen intended to kill Wagner, and then perhaps me. I was able to overpower him and take his gun away."

"Why would your client want to murder you?" a small Hispanic cop asked.

Of all the questions they could have asked, that was as good as any. And one of the toughest to answer.

"He wasn't himself." I inwardly smirked at the double meaning. "He apparently suffered some type of schizophrenic breakdown, as you can see."

I pointed again to Stephen, who looked at us through smeared makeup, heavily-mascara'd eyes, and rosy red cheeks. Not to mention his hairy legs sticking out from under the long, denim skirt.

"Ay-ay-ay, so that's why the güey is wearing a skirt." The Hispanic cop shook his head. "Muy loco."

"What the hell is going on?" the black cop asked again. "I don't get any of this."

"I'm not completely sure myself," I said, and added "Honest!" in response to the sharp look several of the cops shot me. "Look, I was hired by Stephen Davidson to supposedly find his twin sister Stephanie, who'd disappeared from their home when they were kids. Apparently Wagner here broke into the Davidson home with the intention of stealing a historical musket."

"Historical musket?" a previously silent cop asked.

I nodded. "This all started back before the nineteen-sixty-eight Hemisfair world's fair. The Trinity archeologists were in charge of excavating the area around the Alamo. One of their finds was a historic musket, which Chester Davidson took home instead of cataloging with the rest of the relics."

"So he stole it," the black cop said. "Now I'm starting to get it."

"Yes, he did," I said. "Chester Davidson discovered Wagner had broken in to steal the musket for himself, and in the struggle Chester was killed. No one knew what happened to Stephanie. She disappeared."

"So there never was a sister for you to find, and this dude is just crazy?" one of the cop's asked.

"I guess that's as good a description as any. Although I'm still not real clear what's going on, I'm pretty convinced that Stephanie died and sometime between then and now Stephen suffered a psychological breakdown, or at least he developed a second personality—that of his dead twin sister."

Ten pairs of eyes stared at me as if I were the one who'd gone batty. It all sounded pretty lame, even to me, and I was neck deep in it. "Honest!" I repeated. "I'm still trying to wrap my brain around the truth—that my client hired me to find himself. Or herself. Hell, I don't even know the right personal pronouns to use at this point."

"Ms. Mordan.—" the black cop began.

"Morgan."

"Fine. Ms. Morgan. You said there'd been an attempted murder."

"Yes, well, Steph…um, *Davidson* had his gun, her gun, *the* gun pointed at Wagner's head." Now I knew the conversational *Twilight Zone* my California friend Jill had entered when her husband announced he was really a woman and was going to have a sex change operation.

I shook my head, hoping to realign the confused neurons "Davidson had already struck Wagner across the face at least twice and had made specific verbal threats about shooting us both after Wagner was finished confessing. I have no doubt, based upon Davidson's agitated, and obviously confused state, that if I hadn't managed to overpower him, we'd both be dead by now." I heard sighs from several of the cops, probably disappointed that the attempted murder hadn't been more imminent, or at least more dramatic.

"I'd better call one of the campus shrinks." One cop approached Davidson for a closer look.

Me and nine cops nodded in agreement. Even Wagner managed a weak nod.

Davidson just smiled. "Hi, who are you?"

DOUBLE TROUBLE

The best mirror is an old friend.
~George Herbert (1593-1632)

I'd called Judy and Larry as soon as I got home and told them I'd found Stephanie and that I needed to talk and unwind. I couldn't think of better company than my two best friends. Neither had given me much chance to elaborate before deciding we needed to celebrate, although it was still a bit unclear to me exactly what we were celebrating. We spent the better part of that night sitting in my living room, drinking and talking about various forms of insanity.

Two weeks after the showdown in Wagner's office, there was another gathering in my home. This time, Judy, Larry, and I were retelling the whole story to Aunt Louise and Patrick, who was—much to my relief—seemingly quite comfortable in the company of my strange relative.

We'd finished a wonderful homemade Italian dinner that I could already feel settling onto my thighs. It was almost midnight, and we were sitting in my living room, sharing our third bottle of Aunt Louise's expensive cabernet.

She and Larry were sitting on my sofa. Polly and Boggle were snoring in a furry tangle between them. I was curled up on the loveseat with Cooper and Deke on either side of me. In a silent contest for my lap, each had an outstretched paw on one of my thighs, staking their claim for my flesh. Mayfly was laying behind my head, gently kneading the back of my neck with her claws. Oh well, at least I was loved.

Patrick was slouched, catless, in the rocker.

"So?" Aunt Louise asked. "You made us wait patiently through dinner. Now you have to tell all."

She had no idea what she was asking. I grinned. "I was hired by and following the same person."

"Come again?" Patrick said.

I expanded my grin to an ear-to-ear smile—I was going to relish every gap-jawed and befuddled expression Patrick and Aunt Louise made.

"Leave it to Marianna to be hired by a lunatic," Judy said.

"Hey." I raised my chin indignantly. "I'm a fair and impartial private investigator. I accept all cases offered to me, unless they are clearly asking for an illegal service."

"You're just greedy," Larry laughed.

I shrugged and took a big swallow of wine. "I was in double trouble all along and didn't know it. My client was mentally unstable and the subject of my pursuits didn't even exist." I told them about my case, and about the showdown in Wagner's office. I excused myself for a quick potty break, then reclaimed my spot on the loveseat, which Cooper and Deke had completely taken over in my absence.

"Breaks over," Aunt Louise said. "So what happened when the doctor arrived?"

I laughed. "He wasn't sure who the patient was—Davidson or Wagner. He ended up having the police escort both of them to his office in the next building. He wasn't going to let me follow, but I said I represented Davidson, so he begrudgingly obliged. He didn't ask for credentials and just assumed I was Davidson's lawyer."

"You bad girl," Patrick said.

"But as long as you got to hear all the goodies," Aunt Louise added, "do tell…"

I smirked. "Dr. Ramsdell saw Wagner first, since he was the least messed up, at least as far as physical appearance indicated. He gave him something to *help him cope*. After about ten minutes, Wagner was able to do more than babble *not you*, although the first thing he did was start crying. After a few minutes, he calmed down and said he wanted to tell his story, that he'd lived with it too long. Since the police were already there, Wagner just started pouring out a confession to the burglary and even to the murder."

"What about Stephanie?" Patrick asked. "I mean the *real* Stephanie. What happened to her?"

"He accidentally killed her shortly after leaving the Davidson home, although I'm sure he'd eventually have seen he had no choice and would have killed her anyway. She was in the backseat of his car and—in his words—when she came to she started railing on him with her fists and screaming for him to take her home. He pulled over and tried at first to calm her down.

But she just got more agitated, so he slapped her hard, which knocked her out, and then stuffed an old rag in her mouth. Only he didn't notice that he'd stuffed it in too far. She choked to death. When he realized she was dead, he drove to some land his family owns out near Seguin. He buried her, along with the musket."

"He buried the musket?" Aunt Louise asked.

"Sure," Larry said. "Would you try to sell a stolen item that was now linked with a murder and an abduction?"

"Of course not," she responded, and then turned back to me, "But didn't you say he was recently trying to sell the musket? When did he dig it up?"

"He hadn't. Wagner never actually showed it to Mr. Pitt, the antique dealer. He'd just described it to him and promised to return with it a week later."

"Why now, after all this time?" Patrick asked.

"Wagner's land is in the path of the toll road that's going in between Seguin and Austin. He had no choice," I said.

"Where's the musket now?" Patrick asked.

"I'm not sure, but I imagine the police have it at this point. I know Davidson asked that it be donated to the Alamo Historical Society."

"Speaking of Davidson," Judy said, "What's going on with him?"

"He's at the San Antonio State Hospital for psychiatric observation and analysis." I shook my head. "What a head job. There's no doubt in my mind that he's crazy as a bat. I can't figure out how he managed to function on a daily basis. At least I know now what was going on during his Lost Times."

"What exactly happened to him?" Aunt Louise asked.

"I can only tell you what I've learned. This is new to you, too," I nodded to Larry and Judy. "I talked to Dr. Ramsdell, as well as Dr. Kammer, one of the psychiatrists evaluating Davidson at SASH. Dr. Kammer gave me some stuff to read. A lot of it's over my head, but the basics are that he has Dissociative Identity Disorder, what used to be called Multiple Personality Disorder."

"Sybil with a bald head," Judy said as she topped off our wine.

"Something like that." I laughed. "D-I-D normally begins in childhood, like it did with the real Sybil. But sometimes something can trigger the breakdown in an already-fragile adult. Davidson had never gotten over his sister's death, especially since there was no proof she was dead—no body, no nothing. So when his mother died earlier this year, something in his brain just snapped. She was the last woman in his life."

"So it's really the women's fault," Larry quipped.

Judy whopped him with a pillow, then turned back to me. "Did he really have multiple personalities?"

"Thank you." I raised my glass to her. "No, as I was going to say before I was so rudely interrupted," I glared at Larry, "according to Ramsdell, people who suffer from this disorder believe they have multiple personalities, which then take on a life of their own. But the real problem is that the person suffers from dissociative identities. That's why the psychiatric community came up with the new term to be more accurate."

"That poor man." Judy shook her head and frowned.

"Yes, I guess so," I said. "He certainly had a tougher time emotionally than most folks."

"There's one thing I still don't get," Judy said.

"Only one?" Larry teased.

"Well, frankly, I don't understand most of what happened with this case," Judy answered, "but there's one thing that is particularly still bugging me. Wagner knew he'd killed Stephanie, so why did he pretend that it was Stephanie in his office?"

"I can answer that one," Aunt Louise said. "When someone encounters a person who's clearly not what they seem," she emphasized her comment by running her hands down both sides of her pink and white polka dot sundress, "most people go along with the charade because they don't know what's going on. In the case of Stephanie, Wagner knew it wasn't her, and probably also knew it was really Stephen, but he was afraid of what would happen if he confronted the situation, especially with a gun pointed at him."

Patrick nodded. "We receive extensive training in how to handle people who are clearly in a deranged state." At the look Aunt

Louise shot him, he added with a warm smile, "Present company completely excluded, of course."

Aunt Louise smiled back and winked. "So far as you know."

"What's going to happen to Professor Wagner?" Judy asked.

"He's going to be tried for two murders," Larry said. "I checked on him this morning. He's currently in the Bexar County Jail, under a suicide watch, since he's tried twice to kill himself."

"He tried to kill himself?" I asked.

"Yeah," Larry said, "once with a bedspring, which he used to try to puncture his jugular, and once with a strip of bedsheet, which he made into a rather sophisticated noose, or so I was told."

"Geez," Patrick said.

"What he said," I added.

"About damn time he was tried," Aunt Louise said. "He's been walking around for too many years while that poor little girl rotted in the ground."

Judy blanched. Patrick made a soft *urp* sound. I could only smile at Aunt Louise's blunt description.

"I warned you about patterns of two," she continued. "Who would ever have guessed the symbols were pointing to two people in the same body."

Who indeed.

PEACE OF MIND

He that would live in peace and at ease, must not speak all he knows, nor judge all he sees.
~Ben Franklin (1706-1790)

After months of therapy, Davidson was pronounced whole, although he'd probably never know everything he'd done as Stephanie. It'd taken me just as long, lots of wine, and many conversations with Larry, Judy, and even Aunt Louise to forgive him for slaughtering my sweet Georgie. Although my logical mind knew it wasn't really Stephen, convincing my heart was a definite challenge.

Aunt Louise was particularly insistent that forgiveness was important to my own moving on, so I'd reluctantly kept in touch with Stephen by phone and had even visited him a couple of times. In the end, and in spite of everything, I found I actually liked him and wanted to see things turn out for the poor guy.

The previous week, he'd been acquitted of Tom Darnell's murder. Only in Texas was the equivalent of *he needed killing* a good enough defense. In Davidson's case, the jury had decided it wasn't actually Stephen who'd committed the murder, it was Stephanie, who killed him in response to an imminent threat, that of being exposed, which in *her* mind qualified as life-threatening.

Davidson's lawyer had done a bang-up job twisting the jurors heads into tight enough knots with psychobabble that no amount of reasoning by qualified psychiatrists could convince them that Stephen and Stephanie weren't really two completely separate personalities sharing one body. I was glad of the verdict. Davidson *had* killed Darnell, but he hadn't really *known* he was killing him.

In any case, I was standing next to Davidson in front of a display case in the Alamo's artifacts display building. Inside the case was the now-famous Brown Bess, thanks to extensive media coverage of the trial. A small note card next to the musket's stock said *Donated in loving memory of Chester Davidson, 1923-1965.*

"The UT Center for Archeological Research was thrilled when they received the musket for restoration and saw what fine condition it was already in," Davidson said. "I guess I have to at least give Professor Wagner credit for that. He'd emptied out all the gunpowder and then wrapped and taped the musket tightly in the yellow rain slicker before burying it. His actions are what preserved the musket. Even the wooden stock has barely deteriorated."

"Why empty the gunpowder?" I asked

"Mexican gun powder was very unstable. If the musket had remained loaded, it could have gone off any time over the years."

"Wow."

Davidson reached out and traced the shape of the musket on the glass lid of the case. "Maybe now I can put my past to rest. I was finally able to bury my sister's remains, and now I've also been able to return the musket to its rightful location. It was kind of the Alamo Historical Society to allow the dedication card. They don't usually do that for donated items that have a questionable past."

"It's a wonderful tribute to your father's memory."

We silently wandered through the rest of the displays, looking at silver snuff boxes, knives, pistols, other muskets, hats, and a whole host of other relics. Some were from the location of the actual Battle of the Alamo. Others were merely from that same time period and general geographic location.

"I have a date with Patty tonight," Davidson said as we stopped at a display case filled with old books and a yellowed, beaded bag.

"The librarian? That's wonderful." I smiled. "I hope things are going well."

"They are." He nodded. "I'm definitely falling in love with her."

"I'm happy for you. I only had a chance to visit with her that one time at the hospital, but I liked her instantly."

"She has that effect on everyone. Certainly did on me. And she's stood by me through my recovery, the trial, my sister's memorial…" His voice hitched and he gazed into the display case.

I knew we were both trying to find the right way to say goodbye. I put my hand on Davidson's arm. "Please keep in touch. I'd like to hear about the new cat and dog sanctuary you're establishing."

Davidson looked at me with clear, peaceful eyes. He was the happiest I'd ever seen. "I will. And thank you again. You got more than you bargained for with my case, but you stuck through until the end. I owe you for that."

"You're paid in full." I winked, which drew the hoped-for smile in response. I kissed him lightly on the cheek and headed for the door. Outside, I breathed in the cool air as I donned my helmet. I hopped on Pancho Villa, my new royal-blue Suzuki Bandit motorcycle, and headed north.

I was going to take the fast route up the interstate, but instead pointed the front tire toward Marble Falls and the Blue Bonnet Cafe. I figured some chicken fried steak and chocolate cream pie, followed by a winding ride home along FM 1431, sounded just grand. Besides, it was time to put my own ghosts to rest.

Case Closed

For Eric,
my husband and best friend since 1989,
for always believing in me.

For Mom and Dad,
who encouraged me to stretch and grow
and to never accept second best in myself.

For Linda,
who cheerfully took me all over San Antonio as I did
research and who introduced me to a whole
plethora of knowledgable and wonderful people.

ACKNOWLEDGMENTS

So many wonderful people helped me research this book. Thanks to the following for their time, patience, and invaluable contributions:

To John Molin (then) owner of the Snake Farm for the comprehensive tour. I'm sorry I couldn't include a body in the alligator pit.

To Dr. Richard Bruce Winders (Historian and Curator of the Alamo) for the amazing amount of information and help with the Brown Bess musket's history and workmanship, for letting me hold the one in his office, and for letting me also hold the actual bent bayonet tip that inspired this novel.

To Terrell Hills Police Chief Don Davis for an amazing amount of specific information about how emergency services were handled in the mid 60s and how long a search for a missing child would have been conducted (I was surprised by the answer).

To Dr. Karen Bell for her education on various psychological conditions and emotional states that can be brought on by extreme grief.

To Chuck Foreman, licensed private investigator and founder of Center for Search & Investigations (CFSI) for his assistance in helping me keep Marianna authentic.

Made in the USA
Charleston, SC
29 July 2016